M000215983

Gutted

Beautiful Horror Stories

Edited by
Doug Murano and
D. Alexander Ward

Crystal Lake Publishing
www.CrystalLakePub.com

Cover Design:
Caitlin Hackett
https://caitlinhackett.carbonmade.com.

Interior Artwork:
Luke Spooner
www.carrionhouse.com

Interior Layout:
Lori Michelle
www.theauthorsalley.com

Proofread by:
Lisa Childs, Guy Medley,
Paula Limbaugh, Robert Teun

Other titles by Crystal Lake Publishing

The Final Cut by Jasper Bark

Blackwater Val by William Gorman

Devourer of Souls by Kevin Lucia

Tales from The Lake Vol.1

Tales from The Lake Vol.2

Wind Chill by Patrick Rutigliano

Eidolon Avenue: The First Feast by Jonathan Winn

Flowers in a Dumpster by Mark Allan Gunnells

The Dark at the End of the Tunnel by Taylor Grant

Tribulations by Richard Thomas

Writers On Writing: An Author's Guide

Eden Underground: Poetry of Darkness by Alessandro Manzetti

Modern Mythmakers: 35 Interviews with Horror & Science Fiction Writers and Filmmakers by Michael McCarty

Or check out other Crystal Lake Publishing books for your Dark Fiction, Horror, Suspense, and Thriller needs, and join our newsletter while you're there.

Copyright
Acknowledgements

Contents

Foreword by Richard Chizmar i

Stephanie M. Wytovich 1
The Morning After Was Filled with Bone

Brian Kirk 5
Picking Splinters from a Sex Slave

Lisa Mannetti..23
Arbeit Macht Frei

Neil Gaiman...43
The Problem of Susan

Christopher Coake 57
Dominion

Mercedes M. Yardley 79
Water Thy Bones

Paul Tremblay 91
A Haunted House is a Wheel Upon Which Some
Are Broken

Damien Angelica Walters 127
On the Other Side of the Door, Everything Changes

Richard Thomas.......................................143
Repent

Clive Barker 165
Coming to Grief

John F.D. Taff 201
    Cards for His Spokes, Coins for His Fare

Amanda Gowin 239
    Cellar's Dog

Kevin Lucia 263
    When We All Meet at the Ofrenda

Maria Alexander 287
    Hey, Little Sister

Josh Malerman 305
    The One You Live With

Ramsey Campbell 323
    The Place of Revelation

Doug Murano:
*To Rocco, Eva, Luca and Baby Girl: You'll find the
beauty if you decide to look for it.
I hope you do.*

D. Alexander Ward:
*To my wife, my daughter, and my family, who
honor me with their love and support.*

Foreword

MANY YEARS AGO—in the May 1996 issue of *Locus*, to be exact—genre critic extraordinaire, Edward Bryant, wrote the following about my first short story collection, *Midnight Promises*:

"Chizmar certainly believes in—and explores with painful, honest, dead reckoning—human suffering, pain, and occasional transcendence. And that's why he's well worth the reading."

I promise you . . . I don't open this brief foreword with Bryant's words of praise in an effort to boost my own ego, nor to establish an immediate sense of credibility.

In fact, many readers may argue that the above sliver of a review doesn't even fall into the category of "praise." It's more an understanding on Bryant's part, a kind and thoughtful understanding of the engine that drives me as a writer and editor and human being.

And that's my point here, folks, in relation to Bryant's insightful observation and the fine volume of stories you now hold in your hands.

Two simple, yet powerful words:
I understand.

I've written about it before—in essays, and introductions to my own work and the work of others. Most of us writers and editors have done so once we've reached a certain rung in our career ladders; it's practically a rite of passage:

What internal vision drives us as artists and entertainers; how and why do we see the things we see, things others inevitably catch only corner-of-the-eye glimpses of or miss altogether; and perhaps my all-time favorite: my God, wouldn't you rather sit down and write about something happy and filled with golden rays of sunshine?

My response—and the responses of many of my peers—has always been straightforward and bluntly honest: *what makes you think I have a choice?*

Seriously.

It's just how I *see* the world around me, how I see it and *feel* it.

I'm a pretty cheerful guy, living an extremely fortunate life, but when it comes to my writing and enjoying the fictional work of others, I tend to ignore the sunshine and explore the dark shadows and dirty corners instead.

I guess it's just where I feel the most at home, and where my vision is the sharpest.

Take this little exercise for example:

You might stop at a traffic light and glimpse an old man standing on a street corner with a wrinkled paper bag in his hand and think: *aww, how sweet, the old guy's off to the park to feed the pigeons or eat his lunch by the lake.*

I might see something entirely different.

Poor old guy looks sad. Lost. Lonely. Maybe even desperate. I bet his wife died recently. He's unshaven. His pants and shirt are filthy. Is that dirty laundry in the bag and he's on his way across town to the laundry mat . . . or something more sinister? Is that a stain seeping along the bottom of the bag? A scarlet stain?

Yes, sir, that's exactly how I might see it, folks—and as I noted above: what makes you think I have a choice?

There is beauty all around us, and there is horror all around us. Sometimes, it's impossible to tell the difference.

I *see* what I see, and I *feel* what I feel.

I don't really have much of a choice.

I believe it's that way for most of us writers.

I would bet anything it's that way for Stephanie M. Wytovich, whose exquisitely-crafted poem opens *Gutted: Beautiful Horror Stories*.

She writes: "You took everything I had left, but there in that skeletal smile, I've never been more beautiful, even after all the horrible things that I'd done."—and all I can do is nod my head in silent agreement.

She understands.

The editors of *Gutted: Beautiful Horror Stories* are Doug Murano and D. Alexander Ward.

I've never met either gentleman, nor spoken with them on the telephone.

I don't know if they are young (although I'm

betting they are based on their endless enthusiasm, passion, and work ethic) or middle-aged or elderly (like my old man on the sidewalk with the paper bag in his hand).

I don't know if they are married or single, patriarchs or childless, slender or burly, tattooed or pierced, Democrat or Republican.

I don't even know what the "D" stands for in Mr. Ward's byline.

None of this matters a bit to me.

What *does* matter is this: Doug Murano and D. Alexander Ward have assembled a veritable feast for all discerning readers of dark fiction.

Gutted: Beautiful Horror Stories thrilled me and chilled me—and made me *think* about the world around me—in ways not many other anthologies have ever been able to accomplish (which is why I agreed to shoehorn the writing of this foreword into an already overflowing work schedule).

There is darkness and terror and heartbreak to be found in these pages, but also redemption and hope and wisdom. It's a fragile balance, and one to be greatly admired. Every detail, from the careful selection of these fifteen stories and one poem to the thoughtful order in which they appear, is spot on and designed for a finer reading experience.

I could write something about each and every story in the book. I liked them all that much. But I won't. I will leave the amazements—and the terrors—for each of you to experience firsthand. Alone. In the dark.

Instead, I'll tease you about the innovative horrors to be found in Paul Tremblay's "A Haunted House is a

Wheel Upon Which Some Are Broken" and Ramsey Campbell's "The Place of Revelation."

I'll promise you wonder and heartbreak in tales such as Clive Barker's "Coming to Grief" and John F.D. Taff's "Cards for His Spokes, Coins for His Fare," in which Taff successfully channels both Ray Bradbury and Stephen King to weave a splendid dark fantasy all his own.

Finally, I'll hint at the unimaginable shocks waiting for you in Lisa Mannetti's "Arbeit Macht Frei" and even the darkest of love stories in Brian Kirk's "Picking Splinters from a Sex Slave" and Kevin Lucia's "When We All Meet at the Ofrenda" and Maria Alexander's "Hey, Little Sister."

Take my advice: read the stories in the order in which they appear. Take your time to savor them. Think about them. Heal from them.

I don't know a whole lot about Doug Murano and D. Alexander Ward, but I do know this: they've done the horror genre a great service with this book. Readers and writers, alike.

Murano and Ward see a different world than most people see; they *understand*—and I can offer them no higher compliment.

Richard Chizmar
April 12, 2016

The Morning After Was Filled with Bone

STEPHANIE M. WYTOVICH

My bed held an imprint that I wasn't ready to sleep
 with
so I stood in front of my bathroom mirror
applied my favorite shade of red lipstick to my teeth,
teeth that were locked in a permanent smile that held
nothing but words shaped by broken liquor bottles and
 empty ashtrays,
by unfinished poetry and 157 sleeps filled with
 nightmares
and the blankets made of your memory. The cigarette
 smoke
from the circles under my eyes
caused me to bleed soot, to cry ash for so long
that my eyes crawled out of their sockets and rolled
 down the drain,
drowning in the sludge I coughed up from my lungs,
tangled in the hair that no longer brushed against my
 cheeks.
With them, went my lips, tired from too many months
 of promised love,

of forgotten kisses; they crawled off my face
like the worms I hoped would soon eat your body,
like the maggots that bred inside your mouth, that fucked
on the top of your tongue. My lips were poisoned by too many days
of neglect, and I washed them down the sink with the blood
that stained the flesh that covered my skull. It peeled off like soft clay
eager to fall from an unwanted body
where the cold would be forced to embrace it.

I spat at the looking glass that told me I was diseased,
that I was tainted, that I was foul, and I felt for the washcloth
I kept on the rack above the toilet I puked in three times a day. I turned
the faucet to cold, forced it to run ice, and I splashed a baptism
against my bare-bone face while I used the rag to shine my skull. I brushed cobwebs out of the hollows of my sockets, wove blood roses in their place, and in
the spots where I used to blush, I rubbed Gerbera daisies—
I bought them myself—until their burgundy color stained what used
to be my cheeks. And in that bathroom with three lightbulbs burned out,
and a tiled floor sticky with last night's sweat, I tilted my head back and screamed
because death wasn't something I felt, that I carried with me

The Morning After

in the rot in my chest, in the scratch at the back of my
    throat. It was something
that I wore. I ran my hands over the slick sheen of
    bone. I laughed at my blindness
because I could finally see. You took everything I had
    left, but there in that skeletal smile,
I've never been more beautiful, even after all the
    horrible things that I'd done.

Picking Splinters from a Sex Slave

BRIAN KIRK

The box he kept her in was five-and-a-half feet long. I got a glimpse of it as they hauled it from the house, three large policemen lifting on each side as though carrying a heavy coffin to a hearse. Wanting, I suppose, to be a part of history. To take a proverbial brick from the Berlin Wall. They all broke into sheepish grins as the cameras began to flash. Like best men walking down the aisle at a poon hound's wedding. As if they'd done something noble or heroic, rather than finally follow up on the third tip dropped by a neighbor, who they'd locked up several times for petty crimes.

Five-and-a-half feet long. She was four-foot-nine when he took her. Would have been five-seven now if not for the stooped neck. If not for the stunted growth. But I guess her unattained height is the least of my concern. Or maybe it's all summarized in that stolen inch.

Here's how I found out they'd found her. I'm driving home from a gig—I live in Jersey now, I lived in Connecticut then. I'm listening to 96.1 *The Thump* on the FM dial—which was Meagan's favorite station. Back then. The one she made me listen to while driving her to-and-from school. It played six minutes of pop songs sandwiched between sixteen minutes of ads for Clearasil and maxi pads. You'd think I would have stopped listening to the station after she was gone, but I couldn't. In the six years she was missing, the station changed format eight times. Went from pop to oldies to NPR back to pop to sports talk to classic rock back to pop to contemporary rock, which I think just means bland music. It's terrible, but, then again, I'm not really listening.

They interrupted a Bryan Adams song with one of those screeching AMBER alert sounds. Then, from the ethereal airwaves sent from some turnstile station, I hear:

We have breaking news to report to you right now.

Oh my goodness we do.

Yes, my goodness. Meagan Towser, a young girl from the tri-state area who was reported missing six years ago, has just been located.

Amazing, just amazing.

Amazing is right. According to sources on the scene she has been held captive all this time in a house mere miles from the home she was allegedly abducted from.

I imagine the radio waves streaming through the air like some toxic breeze. Birds falling dead from the sky in droves. The voices get huskier, grave and earnest.

Reports indicate she may have been held captive in a box.

Picking Splinters

Oh, God, that's terrible.
Terrible.
Oh, God.
God, that's terrible. Just terrible.
Terrible, God.

I live alone in a tiny condo now, I lived in a ranch home with a family back then. The one Meagan was taken from by a not-too-distant neighbor. It was me, my wife, Debbie, and a dog named Nugget, but Nugget ran away. Nugget smelled like Doritos chips and attic dust, but I loved the little fella. Debbie ran away too. She had smelled more like spring air fabric softener.

Sometimes I wonder if Debbie took Nugget like that not-too-distant neighbor took our little girl. Come to think of it, we crated our dog during the daytime as well. And did so out of love.

Let's get back to the box. Four rough-hewn sheets of plywood bought from Home Depot and cut by one of the store's employees. The planks still had the lumberyard's orange logo painted on each side. Soft wood that splintered easily, evidenced by the back of Meagan's shoulders, arms, and legs. Skin pocked like strawberry seeds from all the untreated splinters.

Say it took her four years to grow to her full height, a span from age thirteen to seventeen. That leaves two years spent with her head thrust up against the top and her feet crunched down below. Her neck cranked forward, knees bent, crammed against the splintered underside of the lid. Pitch dark—he kept her stuffed under his raised bed like a collection of porno mags. Stuffy, dusty. He didn't drill air holes, so she breathed whatever air seeped in through the thin slits on each side. You can hear your breath in a box like that. The hollow sound of every exhale. You can also hear your heart.

I'll skip the sordid details. To be honest, I don't know them anyway. Our conversations, if you can call them that, never involve what went on inside that house. Think I don't want to know? Please. I'm the worst person for this to happen to. A failed comedian filled with morbid curiosity. My twisted mind keeps churning out jokes.

I hate moving, but it's easy with my daughter. She comes packed in her own box.

I hear they're making robotic sex dolls that you can keep in a box. Whatever happened to the good old days when you could just kidnap my daughter?

What's that old equation: Comedy = Tragedy + Time?

I guess you can create a formula like that for everything. Look at the very fabric of reality and you'll see: Love ^{x} You're Fucked = Life.

The karmic irony, if you believe in such things, is that her abductor now lives in a cage, whereas Meagan can roam free. Given, it's not a narrow box cut an inch too short so that his neck stays bent. And he doesn't get raped several times a day. At least, not that I'm aware of. The food's pretty bad, though, from what I understand.

So I hear about her being found through the radio, immediately make the drive back to our old town. Get there in time to see the wannabe pallbearers ushering the box out of the pervert's home. Their shit-eating grins chronicled in camera flash. The whole scene looks like a party that's just winding down. The man who provided the tip is standing amidst a sea of congratulators who all appear drunk or high on crack.

Picking Splinters

Meagan's in the back of an ambulance, a wool blanket that looks just as rough-hewn as the plywood box is wrapped around her torso. If I saw this young lady on the street, I'd pass her by without a second glance. I could buy a Starbucks from her and not think a thing. There's nothing left of my little girl in this nineteen-year-old's gaunt and ruddy face. Those bruised and vacant eyes.

It takes some convincing, but they let me through to see her. All I can feel is a nervous tingling in my testicles. The feeling you get when the roller coaster drops and you promised to keep your hands in the air but you can't. A kind of soundless vertigo. A kind of Zen state. A wash-out of emotion as it collects itself in the seismic undertow and becomes a tsunamic wave. She looks up, sees me. No, sees through me. Looking into her eyes, I doubt she sees anything at all. The wave hits, pulls me under. I drown.

Here's the first night together at home. Not the old home where she was stolen during the daytime like Nugget might have been. The new one that Debbie's never been to, so instead of smelling like spring air fabric softener it smells like moldy parmesan cheese. It's only got one bedroom; I had mentally said goodbye to Meagan years ago. The walls are painted in whatever off-white color they came in. I forgot to buy groceries so the fridge is bare.

"Honey," I say. I used to call her Fish-Face. I used to call her Mug-Head. "We can talk. We can just sit. Maybe we can watch a show? You want something to eat? Maybe I can order something? I don't want to be too pushy." I don't want to leave her alone.

She just stands there. She's still got that scratchy

wool blanket wrapped around her and she keeps cinching it tight. Underneath, she's wearing a tank top undershirt and boxer briefs. She shrugs, stands there some more.

For how small the room is, there seems to be a chasm forming between us. I've never been comfortable around other people. I'm fine on stage, but face-to-face? No. My therapist would call what's happening here exposure therapy. It's when you're forced to do the thing that makes you most uncomfortable so that you can try and get over it. This, I learn, is that thing.

I walk slowly, cautiously, as though approaching a feral cat instead of the daughter whose diapers I once changed. We're next to each other now. Her vacant eyes, I see, are staring at a copy of *Cracked* magazine that is laying by the couch on the floor. Should I do it fast or slow? I don't know, and hardly remember what I decided. Next thing I know my arm is around her, ungainly and stiff, unsure if I feel resistance or acceptance or total indifference. I try to pull her toward me but it's like tugging on the trunk of a tree.

My daughter died in that box. I have to bring her back.

I almost forget I'm supposed to feature for an act at the Improv that night. I wonder if a little comedy could do her some good, but quickly decide it would not. Honestly, I'm frightened of slipping up and telling one of my more inappropriate jokes. Which basically means my whole act.

"Why don't you lie down," I say. "In a warm, comfortable bed for a change."

She nods and I lead her to my room. Her room, now. The only room.

Keeping the blanket wrapped around her, cinching it ever more tightly, she lies down atop the bedspread. Her neck is bent, head thrust forward, so I place another pillow underneath it so that it doesn't just hang in the air. Gaunt and pale with those deep-set eyes staring straight up overhead, Meagan has become a mummy. I watch as her body curls into its accustomed pose. Boxed in atop a king size bed.

I turn on the TV and flip through channels. It's primetime on a Thursday night and guns blaze from every station. I may as well make her watch *Taken* 1, 2, and 3. Then I remember how I kept her books. The ones we used to read to her as a little girl. Maybe that could help soothe her, anchor her in some way to her former self.

"Stay here," I say. "I'll be right back."

The books are in a box in a storage room by the garage. I rip it open and look.

Goldilocks, Hansel & Gretel, Rapunzel, Snow White

Christ, I think with mounting dread. Every story involves some little girl who leaves home and almost gets killed.

Okay, keep it simple. Basic pleasures here: a warm bath, clean clothes, comfort food, a soft bed. She's still my daughter, I'm still her dad. I can do this.

The bathroom is off the bedroom, so I have to pass by her first. I open the door and almost cry out. She's gone. How is that possible? Was she taken again? I run to the bathroom, it's empty.

"Meagan!" I shout so loud it hurts my ears.

Then I hear a muffled voice. Coming from down by the floor. I look and see that the bed skirt is ruffled. I dip to my knees and peek under the bed, and there she is. Her head thrust forward so that her forehead is pressed into the underside of the box spring. That wool blanket pulled so tight I'm surprised she can breathe.

Tired of your daughter forgetting to make her bed? Easy fix. Just have her kidnapped by a man who keeps her in a box and she'll never sleep in it again.

Thank God I didn't perform at that night's show.

Of all people it was the police who saved me, because they sure hadn't saved her. She had written instructions on the underside of the box lid. Had scratched instructions, I mean. With her fingernails. The police used carbon paper to lift all the inscriptions and emailed scanned copies to me. Meagan had scratched into the wood the things she wanted to do when she got free.

Pet animals (I'd never missed Nugget as much as right then)

Swim in the ocean

Something about wanting ice cream or to scream

Never have a boyfriend

Days are nights and nights are days

Please let me suffocate

There was a lot of other stuff. I wouldn't send much of it to the Make-A-Wish Foundation. But it gave me a place to start.

Two weeks and she still hadn't talked. I figured she would have to cry first. Just flush all the toxic sludge that was clogging the pipes. She went to therapy every day, although that didn't seem to do much. The therapist said it would take time: weeks, months, years. She charged $175 per hour.

We're on the way to the zoo. It's 2 p.m. on a Tuesday. August. 96 degrees out, but the heat index says it feels like 99. The index is optimistic. Even still we have to wait in line.

The ticket teller is around Meagan's age, maybe a few years older. She's dressed from head to toe in khaki and wearing a safari hat. Blonde hair with a beautiful face.

Beauty = Symmetry—% of Facial Herpes

If I wasn't with Meagan, I'd try and flirt with this girl. I know I'm a degenerate when I stroke her hand when taking our tickets just so I can touch her skin.

Erection = Impulse to Procreate x Foot Fetish +/- Shame

I know why Debbie left me; I'm not sure why Nugget did.

We walk in to the scent of flamingo shit, and keep going. All I care about is getting her to the panda exhibit. It doesn't matter how down you are; a panda will cheer you up. We pass the warthogs and meerkats and bongos. The howlers and lemurs and orangutans. It's too hot even for the animals. They're all hiding in shadows or covered in mud. Meagan tugs on my shirt while I'm craning my neck to find the emaciated lion; it's the first contact she's initiated on her own. She leads me to a small grey building with a sign that reads, "Mole Rats," and we walk inside.

I'm not a therapist, but I'm seeing the psychology here. These little hairless mutant rats are stuffed in tunnels, buried underground. Just lying there amidst their piss and shit and whatever else. They don't make a playground or a swimming pond or a sports stadium, they just burrow tunnels barely wide enough to fit through that lead to dead end apertures where they lay.

I sigh, reach down and grab hold of her limp hand. "I'm so sorry," I say.

She nods, and I consider that the breakthrough of the millennium. Then she speaks. "Every beautiful creature," she says. "Lives inside a cage."

Meagan used to tell me she thought flipping the bird came from Big Bird only having three fingers, so he was always raising his middle one. That was about as deep as she got. I guess she's had a lot of time to think living inside that box.

It's dark in here and it feels safe. A good place, perhaps, for her to open up.

"Listen," I say, and then the door opens behind us. Harsh, August light blinds us to the three chubby boys who barge through. They're around the same age as Meagan when she was taken.

"Ewww! These fucking things are gross!"

"Look, James! That fat one looks like your grandma!"

Meagan shrivels. I expect to see her clothes fall limp to the ground like when the bad witch of Oz gets dowsed with water. I hurry her out; her legs are stiff; she's stumbling like she's forgotten how to walk. I escort her as fast as I can to the panda exhibit, where I learn that some conditions are immune to a panda's charm.

The next day, she ran away. Or maybe that night, I'm not sure. She tried to go back under the bed and I wouldn't let her. It can't be healthy. It has to be holding her back. Fortunately, finding her was easy. A construction worker found her squeezed inside one of their concrete culvert pipes. Her forehead had an abrasion from rubbing against the rocky underside.

The police brought her home and she wanted to go back under the bed, but again I wouldn't let her.

"Please, just talk to me. Tell me what's going on. How can I help you?"

She won't look at me. There is no possible way for me to catch her eye.

"Meagan, I love you so much. I'm so happy you're home. I'm so sorry for what you've been through. I want to make it all better. You still have a whole life ahead of you to make up for those terrible years."

When she talks now, it's in a kind of mumbling Morse code.

"Nothing . . . can be . . . done."

"Honey," I used to call her Mug-Head, "that's not true. I know it seems like that now, but it'll get better over time."

"Everyone's watching . . . I hate . . . when they look."

"I know it feels that way. But no one around here even knows who you are. You're safe now. I promise you."

"You're . . . watching."

"Yes, but—"

"I don't . . . like it when . . . you look at me."

She's shaking, she's bone white. Terrified or freezing cold, the look is the same. Her chin is tucked deep into her chest trying as hard as she can to hide her face. From me.

I turn and leave the room and listen as she crawls underneath the bed.

She refuses therapy. Doesn't talk when she's there, doesn't want to go. I can't pay $175 for two people to sit in a room in silence. The therapist says she'd like to bring in a specialist who charges twice as much. "Wouldn't we all," I tell her.

I try the beach, find a place that's fairly private. Just one other family a few hundred feet away teaching their toddler son to fly a kite. We walk along the shoreline and the water feels refreshing against my bare feet. Meagan lets it soak her Converse shoes without seeming to notice. I spread out a large blanket and set down the picnic basket containing the combo meals I got from Quizno's. Meagan starts digging in the sand. Slowly, at first, then scooping out large handfuls with both hands. I see what she's doing, and decide to help her. Working together it only takes five minutes to have her buried up to her neck.

"Cover my head," she says.

"No, honey. I can't."

"Please." Her eyes film with tears of anger or frustration.

"Honey, I can't."

"Please!" she screams. Her face is shaking, staring at the ocean with a desperate rage.

I'd brought a beach bucket with us. I grab that and place it on her head and pat it down until it covers her face. Now it just looks like I'm sitting by myself with an overturned bucket beside me. I can hear her crying, for the first time, and it sounds faraway within the hollow inside of the bucket.

"Better?" I ask, as tenderly as I can.

Picking Splinters

The bucket rocks back and forth as she nods her head. Soon the crying stops, and we sit in, what feels like, comfortable silence. This gives me an idea.

The pervert's name is Derrick Patterson. He's a white guy in his fifties. Short, skinny except for a watermelon size beer gut. He had lived with his cousin, and my daughter, in a ramshackle, piece-of-shit house. Guy probably lives more elegantly in prison. For all I know, he may even have a new sex slave. I don't know whether or not to be surprised that he agreed to meet with me. I don't know what I expect to feel when I see him.

My therapist would not recommend this. No one would.

They have me in one of those rooms with little phone booths and a reinforced window separating the people on each end of the line. A door opens and the man who kept my daughter in a box between rapings walks through. Oh, right. One detail I forgot to mention. He doesn't have a neck. It's all just withered scar tissue from the surgery he had to remove cancerous tumors. Stupid fuck still smokes, even though his neck barely looks strong enough to support his stupid head.

I'm already holding the phone. He sits down and picks up his. Raises the voice box to his scooped out throat. He smirks, and I become lost in a fantasy where the reinforced window rolls down and I drag him through to my side and spend the remainder of the day tormenting him in the most sadistic ways my fucked up mind can imagine.

Finally, I come to. "You know who I am?"

His teeth look like chewed-up tootsie rolls. His robotic voice is how a talking insect would sound.

This is something I can't do. Something I can't undo. I skip several questions and get right to the point.

"Tell me how you talked to her," I demand.

"What did you say?

"What did you call her?

"When did you take her out?

"When did you put her back in?

"What did you feed her?

"Was there anything that made her happy? Anything at all?"

His buzz saw voice carved trenches in my brain tissue, but I got the info I needed. Then I got to leave and breathe fresh air while he had to go back and inhale body odor and ball sweat. But that's not nearly enough. Want to know what should happen? They should tie him up and deliver him to me. Leave a guard to make sure it goes my way. Let me take my time, as much as I need. Save the taxpayers a million or two while I enact the only form of punishment that fits the crime. Ruthless, painful revenge.

Instead I find myself at Walmart, buying discount supplies for this plan I've concocted to kidnap my own daughter. There's no equation for this; I've tried. Enter it into a calculator and it'll return: *FAILED TO COMPUTE.*

Ski mask, gloves, sleeping mask, nylon rope. Her sense of smell has gotten much better and I basically wear the same three or four shirts so I buy off-label clothes. Because Lowe's is closer to my house than Home Depot I go there to get the wood. Four rough-hewn boards cut to my exact specifications. I make sure to buy the same cheap brand with the orange logo on the side. Wood so soft I get splinters in my hands loading the planks into the car.

It's hard to remember the Meagan who was taken six years ago. My memories seem idealized now. I imagine reading her stories and going on long walks where I espouse my fatherly wisdom. She runs to me and I lift her up and watch the sun shine through her auburn hair as I twirl her around above me. But, if I'm to be honest, those last couple of years were filled with a lot of confusion, hurt feelings, and shouting. I stopped maturing during my teenage years as well.

I hardly have to prepare. Whether or not she put up a fight back then, I know she won't now. And I'm right. She barely grunts when I break into her room in the middle of the night and pin her against the floor, wrap the sleeping mask over her eyes and stuff the gag in her mouth. She offers zero resistance when I bind her arms behind her and tie them to her legs. I mean none. Taking her to the rental car in the early morning hours is a breeze. I blast loud music while driving in random patterns through town before returning home a couple of hours later. I park in the driveway because I've outfitted the garage, the one room she never spent time in. Her new home.

So here we are, Meagan and me. But she doesn't know it's me. At least, I don't think she does. I guess it doesn't matter. She's happier now than she was before. I've got the room just the way it was the last six years. Her box, an inch too short, is crammed underneath a raised bed. She eats the same food—Ritz crackers and Kraft Easy Cheese. Keeps the same hours. Only difference is she doesn't get raped. Maybe one day she'll want out and I'll let her. Of course I will. My therapist would call this thinking outside the box, which is a terrible joke.

Here we are, her stuffed in her wooden box, me stuffed in my biological one, both condemned to die.

I knock on the lid, scratching my knuckle. It's therapy time.

"Daddy?" Meagan says, just like that pervert said she would. What he trained her to say. Leaning forward, I wonder, if there is a creator, whether He is laughing or if She's crying.

I press the voice box against my throat, so that when I speak it sounds like an insect.

"Shut your mouth you fucking whore."

It's how I say I love you.

Arbeit Macht Frei

LISA MANNETTI

"The women were begging for a little water or a piece of bread. 'Woda . . . khleb.' Two words identified them as Russian. We had heard that so often, we knew 'bread and water' in all the languages of Europe."

—Olga Lengyel

"I had orders to use only the absolute minimum of paper bandages when dressing the wounds of the poor victims of the dogs' fangs and others who had been beaten into unconsciousness."

—Judith Sternberg Newman

"'Don't save him,' one of them said. 'You'll only be prolonging the agony. And you can see for yourself he wanted to escape it now, instead of waiting for the firing squad in a few weeks.'"

—Dr. Miklos Nyiszli

Lisa Mannetti

T he last thing I remember?"

I knew the Red Cross clerk probably meant just before or just after the camp I was in—Waldemar, the Nazis called it—was liberated by the Americans, but so much had happened to me, had happened to the last living member of my family, my mother Kasia, that I thought I'd better start at the beginning. Isn't that the way of it with every important tale?

"Eligia," my mother had always told me—especially when I was being headstrong, or she was urging me to be calm, to be brave—"your name means choice." She'd drilled into me that one could always choose the high road, that it was always best and that it carried meaning—no matter what happened in the end.

So I chose the beginning.

And the clerk, a kindly, patient woman with upswept brown hair let me talk. The talk—and what I would tell her—would be the last thing, I knew, that I would ever choose. The high road, at last.

"We—my mother and I—were taken in Warsaw— the very end of July, 1944—just before the uprising," I began . . .

Like all Polish youngsters, long before it happened, I'd dreamt of the thunderous rattle of Gestapo boots on the stairs. In the dream I would hear that hurried tramp, that deadly cadence punctuated by brutish knocking and furious shouts, the unstoppable upwelling fear of what was about to happen cleaved me instantly awake. In the dark, my heart thudding in my chest, I was aware the dream was no portent: only the playing out of knowing what would inevitably come. We all knew. Heard. Saw it happen a hundred times to neighbors and friends and strangers.

"It was hot that night," I said.

The heat should have stifled the noise, but with the windows open it seemed like that angry leather stamping was coming from everywhere at the same time. Perhaps that hideous deafening echo was ubiquitous: The storm troopers might be raiding every floor of the building at once, simultaneously invading the crumbling apartments next door and across the street and down the block. We were both hidden inside the old wooden armoire that had been her wedding gift from my father. When the noise reached her bedroom, just before they flung open the door, I felt time being sucked away in both the mounting tension and the certainty of discovery. My mother didn't flinch when I dug my fingers into her narrow wrist, she only stiffened and, her head hanging down, bit her lower lip to keep from crying out.

Sounds of chaos—the desk chair kicked aside; the bed hastily thrust up and smashing against the wall; a red glass votive candle in front of the statue of Mary shattering on the floor; flames licking what was left of the dusty curtains; the cupboard door handle finally wrenched open. More shouts. Then the pain of abrasions from floors and carpets, of being pushed and pulled and dragged down three flights to face more loaded rifles on the sidewalk. I looked up and saw dark gray smoke roiling out from my mother's bedroom window. My father, a doctor, had been gone from us for almost five years, and I wondered if I would ever see him again.

Lisa Mannetti

Night-bled sights and sounds of confusion: the crunching of rifle butts against bellies and faces; gunshots; screams. The whole ragged crowd—teenage boys and middle-age women and crying children—whipped and harried by shouts and the shrill barking of infuriated dogs, all of us bullied to the train depot. We'd heard that the Germans forced the Hungarians, the gypsies—and God knew how many others—to march hundreds of kilometers all the way from Budapest to one of the camps in Germany, so that for me (a naive and somewhat rebellious and definitely angry fourteen-year-old), seeing the ailing wooden box car was something of a relief.

Stella Johansson, the Red Cross clerk, had certainly heard about those first insults to the mind and spirit: the callous insanity of cramming eighty, ninety, a hundred or more humans into each car so that there was no room to sit or lie down, no food or water given to us, and she put a consoling hand over mine when I told her how the living were forced to stand and tread upon the dying and the dead . . .

"The selection was at the ramp at Waldemar . . . "

Everyone—by this juncture—knew about the selection process: a bored doctor tipping his finger toward one direction or another. Left, off you went to the gas chambers and the crematoria. Right, a brief respite in hell that included starvation, lice, typhus, and being worked to death—the real, true respite.

Only this time there were brief, whispered words between the doctor (Viktor Freisler, whom I'd come to know) and an *untersturmfurher* who barked,

26

"Any doctors here? Nurses? Medical trainees? Orderlies?"

"Here," my mother called out. "I'm a nurse, sir," she said at the same time she snagged my left arm, adding, "And my daughter, she's sixteen and she worked as an aide in the Catholic hospital, too."

"Where, no doubt, you both hid Jews smuggled out of the ghetto," he said.

My mother kept silent.

He looked me over. "Sixteen? She doesn't look sixteen."

I was tall for my age, but I didn't think I could pass for sixteen.

"It's the war, sir," my mother put in. "The privations—"

"Doesn't *she* speak? How old are you *gnadiges fraulein*?" His words were gracious; his voice was a sneer.

"Sixteen." Even to my own ears my voice sounded hopelessly childish, but he let it pass and my mother and I stood in a clump of three or four people in the dirt road by the boxcars while the multitudes marched away, left and right, to death or death-in-life.

The sign over the camp gate—like the ones at Auschwitz and Dachau—read *Arbeit Macht Frei*. "Work sets you free," my mother whispered. Then I saw her make a tiny cross of her thumb and forefinger and kiss it quickly—as if haste and secrecy would fulfill the intent of her silent prayer.

"There were no real medicines in the hospital," I said, swallowing a lump that had risen uncomfortably in my throat. For now I was on safe ground, but how much was I going to tell this Swedish clerk with the paper nametag and the kind blue eyes? "Coming to the hospital could be a death sentence in itself," I said. She nodded; she knew. "Every now and then word would come down that (for example) there were too many tuberculosis patients in the camp and all of those currently in bed would be sent to the gas chambers . . . to make way—ironically—for new TB victims." I shrugged. Nazi logic was a contradiction—like "exact estimate" or "open secret"—my mother used to say.

"Our lot was only a little better than that of the other inmates, but it was better—at least in some ways. We weren't crammed seven or more to a bunk meant for two; we didn't have to wait in line to use the common latrines—where those who had, say, dysentery accidentally soiled themselves and then were shot for sport that masqueraded as punishment." I paused. "So things were better mostly—but some things were not; some things were harder . . . . 'Canada' was the root, of course: the solution—the salvation— *and* the problem . . . "

"Canada" was the building and its outskirts where— under SS guards—inmates sorted through the vast array of belongings taken from those arriving on the trains. It's almost impossible to describe the house-high heaps of suitcases, clothes, shoes—the mountains of spectacles or Jewish prayer books or felt hats alone, could each have filled an Olympic pool. Anything could be—and was—found by inmates who not only catalogued and heaped up the valuables and the dross from all Europe, but were taught to rummage and snip linings in coats, hidden pockets in books and valises.

It was all there: jewels, money, photographs, candlesticks, pacifiers, toys, rings, bracelets, *mezuzot*—meant to bless now-empty Jewish homes— necklaces, brooches . . . and the food, I thought, instantly feeling saliva womb my tongue. Inmates in just about every *lager* were fed a five- to seven-hundred-calorie-per-day diet that consisted of watery *ersatz* coffee, a few ounces of bread—often moldy— and plumped with sawdust, soup enhanced with weeds and nettles and surprises like mice or insects. Two or three times a week the bread was daubed with a smear of margarine or sugar beet jam; once or twice a week a thin slice of derelict sausage was handed round— nobody bothered to chalk the day's special on a blackboard like a Viennese café on the *Strauchgasse*, that was for sure.

Food haunted us. Not just recollecting ordinary table fare or while dreaming of banquets—though of course it permeated those atmospheres—but during every waking moment. Starvation turned us into ravening animals—just like wealthy, cynical John Slake says in that old primary school story, "Elementals" by Stephen Vincent Benet. Love almost never triumphed. People would—and did—snarl, fight, and *kill* for a crust of trampled mud-covered bread or a rotting potato hidden in a latrine bucket. So "Canada" created a huge, thriving black market—not just for the food smuggled out, but for everything, *anything*. Since all this "bounty" was supposed to go to the Reich, technically the SS posted to "Canada" were stealing, which meant that on a very small scale they overlooked what inmates pilfered, or they made deals with their favorites that went more or less like this: "You find me five high quality diamonds or twenty-five natural pearls, I'll pretend that the wool coat (with its pockets stuffed with who knows what) is yours and it didn't arrive by transport because you've been wearing it since you left Minsk." There were endless permutations of these deals and bargains because everything had a price: a pitcher of water, a bottle of iodine, a neck scarf, a pair of socks, a can of sardines, a slice of fatty, tinned sauerbraten, a cigarette—*a puff on a cigarette*. Stealing from the Reich was called "organization" by the prisoners—no one considered it a moral lapse because it was all stolen from us—from the displaced, brutalized deportees—to begin with anyway. More importantly— to use Nazi doublespeak—this re-allocation of goods saved lives: the camera that became rayon underwear that became aspirin that became half a foil-wrapped *marzipanstollen*—the traditional cake embedded with dried fruit and dusted with powdered sugar—saved lives. It really did.

"'Canada,'" I told Miss Johansson, who'd left off scribbling down clerical notes some time before, "gave the inmates a tiny—no, *infinitesimal* chance. What could we have bartered otherwise? Dirty, vermin-infested striped smocks? Broken heel-less boots?" I shook my head. "The plunder from 'Canada' meant you might have your morale lifted to the point where you could have a ragged form of hope—maybe for one whole day you didn't think about running into the wires of the electric fence or volunteering for the gas chamber." I caught her glance, and she looked away, but she kept listening. "A pair of moth-eaten gloves might mean your hands—after working ten hours in sub-freezing temperatures to dig grave trenches while the *kapos* and the guards whipped, beat, or shot 'slowpokes'—were saved from frostbite that led to infection that led to amputation—generally without anesthesia. ... So, yes, 'Canada' saved us from many a worse hell. It also bred the worst kind of corruption. In the hospital we had access—such as it was—to medical supplies and services so scant as to be near non-existent. It corrupted some of us," I said. "A tiny vial of gentian violet for fungus got you 500 gold marks—or, better still for an inmate who knew which guards could be bribed, a half-kilo of meat ... "

"Sneak it," Ludwicka whispered under her breath. We were in the supply room—a name that might have been a laughable irony a few weeks ago, when it mostly consisted of tottering empty shelves, a few bandages and a cracked beaker labeled "sterile water" to wash out the very worst wounds. Applied with a dropper, the water served to briefly scatter flies drawn to purulence and rot. But the infirmary had changed when Dr. Viktor Freisler—he who'd formerly been in charge of selections—was ordered by someone to conduct a few autopsies here and there. Someone (Himmler? Hoess? Mengele?) wanted to know the precise mechanism by which starvation and dysentery killed prisoners—maybe to speed the death process here and at the other camps. Freisler, perhaps remembering *real* hospital work before the war, and with a certain amount of ego and pride connected to his new duties, commandeered enough instruments and drugs so that the infirmary was now suddenly on a par with the kind of first-aid station you might have found at a resort or a beach in those liberal, carefree years before the war.

"Do you want him to kiss you or not?" Ludi said.

"Well—" I hesitated.

"It's nothing to me, Miss-Sweet-Sixteen-and-Never-Been-Kissed," she said with the loftiness I assumed came from the adulthood conferred by her eighteen years—most of which she'd spent in chic, pre-war Berlin.

My hand stole out toward the bottle marked "Morphine Tablets," my fingertips just about to graze the cool glass. "Isn't this collaborating?"

She shrugged. "It's what's in your heart that counts. Do you think *I* cared when my eaten up old aunts and uncles or spiteful cousins told me it was wrong to dance with Nazis in the supper clubs? Nazis. They're filthy," she made a spitting gesture. "But so what? You can hate them; I did! But a smile and a wink, and then I had pretty clothes and champagne instead of rags and piss-water."

There was something wrong with her logic, I knew, because after all, Ludi was here in Waldemar.

"Who is going to miss *two* lousy quarter-grain tablets of morphine?" Ludi said.

"They count them. My *mother* counts them—"

She flapped a hand. "So big deal. The head nurse counted wrong."

I was shaking my head.

She grabbed my shoulders: "Listen, don't be a fool—haven't you seen what she does?"

I must have looked blank for a moment because she cut in with: "To the new babies?" Her right hand gripped tighter. "To save the mothers!" Ludi meant to jar me out of my daze; instead, even then, I sank deeper.

"Am I the first to tell you this? I mean about the mothers and babies?" I tried to look into Stella Johansson's eyes, but my lids kept fluttering and finally I turned away. I was leaning over the makeshift desk, staring down at my fingers, playing nervously with, of all things, a hook-shaped bobby pin that must have fallen from her upswept hair.

Ludi wore her hair like that, I recalled. *In all that misery and filth, somehow—maybe by contrast—she managed to look glamorous. . . .*

"It's all right," Stella said. "Go ahead." But that didn't tell me whether she already knew.

"The mothers, you see . . . " I paused. "The Germans had a rule. When the babies were born—when the babies *lived,* the mothers had to die . . . "

She nodded. No hint again, but I went on anyway.

"I don't really understand why . . . I mean, was it supposed to be a punishment?" She said nothing. "At any rate, I found out that some of the nurses. . . . They were giving the babies morphine and saying they were stillborn. It was to save the mothers. . . . The Germans were expert at turning ordinary people into murderers. But it was to *save* the mothers—they were weak from childbirth and they were thrown into the ovens while they were still alive. Burned alive . . . unless their babies . . . " I stopped. That's what Ludi told me, but I didn't believe it—and certainly not about my mother (*a nurse! a healer!*)—not for a long time. I was too frightened to believe it . . . afraid the Nazis might kill the infirmary workers—the nurses—if they knew.

"Maybe it was wrong," I told Stella Johansson, "but you could eat better, dress better—*live* better—if you had a boyfriend. Or several. Ludi did at least . . . "

While the rest of us were raking out clumps of hair—whatever had grown back after they shaved our heads—when we combed with our fingers, hers looked . . . looked almost sleek. She pinned it up when she met one of her boyfriends. She had a red dress for dates, she had a *lipstick* . . .

"Max Factor Clear Red," Ludi said. "Just like Hollywood. Just like Rita Hayworth and Maureen O'Hara." She pouted her lips and the golden lipstick tube flashed. "Hold the mirror steady wouldja? And stop moving it; it's small enough already." We were in the supply room again and she positioned my wrist as I gripped the silvery metal handle of a tiny-mirrored dental instrument.

"I don't know why," I said aloud to Stella Johansson, "I didn't think about all those poor people, about how the Nazis yanked their teeth to extract the gold . . . millions of teeth . . . I tried never to look at the mountains of teeth, the heaped up tons of hair when I went past 'Canada.' It hurt to look at them. It hurt because you couldn't help thinking about the millions of people; it hurt because you were scared of losing hair, of losing teeth. Didn't we suffer enough? Did we have to be ugly, too?"

"You turn people into shambling scarecrows, they're not 'people' anymore," Stella said. "You wouldn't hesitate to hang or shoot a scarecrow or throw it in a ditch when you were done with it. It wouldn't bother you to burn a man-shape you no longer considered a man."

"Or a woman, or a child."

She nodded.

"Maybe it was wrong, but I wanted to keep my . . . my woman-shape. Maybe because I was fourteen and never had the chance to be a woman—because of the war, really. I never had a grown-up party dress or went to a dance—all the things in normal times I could have looked forward to in the next year or two . . . and Ludi—everyone really—they all thought I was sixteen, and then it was coming up to April 17th, my fifteenth birthday. Ludi—everyone—thought I'd be turning seventeen . . . "

"Everyone—except Kasia."

"Yes, everyone except my mother," I agreed.

"You're seventeen on the 17th," Ludi said. "That's really something special. And we're going to celebrate."

"What? How?" I kept thinking about how in general, those of us working in the hospital infirmary lived a little better, but still, I'd lost so much weight I had no breasts to speak of. For at least two or three years I'd looked forward to wearing a bra and now I was fifteen and had the nubbins you'd see on a ten-year old child. I'd had one period—my first—back in June, but like most women in the camp, my menses had dried up. My mother said they put something in the food—she didn't know what—and that was why the only pregnant women were the ones that had just arrived on the damn indefatigable trains. I don't know—maybe it was just from being starved—but even if I'd complained back then about the cramps and the low-grade headache, about the messy red napkins and the elastic sanitary belt, even though I griped like my girl cousins and school friends, I'd been secretly pleased when I got my period. Like being admitted to some exclusive club you longed—ached—to get into. But, that had been taken from me, too.

"Up 'til then, even though she said she had Doctor Viktor Freisler wrapped around her little finger, Ludi hadn't been able to convince me to 'organize' the supply room. Oh, I knew she was taking things here and there—bandages, ointments for trench foot—that kind of thing. But she was crafty and she didn't have to rely on stealing from just the infirmary. She had 'Canada,' too. You could buy off an *SS-Totenkopfverbände*—a young German guard—for a half-pint of *schnapps*, or a kiss . . .

"It was about a week before my birthday and Ludi said, 'You've been eating a little better and now that you look a little better, Gia'—she called me that, a nickname for Eligia and I'd never had any nickname before—'and Rudi'—Rudi was one of her swains, 'Rudi has a friend named Frederic, and he would like to spend a little time with you . . . '"

I knew who Frederic was. He had blond hair and green eyes, a grin like my father's. If he weren't German—if he were Polish—I'd have had a hopeless crush on him. Still, he was very good looking, and Ludi said he was nice.

"Take your time," Stella Johansson, said. She could see I was struggling to get this out; she didn't even glance at the thin bracelet watch on her wrist to check how long I'd been talking. She was very pretty; even the weak, intermittent late April sun brought out the golden highlights in her soft brown upswept hair. She was so much like Ludi, I thought maybe I could tell her everything. Tell her how, without meaning to, I betrayed my mother for a pair of red high-heeled shoes. *Red shoes . . .*

Red shoes . . . and a broken tooth.

Stella Johansson was so pretty, I thought she'd understand better—more clearly—if I explained about my father and Ruta and my mother. Surely, as a good-looking *grown-up* woman, she knew the significance—the importance—of physical appearance. "When my father disappeared, there was a postcard," I said.

"Yes," she said, nodding. "That was such a low trick the Nazis played. Giving those early prisoners postcards making them say all was well and that inmates could receive packages. The SS got more goods for the Reich, they got addresses of others who would, in turn, become prisoners. They falsely assured those not yet rounded up that things were not so bad in the camps. All lies . . . and more subterfuge . . . "

Stella was right about the postcards, but the one written in my father's hasty scribble also said "I have seen Ruta in the women's camp." I never understood why he'd tell my mother that he'd seen the woman he left her for in 1939. Maybe he mixed up the cards and meant to send that one to his brother or a close friend—maybe it was a Nazi prank after they'd beaten out of him the names of his colleagues, the details of his life.

All I knew was they'd been arguing for a year or more. He told my mother that she was sad and angry all the time. She was no fun, she'd let herself get unkempt, sloppy—*niechlujny!* he kept shouting at her in Polish. The other nurses at the hospital worked just as hard and they looked all right. Ruta worked with him in the operating room and *she* looked fine. Ruta liked laughing, liked a bit of fun. "The war is going to kill us all," he yelled. He was packing his suitcase. "And I mean to have a little joy, a little beauty! Before the Nazis kill us all, I'm going to have just *one* summer rose. *Tylko jeden zanim umrę!" Just* one *before I die!*

I was angry at her. If she'd just fix herself up, I said over and over, maybe my father would come back. Instead, two years later there was the postcard from Dachau: *I have seen Ruta!*

"I don't know what your situation was during the war," I said to the clerk, "but surely it's a human desire to look your best. A human right—a God-given right." I seemed to notice for the first time there was a tiny diamond ring winking on the third finger of her left hand. "My mother had her chance—but she said it was more important to live—*to work: therefore to live*—good looks would take care of themselves when there was time that belonged to us again."

"What happened, Eligia?"

She's so pretty, I thought. *Whatever she may have suffered during the war, she's attractive again. Desirable. She's engaged. Happy . . .*

But could I really tell her? Tell her that Ludi and I stole three quarter-grain morphine tablets to be exchanged in "Canada" for a certain pair of real Parisian red high-heeled shoes to be worn on a special date in three days' time? That the shoes were safely hidden and I was in a fever of excitement when I broke my tooth the morning of my birthday? Should I tell this kindly Red Cross clerk, whose life was apparently so tidy? Should I tell her . . .

We—Ludi and I—were in the supply room, my confidence was shattered. I had one of the dental mirrors and I was trying to smile so that the broken tooth—the little dog tooth on the lower left—wouldn't show. "Is it very bad? I'm so embarrassed. That lousy bread! If only I'd had a toothbrush or vitamin C tablets—it never would have happened!"

"You can get it fixed later, Gia—the war is almost over. I'm going to dress you up to the nines tonight—lipstick and everything!"

My head was swimming. *A real date. One of Ludi's dresses. High heels—from Paris!*

"Let's take two more of the tablets—you have one, give the other to Frederic—he'll think you're a movie star and you'll be feeling no pain—that's a guarantee!"

As I watched her, she shook out three tablets.

"But, you said *two—*"

There was a fierce rattling sound and the door was flung open.

Standing there, with the angriest look on her face I'd ever seen was my mother.

"What happened, Eligia?" Stella Johansson said again. "Why did we find you—like the female *kapos* and the SS guards who were forced by the Americans—carrying the dead and flinging them into the mass graves?"

It was a punishment detail, I knew—the guards were made to understand what they'd done all during the war and then just before liberation. Running away, leaving thousands to starve, leaving the dead unburied . . . the Americans rounded them up and brought them back.

"What happened? Do you remember?"

But I could not tell her that I stayed mute when Ludi turned my mother in, told the doctor my mother *(a nurse! a healer!)* had been saving other mothers by stilling the lives of their newborn babies. I could not tell her that just two days before the camp was liberated, I saw my mother's face there among the heaps of bodies no one had cleared from the gas chambers . . . .The frenzied attempt by the Nazis to disguise the horrors of what they'd done all those long years. A final solution. I could not tell her that I knew the war was essentially over, that we'd be free soon, but that I kept quiet to wear red heels and lipstick for my birthday date with the young German who would soon no longer be my enemy. I could not tell her that. I could not tell her I was afraid I'd be beaten—or worse—for speaking up. I could not tell her, that I'd realized—too late—that atonement never makes up for the guilt we suffer, for the sins we have committed. I couldn't tell her that nothing is ever enough to make up for the sin of silence, but we have to try.

Pretty as she was, I didn't think she'd understand—*really* understand—what I felt when I looked at the mounds of thousands of the dead, lifted their sagging bodies, inhaled the terrible stench from the pits . . . those beaten, starved, shot, and gassed human scarecrows. She'd never understand, because I didn't understand it myself. I saw my mother's face, head turned, her mouth in a rictus, her body lying on its side near the gas chamber door. Her work was done.

"Why Eligia?" she asked again. Above us, the sun disappeared behind sudden clouds.

"I helped bury the dead . . . because . . . it was the human thing to do," I said, "and I know that from my nurses training, from my work in the hospital."

Arbeit Macht Frei.

Work can set you free.

The Problem of Susan

NEIL GAIMAN

She has the dream again that night.

In the dream, she is standing, with her brothers and her sister, on the edge of the battlefield. It is summer, and the grass is a peculiarly vivid shade of green: a wholesome green, like a cricket pitch or the welcoming slope of the South Downs as you make your way north from the coast. There are bodies on the grass. None of the bodies are human; she can see a centaur, its throat slit, on the grass near her. The horse half of it is a vivid chestnut. Its human skin is nut-brown from the sun. She finds herself staring at the horse's penis, wondering about centaurs mating, imagines being kissed by that bearded face. Her eyes flick to the cut throat, and the sticky red-black pool that surrounds it, and she shivers.

Flies buzz about the corpses.

The wildflowers tangle in the grass. They bloomed yesterday for the first time in . . . how long? A hundred years? A thousand? A hundred thousand? She does not know.

All this was snow, she thinks, as she looks at the battlefield.

Yesterday, all this was snow. Always winter, and never Christmas.

Her sister tugs her hand, and points. On the brow of the green hill they stand, deep in conversation. The lion is golden, his arms folded behind his back. The witch is dressed all in white. Right now she is shouting at the lion, who is simply listening. The children cannot make out any of their words, not her cold anger, nor the lion's thrum-deep replies. The witch's hair is black and shiny, her lips are red.

In her dream she notices these things.

They will finish their conversation soon, the lion and the witch . . .

There are things about herself that the professor despises. Her smell, for example. She smells like her grandmother smelled, like old women smell, and for this she cannot forgive herself, so on waking she bathes in scented water and, naked and towel-dried, dabs several drops of Chanel toilet water beneath her arms and on her neck. It is, she believes, her sole extravagance.

Today she dresses in her dark brown dress suit. She thinks of these as her interview clothes, as opposed to her lecture clothes or her knocking-about-the-house clothes. Now she is in retirement, she wears her knocking-about-the-house clothes more and more. She puts on lipstick.

After breakfast, she washes a milk bottle, places it at her back door. She discovers that the next-door's cat has deposited a mouse head and a paw, on the doormat. It looks as though the mouse is swimming through the coconut matting, as though most of it is submerged. She purses her lips, then she folds her copy of yesterday's *Daily Telegraph*, and she folds and flips the mouse head and the paw into the newspaper, never touching them with her hands.

Today's *Daily Telegraph* is waiting for her in the hall, along with several letters, which she inspects, without opening any of them, then places on the desk in her tiny study. Since her retirement she visits her study only to write. Now she walks into the kitchen and seats herself at the old oak table. Her reading glasses hang about her neck on a silver chain, and she perches them on her nose and begins with the obituaries.

She does not actually expect to encounter anyone she knows there, but the world is small, and she observes that, perhaps with cruel humor, the obituarists have run a photograph of Peter Burrell-Gunn as he was in the early 1950s, and not at all as he was the last time the professor had seen him, at a *Literary Monthly* Christmas party several years before, all gouty and beaky and trembling, and reminding her of nothing so much as a caricature of an owl. In the photograph, he is very beautiful. He looks wild, and noble.

She had spent an evening once kissing him in a summer house: she remembers that very clearly, although she cannot remember for the life of her in which garden the summer house had belonged.

It was, she decides, Charles and Nadia Reid's house in the country. Which meant that it was before Nadia ran away with that Scottish artist, and Charles took the professor with him to Spain, although she was certainly not a professor then. This was many years before people commonly went to Spain for their holidays; it was an exotic and dangerous place in those days. He asked her to marry him, too, and she is no longer certain why she said no, or even if she had entirely said no. He was a pleasant-enough young man, and he took what was left of her virginity on a blanket on a Spanish beach, on a warm spring night. She was twenty years old, and had thought herself so old . . .

The doorbell chimes, and she puts down the paper, and makes her way to the front door, and opens it.

Her first thought is how young the girl looks.

Her first thought is how old the woman looks. "Professor Hastings?" she says. "I'm Greta Campion. I'm doing the profile on you. For the *Literary Chronicle*."

The older woman stares at her for a moment, vulnerable and ancient, then she smiles. It's a friendly smile, and Greta warms to her.

"Come in, dear," says the professor. "We'll be in the sitting room."

"I brought you this," says Greta. "I baked it myself." She takes the cake tin from her bag, hoping its contents hadn't disintegrated en route. "It's a chocolate cake. I read on-line that you liked them."

The old woman nods and blinks. "I do," she says. "How kind. This way."

Greta follows her into a comfortable room, is shown to her armchair, and told, firmly, not to move. The professor bustles off and returns with a tray, on which are teacups and saucers, a teapot, a plate of chocolate biscuits, and Greta's chocolate cake.

Tea is poured, and Greta exclaims over the professor's brooch, and then she pulls out her notebook and pen, and a copy of the professor's last book, *A Quest for Meanings in Children's Fiction*, the copy bristling with Post-it notes and scraps of paper. They talk about the early chapters, in which the hypothesis is set forth that there was originally no distinct branch of fiction that was only intended for children, until the Victorian notions of the purity and sanctity of childhood demanded that fiction for children be made . . .

"Well, pure," says the professor.

"And sanctified?" asks Greta, with a smile.

"And sanctimonious," corrects the old woman. "It is difficult to read *The Water Babies* without wincing."

And then she talks about ways that artists used to draw children—as adults, only smaller, without considering the child's proportions—and how the Grimms' stories were collected for adults and, when the Grimms realized the books were being read in the nursery, were bowdlerized to make them more appropriate. She talks of Perrault's "Sleeping Beauty in the Wood," and of its original coda in which the Prince's cannibal ogre mother attempts to frame the Sleeping Beauty for having eaten her own children, and all the while Greta nods and takes notes, and nervously tries to contribute enough to the conversation that the professor will feel that it is a conversation or at least an interview, not a lecture.

"Where," asks Greta, "do you feel *your* interest in children's fiction came from?"

The professor shakes her head. "Where do any of our interests come from? Where does your interest in children's books come from?"

Greta says, "They always seemed the books that were most important to me. The ones that mattered.

When I was a kid, and when I grew. I was like Dahl's *Matilda*. . . . Were your family great readers?"

"Not really. . . . I say that, it was a long time ago that they died. Were killed. I should say."

"All your family died at the same time? Was this in the war?"

"No, dear. We were evacuees, in the war. This was in a train crash, several years after. I was not there."

"Just like in Lewis's *Narnia* books," says Greta, and immediately feels like a fool, and an insensitive fool. "I'm sorry. That was a terrible thing to say, wasn't it?"

"Was it, dear?"

Greta can feel herself blushing, and she says, "It's just I remember that sequence so vividly. In *The Last Battle*. Where you learn there was a train crash on the way back to school, and everyone was killed. Except for Susan, of course."

The professor says, "More tea, dear?" and Greta knows that she should leave the subject, but she says, "You know, that used to make me so angry."

"What did, dear?"

"Susan. All the other kids go off to Paradise, and Susan can't go. She's no longer a friend of Narnia because she's too fond of lipsticks and nylons and invitations to parties. I even talked to my English teacher about it, about the problem of Susan, when I was twelve."

She'll leave the subject now, talk about the role of children's fiction in creating the belief systems we adopt as adults, but the professor says, "And tell me, dear, what did your teacher say?"

"She said that even though Susan had refused

Paradise then, she still had time while she lived to repent."

"Repent *what*?"

"Not believing, I suppose. And the sin of Eve."

The professor cuts herself a slice of chocolate cake. She seems to be remembering. And then she says, "I doubt there was much opportunity for nylons and lipsticks after her family was killed. There certainly wasn't for me. A little money—less than one might imagine—from her parents' estate, to lodge and feed her. No luxuries . . . "

"There must have been something else wrong with Susan," says the young journalist, "something they didn't tell us. Otherwise she wouldn't have been damned like that—denied the Heaven of further up and further in. I mean, all the people she had ever cared for had gone on to their reward, in a world of magic and waterfalls and joy. And she was left behind."

"I don't know about the girl in the books," says the professor, "but remaining behind would also have meant that she was available to identify her brothers' and her little sister's bodies. There were a lot of people dead in that crash. I was taken to a nearby school—it was the first day of term, and they had taken the bodies there. My older brother looked okay. Like he was asleep. The other two were a bit messier."

"I suppose Susan would have seen their bodies, and thought, they're on holidays now. The perfect school holidays. Romping in meadows with talking animals, world without end."

"She might have done. I only remember thinking what a great deal of damage a train can do, when it hits another train, to the people who were traveling inside. I suppose you've never had to identify a body, dear?"

"No."

"That's a blessing. I remember looking at them and thinking, *What if I'm wrong, what if it's not him after all?* My younger brother was decapitated, you know. A god who would punish me for liking nylons and parties by making me walk through that school dining room, with the flies, to identify Ed, well . . . he's enjoying himself a bit too much, isn't he? Like a cat, getting the last ounce of enjoyment out of a mouse. Or a gram of enjoyment, I suppose it must be these days. I don't know, really."

She trails off. And then, after some time, she says, "I'm sorry dear. I don't think I can do any more of this today. Perhaps if your editor gives me a ring, we can set a time to finish our conversation."

Greta nods and says of course, and knows in her heart, with a peculiar finality, that they will talk no more.

That night, the professor climbs the stairs of her house, slowly, painstakingly, floor by floor. She takes sheets and blankets from the airing cupboard, and makes up a bed in the spare bedroom, at the back. It is empty but for a wartime austerity dressing table, with a mirror and drawers, an oak bed, and a dusty applewood wardrobe, which contains only coat hangers and a cardboard box. She places a vase on the dressing table, containing purple rhododendron flowers, sticky and vulgar.

She takes from the box in the wardrobe a plastic shopping bag containing four old photographic albums. Then she climbs into the bed that was hers as a child, and lies there between the sheets, looking at the black-and-white photographs, and the sepia photographs, and the handful of unconvincing color photographs. She looks at her brothers, and her sister, and her parents, and she wonders how they could have been that young, how anybody could have been that young.

After a while she notices that there are several children's books beside the bed, which puzzles her slightly, because she does not believe she keeps books on the bedside table in that room. Nor, she decides, does she usually have a bedside table there. On the top of the pile is an old paperback book—it must be more than forty years old: the price on the cover is in shillings. It shows a lion, and two girls twining a daisy chain into its mane.

The professor's lips prickle with shock. And only then does she understand that she is dreaming, for she does not keep those books in the house. Beneath the paperback is a hardback, in its jacket, of a book that, in her dream, she has always wanted to read: *Mary Poppins Brings in the Dawn*, which P. L. Travers had never written while alive.

She picks it up and opens it to the middle, and reads the story waiting for her: Jane and Michael follow Mary Poppins on her day off, to Heaven, and they meet the boy Jesus, who is still slightly scared of Mary Poppins because she was once his nanny, and the Holy Ghost, who complains that he has not been able to get his sheet properly white since Mary Poppins left, and God the Father, who says, "There's no making her do anything. Not her. *She's* Mary Poppins."

"But you're God," said Jane. "You created everybody and everything. They have to do what you say."

"Not her," said God the Father once again, and he scratched his golden beard flecked with white. "I didn't create her. She's Mary Poppins."

And the professor stirs in her sleep, and afterward dreams that she is reading her own obituary. It has been a good life, she thinks, as she reads it, discovering her history laid out in black and white. Everyone is there. Even the people she had forgotten.

Greta sleeps beside her boyfriend, in a small flat in Camden, and she, too, is dreaming.

In the dream, the lion and the witch come down the hill together. She is standing on the battlefield, holding her sister's hand. She looks up at the golden lion, and the burning amber of his eyes. "He's not a tame lion, is he?" she whispers to her sister, and they shiver.

The witch looks at them all, then she turns to the lion, and says, coldly, "I am satisfied with the terms of our agreement. You take the girls: for myself, I shall have the boys."

She understands what must have happened, and she runs, but the beast is upon her before she has covered a dozen paces. The lion eats all of her except her head, in her dream. He leaves the head, and one of her hands, just as a housecat leaves the parts of a mouse it has no desire for, for later, or as a gift.

She wishes that he had eaten her head, then she would not have had to look. Dead eyelids cannot be closed, and she stares, unflinching, at the twisted thing her brothers have become. The great beast eats her little sister more slowly, and, it seems to her, with more relish and pleasure than it had eaten her; but then, her little sister had always been its favorite.

The witch removes her white robes, revealing a body no less white, with high, small breasts, and nipples so dark they are almost black. The witch lies back upon the grass, spreads her legs. Beneath her body, the grass becomes rimed with frost.

"Now," she says.

The lion licks her white cleft with its pink tongue, until she can take no more of it, and she pulls its huge mouth to hers, and wraps her icy legs into its golden fur. . . .

Being dead, the eyes in the head on the grass cannot look away.

Being dead, they miss nothing.

And when the two of them are done, sweaty and sticky and sated, only then does the lion amble over to the head on the grass and devour it in its huge mouth, crunching her skull in its powerful jaws, and it is then, only then, that she wakes.

Her heart is pounding. She tries to wake her boyfriend, but he snores and grunts and will not be roused.

It's true, Greta thinks, irrationally, in the darkness. *She grew up. She carried on. She didn't die.*

She imagines the professor, waking in the night and listening to the noises coming from the old applewood wardrobe in the corner: to the rustlings of all these gliding ghosts, which might be mistaken for the scurries of mice or rats, to the padding of enormous velvet paws, and the distant, dangerous music of a hunting horn.

She knows she is being ridiculous, although she will not be surprised when she reads of the professor's demise. *Death comes in the night,* she thinks, before she returns to sleep. *Like a lion.*

The white witch rides naked on the lion's golden back. Its muzzle is spotted with fresh, scarlet blood. Then the vast pinkness of its tongue wipes around its face, and once more it is perfectly clean.

Dominion

CHRISTOPHER COAKE

Friday night they all camped by the lake, as planned, and then what happened with Mason happened, and the next day, Saturday, while the others hiked up a nearby ridge, Hannah lay alone in her tent, trying to think of a way out. She came up with nothing. Would anyone even believe her, if she told? Kyle was Mason's older brother, and Beth was engaged to Kyle, and constantly stoned. Hannah was in the middle of the Nevada desert, a hundred miles from Reno, and her cell phone didn't get coverage, and instead of figuring out any kind of plan, she kept falling back into telling herself how stupid she was, how she'd made all the dumb choices she'd spent her life trying not to make, and now what could she even do?

When the others came back from their hike, she rose, reluctantly, to meet them. Mason grabbed her around the waist and kissed her cheek, smelling of sweat and dust. Maybe Beth saw the dismay on her face.

Not feeling any better? Beth asked. Hannah had told them she was hung over.

Say it, say it, Hannah told herself. But instead her mouth opened and out came, I guess.

Kyle grinned. I told you to go easy on the booze, but did you listen?

She said nothing, and so she watched, sick at heart, as they went ahead with their plans. They packed their tents into the Jeep, and Kyle drove them down from the lake, then farther into the desert, toward the abandoned town, where they were going to explore and camp a second night, where Hannah would be even more alone.

In the back seat, Hannah curled around her backpack and pretended to sleep, her face to the window. Mason sat beside her, and she swore she could feel it every time his eyes landed on her, like fingers touching her, hands pressing her down.

She was younger than the others: seventeen, though she'd been told she looked—acted—older. Mason was nineteen; Kyle and Beth were twenty-five. The three of them worked together at a restaurant downtown, but Hannah figured they made a lot more money moving drugs; they certainly never lacked for good weed, or molly. She'd been proud of herself for figuring it out. (She was smart—people told her that, too.) When Mason had invited her camping with them for the weekend, she'd been even prouder, had felt a fierce and soaring freedom as they hurtled east out of Reno, hip-hop they let her choose playing on the Jeep's stereo, Mason's hand on her thigh. This, she had thought, was how she wanted her life to be.

She'd met Mason three weeks before. He had come up to her at a house party, walking past girls who were older and prettier. He was beautiful: full-sleeve tats and laughing eyes; a beard thick enough to twine her fingers into. He knew how to dance. His presence seemed to make her high.

When her mother met him, she said, That boy's bad news.

But her mother hung out with bikers, and was sometimes gone for days at a time; her life was a mess, her judgment worse. Hannah had sworn to do better. She got okay grades; she liked to party, sure, but she was—had always been—careful with boys. Her girlfriends made fun of her for being a virgin, but, god—Hannah knew better than any of them that if you weren't careful, you'd end up living in a shitty apartment in a shitty Reno neighborhood, with a teenager of your own, dealing blackjack, your life never again your own. Hannah was going to graduate high school; she was going to go to Portland State, study design.

Last weekend, she and Mason had fooled around a little on her bed. When she'd told him she wanted to take things slow, he'd laughed and said, Really?

Really, she said, re-buttoning her blouse.

An old-fashioned girl, huh?

She didn't tell him about her virginity; she didn't like people, let alone boys, knowing she was afraid of anything. She pushed him back on the bed and gave him a hand job—she knew how—and that seemed to make him happy.

After kissing her goodnight, though, he said, I'm not a very old-fashioned guy, you know?

I know, she said. She kissed him again, made up her mind, and said, Soon.

The abandoned town was named Dominion, and was a long way from anywhere inhabited—they'd driven for eighty miles on two-lane blacktop without seeing any life but a couple of distant ranches, and big rigs headed north to Idaho. The town wasn't even marked by a sign. Kyle simply turned off the highway onto a rutted dirt road that curved slowly away to the east, around the base of a craggy mountain. Dominion was two miles farther along, a small clump of structures and trees circled by a high chain-link fence and bullet-pocked NO TRESPASSING signs. Kyle parked in front of the fence's gates and turned off the engine. To the west were the mountain's abrupt gray cliffs; to the east was a vast, bone-white playa, followed by another swell of mountains, all of it as empty of people as an ocean.

Hannah knew about the town—a few Reno kids every year came out here to get drunk or stoned and scare themselves, or camp overnight, or both. It was a thing to do, and now they were doing it too.

It's spooky, but it's cool, Mason had told Hannah, when he'd invited her along. He and Kyle had been there before. You can find all kinds of weird stuff out there in the houses.

He told her the town had been built by a mining company in the 1950s, after they'd discovered a gold seam, a big one, under the mountain. The mine hired a few dozen men from Reno to work the vein, and built a suburb for them, with its own school and churches and store and golf course, so the men could bring along their families.

Then in the 70s the gold had dried up, and just like

that the town was dead, the residents moved out. The company cared enough about the property to erect a fence around the entire town, and the mineworks another mile away, but not enough to guard it. A liability thing, Mason had told her, in case some idiot dies out there. Every once in a while a highway patrolman might drive by and report damage to the fence, but that was about it.

Hannah climbed now out of the ticking Jeep, looking at the decay on the other side of the fence, hearing—behind the noise of Kyle and Mason unloading—the deeper silence of the desert, the uncanny absence of motors and electricity.

People had died in Dominion, Mason had said. A couple of kids who OD'd on something; and a lone hiker, who'd fallen while exploring a house and had broken his back.

Sounds like a blast, she'd said.

Hey, he said. Don't worry. I'll protect you. You'll have a good time.

But he'd lied.

They'd spent all day yesterday at a little mountain lake a couple of mountain ranges southeast of Reno, swimming first and then setting up tents for the night. They'd all gotten drunk and stoned around their fire pit, and then they'd gone to bed.

In their tent, she'd made out with Mason, laughing and tickling at first, then on to more serious stuff. One of the ways she ached, now, was remembering that she'd been ready, for a little while there, to go all the way. She'd gone to bed intending it.

If she had, would she have ever found out what Mason was really like?

While kissing her he'd said, Shh, and laughed against her neck, and Hannah heard it too: soft moaning, coming from the other tent. Beth's voice, thrilled and tender.

She heard more than moans, and she realized: they'd be able to hear *her*, too.

She told Mason, I can't, not here, and he'd laughed, as though she was joking. She pushed his hand away.

Christ, he'd said, seriously?

He was sulky after that. Her head swam with drink; she curled up alone and tried to sleep, and Mason left the tent; later she heard him talking with Kyle, the two of them popping beers and flicking lighters; their laughter sounded cruel, and she imagined Mason telling Kyle how skittish she was, how young, how *old-fashioned*.

Even so, she went to sleep.

Then Mason was back in the tent, and he was kissing her, hard, his mouth tasting of beer and something else metallic and awful, and she kissed him back, but then he had his hands under her t-shirt. He was panting through his nose, a heavy shadow above her. Then he was pulling off her shorts. She yelped, suddenly terrified, but he pressed his mouth down on hers and spread her legs with his knees.

Shh, he said, during, a hand over her mouth. It's okay.

Afterwards, he said, God*damn*, and kissed her cheek. Thank you.

Soon he was asleep, snoring, and she lay aching beside him, pinned beneath his big arm, too hurt and terrified to move, even to wipe herself off.

Dominion

In the morning, when he'd gone hiking with the others, and she was alone, she'd waded into the lake—it was the closest she could get to a shower. Shivering in the silvery water, she'd found bruises on her wrists, each one the size of his fingertips.

Kyle and Mason cut a flap of the fence open with bolt cutters—they were suspiciously good at it—and shuttled their things inside the town. Soon they'd set up camp behind Dominion's old, dark, boarded-up church, not far from the gates, near a fire pit some past visitors had made out of old sheet metal. Mason filled it with branches and boards they pulled off the walls of the church; the fire was now catching, rising and flickering. The sun had dropped behind the mountain, and the playa outside the fence was golden, deepening into mauve. On the other side of the fence, up on the mountainside, a coyote let out its liquid, gulping cry, and was answered.

They were in what had once been the downtown. Next to their church was a small, boxy brick school building that still had the word *Dominion* painted in yellow above its entrance. *Home of the Nuggets!* Across the street from the school was an old store with a gas pump. Every building had its doors and windows boarded shut, though here and there boards had fallen, or been pried away, leaving dark holes.

Past the school, to the north, the old neighborhoods began, dozens of sagging, shuttered bungalows clustered around culs-de-sac; that was where Kyle and Mason wanted to explore, later.

In the meantime, Hannah sat cross-legged on an

old door, just outside the tent. She didn't want to go exploring, but she didn't want to be left alone, either. Or, later, to be alone in the tent with Mason. Unless she told them she was sleeping in the Jeep, or in one of the houses, that was her fate.

Beth had given her a headlamp on an elastic band; she put it on, but kept the light off and watched the fire.

Mason dropped down beside her; she froze.

He said, Dude, please tell me what's wrong. You've been weird all day.

Like she should confide in him, like she had a problem they could just talk through.

Beth and Kyle were standing close together in the tall grass beside the school, smoking and laughing, too far away to hear.

I just can't believe you did that, she said.

He kicked at the dirt with his Tevas. Did what?

She was stunned.

He laughed, but it was a fake laugh, an acting-laugh. He reached for her hand.

Are you talking about last *night?*

What do you think I'm talking about?

What—didn't you like it?

She pushed away, stood, walked quickly through the grass, toward Kyle and Beth. The fire behind her threw her shadow across the schoolhouse's faded, dusty bricks.

Hey, kiddo, Kyle said.

She was angry, now. She'd never been so angry before in her life.

Beth studied her face, then held out the joint she'd been smoking. You want a hit?

Mason had followed her; he joined them, his face shadowed by the fire. Hannah took the joint and turned her back to him, then pulled the smoke in deep. Maybe, at least, her hands would stop shaking.

Easy there, Kyle said. Special blend. It's laced with some extras.

What extras? she said.

Kyle laughed. Not sure, exactly. Got it from a chemist at Burning Man, said it was proprietary. You're gonna feel real good, I can tell you that much.

Hannah looked at the joint, then at Beth, who smiled, kindly; she was already stoned. So was Kyle. They were no help. Nobody was going to be any help.

God. She took another hit, and then another, thinking about the way her mother put back beers, and Beth laughed.

When Hannah turned around Mason had returned to the fire, his shoulders tight, his hands in his pockets. He seemed hurt.

Good, she thought. She exhaled smoke.

II.

Imagine what it would be like to live here, Kyle said, later, the first joint gone, and a second one too. They were all sitting around the fire, wearing their headlamps in the darkness; Kyle and Beth had been talking about exploring, filling the silence left by Hannah and Mason, but no one had stood.

God, Beth said, looking at the school, I think I'd kill myself.

Hannah said nothing. Her brain was light, cottony. When she moved her head the buildings and the old light poles and Kyle and Beth and Mason—sitting by himself, sullenly, on the other side of the fire—all stretched and smeared. Kyle hadn't lied about whatever was in that joint.

She thought about telling Beth, I know exactly what it's like to live here.

It would be a nightmare, she could say. Wouldn't it? To have nowhere to go and no one new to meet, and nothing to see but the endless desert and the stars in the sky. And the people you were stuck with. The people you'd chosen to follow out here.

You'd be trapped, she could say. Stuck, like the woman watching them from the street, the one in the sundress, pushing the stroller.

Hannah stood.

She's so sad, she said, her tongue thick, and their headlamps swung to her.

Who's sad? Beth asked.

There were several others, now. They wore long dresses and high-heeled pumps and sunhats, and they stood in bunches outside the school, and on the steps of the church, and they were walking in and out of the store holding bags, striding away down the road toward the houses, holding the hands of small children, or walking beside the men.

Beth said, hurt, God, hers kicked in *fast*, I barely feel anything.

She's pretty tiny, Kyle said, and Hannah wanted to tell him, No I'm not, I'm five foot eight in heels, I'm nearly as tall as Nick—

She flushed; her forearms and cheeks and the small of her back prickled with sweat.

Mason said, Who the fuck is Nick?

Kyle—his voice odd, full of wonder—said Oh my *god*. Over the church.

Hannah heard them first: several pops, like gunshots, and then a crackle and sizzle—and then streams of light and smoke coming down from the sky overhead, and the boy in the stroller in front of her laughed and clapped and laughed. She might have too, except for the hand at the small of her back. *His* hand.

Dude, he said, what's wrong with you?

Wow, Beth said. *Wow*. What's happening here?

Hannah walked past the church, onto the street, away from Mason. Down the road, between the branches of the trees that separated one cul-de-sac from the next, Hannah saw flickering lights, golden, like flames.

The woman was walking along the sidewalk, away from her, toward the flames, pushing a stroller.

Hannah followed.

Then she was on the old residential streets, lined by black, grasping trees; the asphalt was shattered, sometimes upheaved into jags, elsewhere collapsed into pits and craters caked with dried mud. Her feet were numb; she had to be careful. Her whole body felt jerky, malfunctioning, like a puppet's.

Where are you going? Mason called, behind her.

Behind them, a pop, a sizzle. The asphalt glowed a dark red, then a shuddery blue. Her shadow stretched out, wheeled, as the fireworks soared and then dropped.

The woman was walking in stride with her now along the sidewalk, in sudden, warm sunshine, smiling oddly, curiously at her; she was wearing a blue dress with a wide skirt and white flat shoes. She was Hannah's age, or not much older—so young, and so beautiful; Hannah liked the way her dark hair curled around her ears, liked her broad hat and the smile on her face, which was soft, trusting, and Hannah felt the urge to tell her, Don't trust anyone, before it's too late, and before she could say this the woman stopped, and her face changed.

Jesus, Hannah, Mason said. He grabbed her wrist, the one he'd bruised. He was breathing hard.

I saw a woman.

No you didn't—

But then he sounded doubtful.

A shape flew low overhead, big and heavy, and settled on a nearby branch. It let out a soft hoo.

The night was dark again, and colorful. Hannah turned to look behind them, and the fireworks were stuck in the sky, tendrils of light and smoke dropping in permanent, sparkling ropes behind the spire of the church. She heard laughter, applause. She heard a harsh, flat pop. Then another.

She smelled smoke, drifting low and insidious between the tree trunks.

Behind them, Beth let out a whoop, and Kyle laughed. This is *amazing!*

We shouldn't be alone back here, Mason said.

Why? she asked him. She felt light, serene. What are you afraid of?

God! I'm not afraid of—

The woman was up ahead, crossing the street; she was pushing her stroller.

She pulled away from Nick's grasp, and ran to

catch up, even though this would make Nick angry, but what could she do? Everything made Nick angry. She heard him behind her, his heavy footfalls, a curse as he stumbled in the dark.

Then she was in the center of a cul-de-sac, ringed by four squat two-story bungalows. The woman was standing on the walk in front of the rightmost house, in dappled sunshine. She was wearing a different dress, white with yellow flowers and a big bell of a skirt, and next to her was Mason—no, not Mason; the man's cheeks and eyes and beard were like Mason's, but he had blond hair. He was wearing jeans and boots and a flannel shirt and his arm was around the woman's shoulders. She was pregnant, Hannah saw, her stomach a taut ball. In the woman's eyes were the reflections of fireworks, and then it was night again and lights were on through the windows of the house and the woman was standing in the doorway, looking out, at Hannah.

She retreated inside, but the door hung open behind her.

Hannah, Mason called, come back here.

Hannah forced her legs to move toward the woman's house.

Both their headlamps were pointed at it: the rightmost bungalow, its windows boarded, its siding dark—at first Hannah wondered, Why would someone paint their house black? But then she saw: the house had burned.

That couldn't be, though, because behind a picture window was a lit dining room, and the woman too—she was setting down a plate of food, smiling, in front of the blond man, but something was wrong with him, in the hunch of his shoulders, the muscles working in his jaw. Quick as a snake he caught hold of the woman's wrist, and her eyes touched Hannah's through the glass.

Somewhere behind them Kyle hooted, and then Mason's arm was rough and muscled around her waist. Jesus, you're fucked up, he said. The owl settled on a tree branch in front of the woman's house, its eyes tracking them, yellow and translucent, like hard lemon candies.

Mason turned her, held her cheeks in between his hands. *Hannah*, he said.

He'd done this last night, too, after, when she'd been crying, not wanting to look him in the eyes. He'd held her head like this and kissed her.

Her body broke free from his grip and she ran toward the open door of the house, and the woman she could see inside of it, drifting back from the doorway, beautiful and kind and terrified, inviting her in.

The ruined door pushed gently open at her touch, and with it came sunlight; it threw her shadow ahead of her, swinging it across the room as if on a hinge.

What a lovely house! Directly ahead, narrow stairs climbed into shadow. The living room, just to her left, was already furnished. Nick had shipped out a couch and two matching armchairs and a coffee table; they were arranged neatly on the thick brown carpet. There was no television, but he'd warned her about that: he could afford one, sure, but this far out you couldn't get a signal. To her right was the dining room; in its center was a long table and six chairs with high backs. She would have friends, she would have people over, she would *entertain*.

She could live in a place like this. The dining room window looked out over the cheerful cul-de-sac, and while the trees the mine had planted were only saplings, now, they'd grow in, and before long they'd provide shade, and she wouldn't see the mountain on the horizon while cooking. This house would be like any house back in the city. And Nick was standing in the kitchen, smiling at her—but his eyes bore into her, gave her that feeling she could not put a word to, a fear and a pride and a quickening in her breath, and she went to him and he kissed her, he was grabbing at her dress, and then it was dark out and he was standing over her, and her cheek was burning, and Hannah was gasping in the cold, she'd tripped over the torn old linoleum of the kitchen floor, and her head swum and her nostrils stung with mold and soot and her breath clouded in the beam of her headlamp and outside Mason called, Hannah, what the fuck are you *doing*?

The woman stood on the other side of the kitchen, smiling down. She was holding a can of gasoline.

Then she drifted away, into the hallway behind her.

Hannah climbed to her feet. She crossed the kitchen. Where the woman had stood the air smelled of smoke, of the dry dust that blew up from the pages of old books.

Hannah! Mason called. He was angry, now, she could hear it; she remembered him in the tent, the fear and the pain, and her heart pounded.

She wanted to tell the woman, We can't let him in.

The woman was entering a dark doorway, halfway down the hall.

Hannah crept to the door and looked through it after her. In the beam of her headlamp was a four-poster bed. The woman lay beneath the man, her face tilted toward the door. He was naked; thrusting; the woman's legs were wrapped around his hips; Hannah couldn't watch them, it made her hurt to watch them, but she did. The woman wanted her to. The woman's cheeks were wet. The bed thumped against the wall. Her eyes, soft and deep, locked with Hannah's.

The fireworks popped like gunshots over the church. Upstairs, wings fluttered like flames, catching and spreading.

She heard Mason say, Who's there?

He said, Who are *you*?

The bed was empty, now, lit blue and cold by her headlamp. The sheets and comforter were pulled halfway down. The mattress was darkened along one side, stained wet and black in the shape of a crescent. Smoke was pooling around her ankles.

The woman was at her left, now, at the end of the hallway, where it joined the living room. Mason was in the house—the dining room, she thought. The woman had her hands on the shoulders of a young boy. His face was heartbreakingly pretty and pale and his hair was blond and he was crying—

Jesus Christ, Helen, Mason said. His voice odd. Deeper. Don't make me come find you.

The woman had gone. Hannah crossed the living room, her feet barely touching the floor, listening, keeping herself at all times on the opposite side of the house from Mason. Now she was near the front doorway again, at the foot of the stairs. The woman stood near the top, smiling down at her.

Dominion

Hannah lifted her feet, placed them, pushed down. The wooden steps had give to them; old nails groaned.

Mason said, Woman, I'm gonna stripe your ass, and Hannah didn't know what that meant, but she did. She climbed more quickly.

His footfalls—he must be in the kitchen—were heavy, narcotic, his words slurred and too loud. Hannah pulled closer to the woman with every step, even though the air, here, was buzzing and thick with dust. Hannah gagged. And then the woman was just above her, and Hannah could not, would not, look at her face; she did not want to know what the woman really looked like—because though the woman was kind and beautiful and smiling, another face lay beneath that one; she knew, deep down, that she could not bear to see it, because she knew that the house had burned—the woman had burned it, after—she knew how all this ended, and the woman needed her to, and smoke was in the air and she smelled—

In the back hallway Mason said, Fucking Christ, Helen, tell me why I married you if you're going to be like this. Each word sharp and full of hatred.

They were in the upstairs hallway, now. The hall was short; one door to the right, and one to the left. The woman stopped, stricken, in front of the closed right door. John was playing in there, and had angered him. John always angered him. Through the door she heard Nick shouting, she heard the boy's cries, heard her own name being called—

Then the woman was carrying the child in her arms, through the doorway to the left.

Helen! Mason bellowed, from down below, in the living room.

Hannah followed the woman and stood in the doorway. In her headlamp's beam was a small bed, and over the bed was a model biplane, or an owl, hanging from a thread, and behind it, in the sky, fireworks burst, and below on the bed was the boy, lying on his back atop the covers, and beside the bed knelt the woman, and Hannah joined her, gagging, and John's face was swollen and red, blood crusting his nose and lips, and the woman stroked his hair and kissed his forehead, remembering unbidden his tiny mouth at her breast—at once gentler and more forceful than Nick's mouth had ever been; she remembered pushing the boy through and out of her, she remembered the smell of his hair and the way his cries became a fishhook in her heart, moving her from place to place; she remembered taking him, every year, to see the fireworks; she thought that even now, like this, he looked more like his father than her, and how unjust that was, that he would have *this* father, this father who—

I'm gonna make you sorry you were born, Mason said, from the foot of the steps—

A man was bending over the bed; he was lifting a stethoscope from the boy's chest.

Then he was passing his hand over the boy's eyes, first one and then the other.

And Hannah knew, then: this was why you stayed forever, because after this, where could you ever go?

The sound that tore from Hannah's throat was both hers and not hers; the sound had substance, a beak and feathers, and it left her, hunting.

Dominion

She stepped from the room back into the hallway. He was thumping up the steps. Outside the fireworks boomed and sizzled and whined, and Hannah heard the people of the town clapping and cheering—the same women who'd brought her flowers and casseroles and held her hand in church, who told her, You have to endure, who told her, It'll be all right; but they didn't have to be with him, they didn't have to share a bed with him, even now, lying awake in the night thinking of the pistol he kept in the nightstand, waiting for him to fall asleep—

Not one of them wanted to see what was happening to her. What she had to endure.

She followed the woman down the hallway, as far as she could from the stairs. The woman pointed at the floor, and Hannah saw, then, the sagging, rotted floorboards in the center of the hall; she edged around them to the left, then stood with her back pressed against the charred wallpaper.

The fireworks sounded like gunshots, like her heart beating.

She could only see the light on his forehead as he reached the top of the steps. Just as he could see hers, at the end of the hall, blinding and obscuring.

His voice was clotted, at once angry and terrified.

Hannah? Is that you?

She thought of him in the tent, pressing her down.

It's me, she said. I'm here.

He walked to her, his footsteps heavy. The floorboards cracked and broke beneath him, and he dropped away into darkness as though yanked there by a hand.

She descended the stairs, her palm flat against the ashy wallpaper. She could barely breathe; her throat was coated with dust and smoke.

Outside Kyle and Beth were laughing, calling for them.

She was tempted to go to them right now, to tell them there'd been an accident. But she had to see. She owed him that.

She picked a path through the living room to the rear of the house. Her feet and hands tingled, as though waking. Her headlamp revealed the charred carpet, the scars in the burned beams and exposed bracing, the rot and muck. She entered the back hallway, went to the doorway of the room with the stained bed. But the bed was gone—there was only a jumble of wood and plaster in the center of the room, and on top of it was Mason, his limbs as broken as the boards beneath him. A cut across his forehead had slicked his face with blood. In his fear he looked younger than he was. A boy, not much older than her.

The woman was kneeling beside him.

Please, he said. Don't.

She was running from the house, now, toward Kyle's and Beth's voices; her footfalls and her body had weight again; what a relief it was to be herself again, to fill her lungs with air, and she told herself she must always remember it; the woman had given her this; it was a gift.

She'd given a gift in return, too. She must always remember that as well.

Dominion

Mason, his breath quickening; the laughter and fireworks in the distance; the woman bending close, her hair made of smoke.

Mason seeing her face, knowing her, truly knowing her, as she reached down and gently passed her hand over each of his eyes.

Water Thy Bones

MERCEDES M. YARDLEY

There's a loveliness to bones. Their shape. Their weight. Their strength and fragility.

A body uses them to run. Uses them to stand timidly against a wall. They hold a person upright, if they're working correctly. They're a framework for an entire system, a complete body, and the significance of that is very nearly overwhelming

Yet at the same time, bones are so exceptionally frail. They can be broken. Sawed through. Pulverized. Bleached. Painted. Kept. Valued. Destroyed.

Remembered.

Taken.

Oh, yes, they can be taken. While the victim still hangs on them, a skinsack of meat. Veins still connect, blood still carries oxygen back and forth like it's a precious thing, and at that point it still is.

That's when their beauty becomes something real. When bone is exposed to the air for the first time, and the marrow gasps as it breathes in deep. The rest of it, the tissue, gristle, and muscle is pulled away, and the skeleton is allowed to be free.

That's the part Michael Harrison liked the best.

Peeling away the stinking red refuse and letting the white parts glitter and shine through. It's the most awe-inspiring kind of birth, the most natural. Give all of us time and nature will do it for us. But sometimes nature needs a push.

Nikilie was a strong, beautiful thing. She suffered from pain that pressed behind her eyes like delphiniums, but she still got out of bed and moved around the world as living things do. Her tongue was red and her eyes the warmest of browns. Eyes you could fall into, dark skin smooth as butter. It invited the unwanted stares and hands of men and women everywhere she went. At least it used to, until she started taking razor blades and serrated knives to her body in the dim quiet of her bathroom.

"You're so lovely, Nikilie," friends told her. She cut and sawed at the skin on her thigh, leaving tight, slim lines beaded with blood. Jewels on the skin of a goddess. That was beauty. That was purity, right there.

"Baby, come here." Cat calls on the street and lascivious glances turned into something genteel, something finer under her blade.

"I want you," her boss told her behind his office door. He was one of many, simply another person abusing authority. His hand slid up and under her shirt. "A gorgeous woman such as yourself should never be lonely."

"I never am," she replied, but her whispers disappeared under the sound of fabric ripping, her favorite top turned into rags. Her words, though, shone as she carved them into her skin in the silence of night.

Water Thy Bones

Never lonely. Never. Never never never.

Fabric can be rent, and so can skin, but at least she made the choice this time. Pried under the coating. Saw what lay underneath.

She wasn't simply her face or her skin or the smooth Island accent of her words. She was herself. Nikilie. She was what ran under her skin, not merely the features built out of it. She wanted somebody who would love her from the inside out.

The first time Michael saw Nikilie, he stopped and stared at the aggressive way her skull pressed against the paper-thin skin of her face. She pursed her lips and worked her jaw, the bones moving in such a way that Michael had to stifle a groan.

"What is your name?" he asked her. She sat on the hard, plastic seat of the subway, an exotic flower growing from the cracks in the pavement. He stood next to her, holding loosely to the straps above.

"Trudi," she said, not meeting his eyes.

"I don't blame you for lying. I'm a stranger on the subway. My intentions may not be honorable."

Her eyes flicked up, then, warm and wet. He saw moss and flowers and lovely things growing in their humidity. A tropical paradise.

"You're not from New York," he said, and then blushed.

This made her laugh, and she scratched at her wrist. It always itched.

"No, I'm not. But you are. And yet you're easily embarrassed. How can this be?"

He shrugged, grinning, and she smiled back. Beautiful white teeth, strong, and one overlapped the other just a bit. Perfection.

He wanted to run his fingers across them. He wished to wear them as pearls.

"I'm awkward," he said, and lifted his shoulders again. A *what can I do?* gesture. The self-realization of a different man. "I say what I think instead of saying what I should. I don't mean to make people uncomfortable. I just do. I'm no good at small talk."

"Why is that? If you realize it makes it difficult to fit in?"

The movement of the subway shook them, made him dance and sway with unusual grace. His suit coat looked like bird feathers. He was something exotic, something from the islands, and for a second a look of recognition, of delight, shone from Nikilie's eyes. *Ah, yes,* her eyes seemed to say. *This is something I've seen before.*

"Life is too short, I suppose," he answered. "There seems to be so little time. Yet we're supposed to dance around this and barely mention that. I don't understand it. In two minutes I'll step off this platform and will most likely never see you again, so why shouldn't I say what I'm thinking instead of wasting that time with faux pleasantries?"

"And what are you thinking?"

He could read her expectations in the lift of her brow, in the tiredness that suddenly came into her eyes. *You're beautiful. Could we go out for coffee?* Or perhaps, *Such an exquisite face you have.* Something about her face, her lips, her eyes. About her body or long, long limbs. But he had caught sight of the black, healed skin on her wrists, under her bangles, and when her shirt fell off her shoulder just a bit, before she automatically pushed it back up, he saw the fresher wounds there.

"Your bones," he said, and gestured with one hand. "Your elbows and knees. The things that make you *you,* underneath everything else. I've never seen anything more striking."

Nikilie's mouth fell open. The subway stopped and Michael was gone in a flurry of suit coats and umbrellas, moon boots and patchouli.

Nikilie stared at the floor for the remainder of her ride. That night she took a razorblade to her inner thigh, but the cuts were heartless and shallow.

They had coffee at a safe, generic, neutral spot. Nikilie thought about discussing the weather, but Michael had no interest in such niceties.

"Did you ever break your leg?" he asked. "You have a slight limp."

She had, indeed, broken her leg a few years ago. Skiing, she told him.

"An island girl on skis is just as tragic as you'd think," she told him, and when he laughed, she saw the fillings in his teeth. It made her heart hug close, just a little.

"When you are dead and gone," he said, "they'll look at your skeleton and be able to see that break. How it healed itself over. People will hold your bones and wonder what caused it. Running from a predator, perhaps? Or something that happened as a child? No, it didn't heal correctly for that. It must have happened when you were a strong, adult woman. I bet they wonder. I bet they speculate. You'll give them pause, and joy, and something to puzzle over."

Michael talked so tenderly, so gently, of strangers

holding and caressing her bones. It nearly made her frown. It made her want, and she wasn't a woman accustomed to wanting.

"What's wrong, Nikilie? Am I disturbing you with this talk?"

His eyes were open and very nearly alarming in their earnestness. She should demure. She should excuse herself and go back to her hopeless, helpless life. That's the way society worked. That's the way the script played out.

"No, you're not," she said, and the boldness and sheer honesty of her words shocked her. "It sounds strangely wonderful. Isn't that an odd thing?"

"Not at all," he said reverently. "You want to be loved and worshiped the way a woman should be. Not because of your airs or your face. Not because of the fine clothes and jewelry you wear. But because of you. Who you are at the heart. At your very center."

His talk tasted so sweet that she turned down her boss the next time he made advances.

"What's wrong, baby?" he asked. "Don't be like this, a beautiful woman like you."

"This bag of flesh is the very least of me," she said, and quitting her job felt like the best thing in the world. She walked out of the building and blinked in the cold New York sunshine. She took off her high heels and walked all the way home.

Nikilie and Michael began to visit zoos and aquariums. Cemeteries. They twined their thin fingers close, bone rubbing against bone. When she curled up with her feet in his lap, he ran his hand down her ankles, caressing the tendons and scarring there.

"Tell me why you cut yourself."

No judgement. No sad-eyed face of faux concern. Her Michael Harrison wasn't like that, and he would never be like that. He just wanted to know, and Nikilie found she wanted to tell him.

"A few reasons, I guess. It makes me feel better."

"How so?"

"My skin itches, for one thing. It tickles from underneath. Like there's something below that is trying to break through the crust."

"Like what?" His eyes were bright, dilated with interest and the strangest type of arousal. Nikilie briefly thought she should feel stupid or embarrassed, but she didn't. She watched Michael run his tongue over his lips unconsciously, and she swallowed any would-be embarrassment away.

"Rivers, perhaps? Oceans. Stars. Lianas, maybe. May I have a drink of water?"

"Of course," he said, and poured her a glass from the pitcher he always kept nearby for her. "Why else?"

She drank the entire glass of water without pausing, and then held the cool cup to her cheek.

"What? Oh. I . . . "

The words really did fade away, then, because she simply didn't know what to say. *Beauty is a curse,* perhaps, although that sounded so terribly arrogant. More importantly, it wasn't what she meant. *I hate all of the trappings of being human* didn't make sense, either, although it was closer. *I want to scrape it all off and be free.* That was the closest yet, but it made her feel quite mad and restless inside, even as the thought thrilled her.

So instead she sighed, and that was the best she could do. Sighed and fluttered her hand to her scars uselessly. She shook her head and searched out Michael's eyes.

They blazed. They contained passion and desire and exquisite care and something so akin to purpose that Nikilie's breath caught in her throat with hope.

"You're trapped by something that covers you. Beauty, yes, but it's like a cold, wet blanket draped over your true self. There's something superb inside, the true you, but it's shrouded in fluff and perfume and bubbles. Is this how you feel?"

Nikilie felt something move, deep within her bones. Her marrow uncurled and stretched. Something bloomed. It felt like Hibiscus.

"Yes," she whispered, and her voice didn't shake. It felt *alive*. It climbed from her throat and wound around Michael's hand, searching for sunlight.

"Beneath your skin, which is indeed fine, and subcutaneous layers of fat, there are veins and ropes of nerves. Meat and muscle. All of this excess. So much bloat! Ah, but under that? At the very core of you?"

If her eyes were alight, then his were on fire. They burned. Sparked. Two delirious gorgeous infernos of famine and desire, burning away the refuse of her body to get to the bare essence underneath.

He saw the basics of her, the very base, and that's what he wanted. Not the trappings. Not the prettiness. He wanted the deep and dark and ugly. The most honest and primal parts.

You are everything I ever wanted, she told him. She didn't say a word, but she felt his grip tighten on her bony wrist and knew he understood.

Her hand shook, but not in self-loathing this time. It was a wondrous thing. She cleared her throat.

Water Thy Bones

"Could you hand me my purse?"

He did, his eyes never leaving hers. They radiated sunlight, and she felt a physical itch under the skin on her wrist.

She reached into her bag and pulled out a small box. Inside was a tissue-wrapped razor.

"Just in case," she said, and when she smiled, the island erupted in full bloom.

He was hungry, starving, and watched her like any predator watches its prey. It was, perhaps, the first time she had ever desired to be consumed.

The razor glistened in the light like ice in a polar cave. The aurora borealis held between her fingers. A wishing star fallen to earth and seeking to sup from her veins.

"Shall I feed it?"

Nikilie's voice held the slightest hint of teasing, but underneath the playfulness, it carried so much more.

Shall I? Shall I do this now, here with you, and will we both accept the consequences that come with it?

He didn't reply, but touched her face softly. He traced her jawline, felt down her neck, and ran his fingers across her collarbone. That's where he let his fingers rest, and the warmth of them felt volcanic to Nikilie.

"There," she said, and placed her hand atop his. "This bone specifically belongs to you. It's yours, always."

"You know I'll treasure it," he said, and his voice was thick and heavy.

"I know you will. You genuinely will. You're the only one who loves me from the inside out."

The first cut went deeper than planned, the blade

ice cold and giving her that momentary instant of surprise. Her mind went blank, her body confused, her nerves short-circuiting and her mouth curling in a soft "oh" of surprise. Then the pain hit, and she closed her eyes against the glorious rush.

Michael sank to the ground and held his arms out to her. She crawled into his lap, and he wrapped himself around her. Blood soaked into his sweater.

"Are you all right, my love?" he asked, and her lips curved in response.

"I have never felt so alive," she answered, and cut again.

No holding back. No fits of guilt or shame, of wondering how she should hide her wounds, of cradling her head in her bloody hands and sobbing. She only felt euphoria. Excitement. She was unearthing the deepest, best parts of herself, and most precious of all, she wasn't doing it alone.

She grew too weak to cut with the force necessary, and she blinked sunny, Caribbean eyes at Michael.

"Would you?"

She spoke so softly that he leaned forward to hear her, but with such love that her words reverberated through him.

"Of course."

He guided her fingers, and they both gasped as something green and fresh unfurled from her vein.

"I knew it," she breathed.

She was fading fast, her voice nearly gone, and Michael helped her go deeper, discovering the cosmos and Garden of Eden hidden away all of these years. Before the light in her eyes went out, she wanted to see everything, to see the value and gold hidden at her very center.

"Hang on just a little longer, love," he said, and worked furiously until lilies spilled from her wrists, and heliconias, orange and gay, and vines, and all of the flowers she had ever seen. Cereus bloomed furiously, reminding her of the moon at night.

"You make me feel not so alone," she said, and then the vines overtook her, covering her frail neck, twisting into her mouth and twirling over her eyes. Petals bloomed and fell. Michael was left holding something delicate and wonderful, beautiful from within as well as without.

"You'll never be alone. Never. I'll always, always be with you. I promise."

A girl missing in the city didn't retain the public's attention for long. But Michael was a man who cherished a special thing, the inner wholeness of a person. He tenderly unwrapped flowers and leaves until he found skin and flesh, and then he looked deeper. He cut, scraped, and boiled until he was left with bone. It was white and fresh and pure, with life blooming from the marrow. He held each flowering vertebra gently in his hands, and kissed each and every rib.

His garden was exquisite, a thing of wonder and beauty. Flowers bloomed from eye sockets, thrived from femurs. Nikilie was broken down into the most astounding of parts. True to his word, Michael never forgot her. He watered her bones daily.

A Haunted House is a Wheel Upon Which Some Are Broken

PAUL TREMBLAY

ARRIVAL

Fiona arranged for the house to be empty and for the door to be left open. She has never lived far from the house. It was there, a comfort, a threat, a reminder, a Stonehenge, a totem to things that actually happened to her. The house was old when she was a child. That her body has aged faster than the house (there are so many kinds of years; there are dog-years and people-years and house-years and geological-years and cosmic-years) is a joke and she laughs at it, with it, even though all jokes are cruel. The house is a New England colonial, blue with red and white shutters and trim, recently painted, the first floor windows festooned with carved flower boxes. She stands in the house's considerable shadow. She was once very small, and then she became big, and now she is becoming smaller again, and that process is painful but not without joy and an animal-sense of satisfaction that the coming end is earned. She thinks of endings and beginnings as she climbs the five steps onto the front porch. Adjacent to the front door and to her left is a white historical placard with the year 1819 and the house's name. Her older brother, Sam, said that you could never say the house's name out loud or you would wake up the ghosts, and she never did say the name, not even once. The ghosts were there anyway. Fiona never liked the house's name and thought it was silly, and worse, because of the name preexisting and now post-existing it means that the house was never hers. Despite everything, she wanted it to always be hers.

Fiona hesitates to open the front door. Go to pg 93 THE FRONT DOOR.

Fiona decides to not go inside the house after all and walks back to her car. Go to pg 121 LEAVING THE HOUSE.

A Haunted House

THE FRONT DOOR

It's like Fiona has always and forever been standing at the front door. She places a hand on the wood and wonders what is on the other side, what has changed, what has remained the same. Change is always on the other side of a door. Open a door. Close a door. Walk in. Walk out. Repeat. It's a loop, or a wheel. She doesn't open the door and instead imagines a practice-run; her opening the door and walking through the house, stepping lightly into each of the rooms, careful not to disturb anything, and she is methodical in itemizing and identifying the ghosts, and she feels what she thinks she is going to feel, and she doesn't linger in either the basement or her parent's bedroom, and she eventually walks out of the house, and all of this is still in her head, and she closes the door, then turns around, stands in the same spot she's standing in now, and places a hand on the wood and wonders what is on the other side, what has changed, what has remained the same.

Fiona opens the door. Go to pg 94
ENTRANCEWAY.

Fiona is not ready to open the door. Go to
pg 93 THE FRONT DOOR.

Fiona decides to walk back to the car and
not go inside the house. Go to pg 121
LEAVING THE HOUSE.

ENTRANCEWAY

Fiona gently pushes the front door closed, watches it nestle into the frame, and listens for the latching mechanism to click into place before turning her full attention to the house. The house. The house. The house. Sam said because the house was so old and historical (he pronounced it his-store-ickle so that it rhymed with pickle) there was a ghost in every one of the rooms. He was right. The house is a ghost too. That's obvious. That all the furniture, light fixtures, and decorations will be different (most of everything will be antique, or made to look antique; the present owners take their caretakers-of-a-living-museum role seriously) and the layout changed from when she lived here won't matter because she's not here to catalogue those differences. She'll only have eyes for the ghost house. Fiona says, "Hello?" because she wants to hear what she sounds like in the house of the terrible now. She says hello again and her voice runs up the stairs and around banisters and bounces off plaster and crown molding and sconces, and she finds the sound of the now-her in the house pleasing and a possible anecdote to the poison of nostalgia and regret, so she says hello again, and louder. Satisfied with her re-introduction, Fiona asks, "Okay, where should we go first?"

Fiona turns to her right and walks into the living room. Go to pg 96 LIVING ROOM.

A Haunted House

Fiona walks straight ahead into the dining room. Go to pg 98 DINING ROOM.

The weight of the place and its history and her history is too much; Fiona abruptly turns around and leaves the house. Go to pg 121 LEAVING THE HOUSE.

Paul Tremblay

LIVING ROOM

Dad builds a fire and uses all the old newspaper to do it and pieces glowing orange at their tips break free and float up into the flue, moving as though they are alive and choosing flight. Fiona and Sam shuffle their feet on the throw rug and then touch the cast iron radiator, their static electric shocks so big at times, a blue arc is visible. Mom sits on the floor so that Fiona can climb onto the couch and jump onto her back. A bushel and a peck and a hug around the neck. The fire is out and the two of them are by themselves and Sam pokes around in the ashes with a twig. Sam says that Little Laurence Montague was a chimney sweep, the best and smallest in the area, and he cleaned everyone's chimney, but he got stuck and died in this chimney, so stuck, in fact, they would not be able to get his body out without tearing the house apart so the home owners built a giant fire that they kept burning for twenty-two days, until there was no more Little Laurence left, not even his awful smell. Sam says that you can see him, or parts of him anyway, all charred and misshapen, sifting through the ash, looking for his pieces, and if you aren't careful, he'll take a piece from you. Fiona makes sure to stay more than an arm's length away from the fireplace. Of all the ghosts, Little Laurence scares her the most, but she likes to watch him pick through the ash, hoping to see him find those pieces of himself. There are so many.

Fiona curls into the dining room. Go to pg 98 DINING ROOM.

A Haunted House

Fiona walks to the kitchen. Go to pg 100 KITCHEN.

This is already harder than she thought it was going to be; impossible, in fact. Fiona doesn't think she can continue and leaves the house. Go to pg 121 LEAVING THE HOUSE.

DINING ROOM

Fiona and Sam are under the table and their parents' legs float by like branches flowing down a river. The floor boards underneath groan and whisper and they understand their house, know it as a musical instrument. Dad sits by himself and wants Fiona and Sam to come out from under the table and talk to him; they do and then he doesn't know what to say or how to say it; her father is so young and she never realized how young he is. Mom isn't there. She doesn't want to be there. Sam says there was an eight-year-old girl named Maisy who had the strictest of parents, the kind who insisted children did not speak during dinner, and poor Maisy was choking on a piece of potato from a gloopy beef stew and she was so terrified of what her parents would do if she said anything, made any sort of noise, she sat and quietly choked to death. Sam says you can see her at the table sitting there with her face turning blue and her eyes as large and white as hard boiled eggs and if you get too close she will wrap her hands around your neck and you won't be able to call out or say anything until it's too late. Of all the ghosts, Maisy scares Fiona the most, and she watches in horror as Maisy sits at the table trying to be a proper girl.

Fiona walks straight ahead and into the kitchen. Go to pg 100 KITCHEN.

Fiona turns right and walks into the living room. Go to pg 96 LIVING ROOM.

A Haunted House

Fiona by-passes the kitchen entirely and goes to the basement. Go to pg 102 BASEMENT.

This is harder than she thought it was going to be; impossible, in fact. Fiona doesn't think she can continue and leaves the house. Go to pg 121 LEAVING THE HOUSE.

KITCHEN

Dad cooks fresh flounder and calls it "fried French" and not fish so that Fiona will eat it. The four of them play card games (cribbage, mainly) and Fiona leaves the room in tears after being yelled at (Dad says he wasn't yelling, which isn't the same as saying he's sorry) for continually leading into runs and allowing Sam and Mom to peg. Mom sits at the table by herself and says she feels fine and smokes a cigarette. Her mother is so young and Fiona never realized how young she is. Sam screams and cries and smashes glasses and dishes on the hardwood floor and no one stops him. Fiona and Mom stand at the back door and look outside, waiting for the birds to eat the stale bread crumbs they sprinkled about their small backyard. Sam says there was a boy named Percy who was even smaller than Little Laurence. He was so small because the only thing he would eat was blueberry muffins, and he loved those muffins so much he crawled inside the oven so that he could better watch the muffin batter rise and turn golden brown. Sam says that you can see him curled up inside the oven and if you get too close he'll pull you in there with him. Of all the ghosts, Percy scares Fiona the most because of how small he is; she knows it's not polite but she can't help but stare at his smallness.

Fiona saves the basement for later and walks through the dining room, the living room, and then into the den. Go to pg 103 DEN.

A Haunted House

Fiona backtracks into the dining room. Go to pg 98 DINING ROOM.

Fiona goes to the living room. Go to pg 96 LIVING ROOM.

Fiona goes into the basement. Go to pg 102 BASEMENT.

This is harder than she thought it was going to be; impossible, in fact. Fiona doesn't think she can continue and leaves the house. Go to pg 121 LEAVING THE HOUSE.

BASEMENT

Fiona is not ready for the basement, not just yet.

Fiona saves the basement for later and walks through the dining room, the living room, and then into the den. Go to pg 103 DEN.

Fiona goes into the kitchen. Go to pg 100 KITCHEN.

The idea of going into the basement is enough to make her abandon the tour and leave the house. Go to pg 121 LEAVING THE HOUSE.

A Haunted House

Sam is never delicate closing the French doors and their little rectangular windows rattle and quiver in their frames. Fiona rearranges the books in the built-in, floor-to-ceiling bookshelves; first alphabetical by author, then by title, then by color-scheme. Dad shuts the lights off in the rest of the house, leaving only the den well lit; he hides, and dares his children to come out and find him, and he laughs as they scream with a mix of mock and real terror. Dad and Mom put Sam and Fiona in the den by themselves and shut the French doors (controlled, and careful) because they are having a private talk. Mom sits on the couch and watches the evening news with a cup of tea and invites Fiona and Sam to watch with her so that they will know what's going on in the world. Sam and Fiona lay on the floor, on their stomachs, blanket over their heads, watching a scary movie. Sam stands in front of the TV and stiff-arms Fiona away, physically blocking her from changing the channel. Mom lets Fiona take a puff of her cigarette and Fiona's lungs are on fire and she coughs, cries, and nearly throws up, and Mom rubs her back and says remember this so you'll never do it again. Sam says there was a girl named Olivia who liked to climb the bookcases in the walls and wouldn't stop climbing the shelves even after her parents begged her not to, and in an effort to stop her, they filled the bookcases with the heaviest leather-bound books with the largest spines that could squeeze into the shelves. Olivia was determined to still climb the shelves and touch the ceiling like she'd always done, and she almost made it to the top again, but her feet slipped, or maybe it was she couldn't get a good handhold anymore, and she fell and broke her neck. Sam says you can see Olivia high up, close to the ceiling, clinging to the shelves, and if you get too close Olivia throws books at you, the heaviest ones, the ones that can do the most damage. Of all the ghosts, Olivia scares Fiona the most, but she wants to read the books that Olivia throws at her.

Fiona goes back to the entranceway and to the front stairs. Go to pg 105 THE STAIRS.

Fiona goes into the kitchen. Go to pg 100 KITCHEN.

The first floor is enough. Fiona doesn't think she can continue and leaves the house. Go to pg 121 LEAVING THE HOUSE.

A Haunted House

THE STAIRS

Sam ties his green army men to pieces of kite string and dangles them from the banister on the second floor and Fiona is on the first floor, pretending to be a tiger that swipes at the army men, and if foolishly dropped low enough, she eats the men in one gulp. Fiona counts the stairs and makes a rhyme. Dad falls down the stairs (after being dared by Sam that he can't hop down on only one foot) and punches through the plaster on the first landing with his shoulder; Dad brushes himself off, shakes his head, and points at the hole and says, "Don't tell Mom." Mom walks up the stairs by herself for the last time (Fiona knows there's a last time for everything), moving slowly and breathing heavy, and she looks back at Fiona who trails behind, pretending not to watch, and Mom rests on the first landing and says there's a kitty cat that seems to be following her, and she says that cat is still with her when she pauses on the second landing. Sam says there was a boy named Timothy who always climbed up the stairs on the outside of the railings, his toes clinging to the edges of treads as though he was at the edges of great cliffs. Climbing over the banister on the second floor was the hardest part, and one morning he fell, bouncing off the railings and he landed head-first in the entranceway below, and he didn't get up and brush himself off. Sam says that Timothy tries to trip you when you are not careful on the stairs. Of all the ghosts, Timothy scares Fiona the most, but she still walks on the stairs without holding onto the railings.

Fiona walks up the stairs without holding the railing (and actually smiles to herself), and then goes into her bedroom. Go to pg 107 FIONA'S BEDROOM.

The stairs make Fiona incredibly, inexplicably sad and Fiona doesn't think she can continue and leaves the house. Go to pg 121 LEAVING THE HOUSE.

A Haunted House

FIONA'S BEDROOM

She spies out the window, which overlooks the front door, and being that their house is on top of a hill, it overlooks the rest of the town, and she picks a spot that is almost as far as she can see and wonders what the people there are doing and thinking. Dad reads her the *Tales of Mr. Jeremy Fisher* using a British accent; it's the only storybook for which he uses the accent. Mom takes the cold facecloth off of Fiona's forehead, thermometer from her mouth, and says scoot over, I'll be sick with you, okay? That night, Dad isn't allowed in her room and he knocks quietly and he says that he's sorry if he scared her in the basement and he's sorry about dinner and he's making it right now and please open the door and come out, and he sounds watery, and she's not mad or scared (she is hungry) but tells him to go away. Sam is not allowed in her room but he comes in anyway and gets away with it and he smiles that smile she hates. She misses that smile terribly now for as much of a pain in the ass as he was as a child, he was a loyal, thoughtful, sensitive, if not melancholy, man. Sam says that there is the ghost of a girl named Wanda in her closet and no one knows what happened to her or how she got there because she's always been there. Of all of the ghosts, Wanda scares Fiona the most because try as she might, she's never been able to talk to her.

Fiona will go to all of the second floor rooms in their proper order, waiting until she's ready to go to her parents' bedroom. Go to pg 109 SAM'S BEDROOM.

Go to pg 109 SAM'S BEDROOM.

———

The second floor is indeed too much. Fiona doesn't think she can continue and leaves the house. Go to pg 121 LEAVING THE HOUSE.

A Haunted House

SAM'S BEDROOM

Fiona sits outside Sam's room and the door is shut and Sam and his friends are inside talking about the Boston Red Sox and the Wynne sisters that live two streets over. Fiona finds magazines filled with pictures of naked women under his bed. Dad is inside Sam's room yelling at (and maybe even hitting) Sam because Sam hit Fiona because Fiona took some of his green army men and threw them down in the sewer because Sam wouldn't play with her. Sam lets Fiona sleep on the floor in a sleeping bag (she always asked to do this) because they watched a scary movie and she can't sleep but isn't scared and tries to stay awake long enough to notice how different it is sleeping in Sam's room. Mom hides under Sam's piled bed sheets and blankets and they trick Dad into going into Sam's room and she jumps out and scares him so badly he falls down on the floor and holds his chest. Sam tells Fiona to come into his room and she's worried he's going to sneak attack, give her a dead arm or something, and instead he's crying and says that they aren't going to live in this house anymore. Sam says that there aren't any ghosts in his room and tells her to stop asking about it so Fiona makes one up. She says that there's a boy who got crushed underneath all of his dirty clothes that piled up to the ceiling and no one ever found the boy and Sam never takes his dirty clothes downstairs because he's afraid of the boy. Of all the ghosts, this one scares Fiona the most because she forgot to name him.

Fiona goes into the bathroom. Go to pg 111 BATHROOM.

The second floor is indeed too much. Fiona doesn't think she can continue and leaves the house. Go to pg 121 LEAVING THE HOUSE.

A Haunted House

BATHROOM

Dad leaves the bathroom door open when he shaves his face and he says there goes my nose and oops no more lips and I guess I don't need a chin. The shaving foam is so white and puffy when Fiona puts it on her face, and she greedily inhales its minty, menthol smell. Sam is in the bathroom for a long, long time with what he says are his comic books. Mom is strong and she doesn't cry anywhere else in the house, certainly never in front of Fiona or Sam, but she cries when she's by herself and taking a bath and the water is running; the sound of a bath being run never fails to make Fiona think about Mom. Everyone else is in her parents' bedroom and to her great, never-ending shame, Fiona is in the bathroom with the door shut, sitting on the floor, the tile hard and cold on her backside, the bath running, the drain unstopped so the tub won't fill, and she cries, and Dad knocks gently on the door and asks if she's okay and asks her to come back, but she stays in the bathroom for hours and until after it's over. Sam says that there was a boy named Charlie who loved to take baths and stayed in them so long that his toes and feet and hands and everything got so wrinkly that his whole body shriveled and shrank he eventually slipped right down the drain. Sam says that if you stay in the bath too long Charlie will suck you into the drain with him. Of all the ghosts, Fiona finds Charlie the least scary, but she talks to him in the drain.

Fiona goes into the hallway stands in front

of her parents' bedroom. Go to pg 113
PARENTS' BEDROOM DOOR).

———

Fiona stays in the bathroom, like she did
those many years ago. Go to pg 111
BATHROOM.

———

Fiona doesn't think she can continue and
leaves the house. Go to pg 121 LEAVING
THE HOUSE.

A Haunted House

PARENTS' BEDROOM DOOR

The door is closed. It's the only door in her haunted house that is closed. Even the door to the basement in the kitchen is open. The door is closed. It's a Saturday afternoon and the door is closed and locked, and Fiona knocks and Mom says please give them a few minutes of privacy and giggles from deep, down somewhere in her room, and Fiona knocks again and then Dad is yelling at her to get lost. The door is closed because it's almost Christmas and she doesn't believe in Santa anymore but hasn't said anything, and she knows she can't go in there because their presents are wrapped and stacked along one bedroom wall. The door is closed and Mom's smallest voice is telling her that she can come in, but Fiona doesn't want to. Fiona places a hand on the wood and her hand is a ghost of her younger hands. She wonders what is on the other side, what has changed, what has remained the same. Change is always on the other side of a door. Open a door. Close a door. Walk in. Walk out. Repeat. It's a loop, or a wheel. Of all the ghosts, the ones in her parents' bedroom scare her the most because maybe nothing ever changes and even though she's an adult (and likes to think of herself at this age as beyond-adult because its connotations are so much more dignified and well-earned than the title elderly) she's afraid she'll make the same decisions all over again.

Fiona opens the door. Go to pg 115
PARENTS' BEDROOM.

Fiona returns to the bathroom. Go to pg 111 BATHROOM.

Fiona doesn't think she can continue and leaves the house. Go to pg 121 LEAVING THE HOUSE.

A Haunted House

PARENTS' BEDROOM

Sam and Fiona wrestle Dad on the bed with his signature move being a blanket toss over their bodies like a net so that he can tickle them with impunity. Fiona tells Mom that Dad shouldn't have hit Sam because she kind of deserved what he did to her for throwing his army men in the sewer. Mom stands in the room wearing only a loose-fitting bra and underwear, and she yells at her clothes, discarded and piled at the edge of the bed, saying nothing she has fits her anymore, and she says it's all just falling off of me. It's Christmas morning and Sam and Fiona sit in the dark and on the floor next to Mom's side of the bed, watching the clock, waiting for 6 a.m. so that they can all do downstairs. Mom is in bed; she's home from the hospital and she says she is not going back. Despite the oppressive heat, Fiona sleeps wedged between her parents during a thunderstorm, counting Mississippis after lightning strikes. Fiona gives Mom ice-chips because she can't eat anything else and Mom says thank you after each chip passes between her dried, cracked lips. Dad sets up a mirror opposite the full-length mirror and takes pictures of Fiona and her reflections from different angles with his new camera (she doesn't remember ever seeing the photos). Mom's skin is a yellow-ish green, the color of pea soup (which Fiona hates) and her eyes, when they are open, are large and terrible and they are terrible because they are not Mom's, they are Maisy's eyes, and her body has shriveled up like Charlie's and pieces of her have been taken away like she was Little Laurence and she says nothing like Maisy and Wendy say nothing, and Sam is standing in a corner of the room with his arms wrapped around himself like boa constrictors and Dad sits on the bed, rubbing Mom's hand and asking her if she needs anything, and when a nurse and doctor arrive (she doesn't remember their names and wants to give them ghost names) Fiona does not stay in the room with her family, she runs out and goes to the bathroom and sits on the floor and runs a bath and she hasn't forgiven herself (even though she was so young, a child; a frightened and heartbroken and confused and angry child) for not staying in the room with Mom until the end. Sam says there was a girl named Fiona that looked just like her and acted just like her, and her parents stopped caring for her one day so Fiona faded away and disappeared. Sam says that if Fiona doesn't stop going into Mom's and Dad's room that the ghost-Fiona will take her over and she'll disappear, fade away. Of all the ghosts, ghost-Fiona scares her the most, even though she knows Sam is just trying to scare her out of the room so that he can wrestle Dad by himself, and she thinks that there are times when that ghost-Fiona takes over her body and the real-her goes away, and sometimes she wishes for that to happen.

Fiona is determined to finish her tour and she walks downstairs, walks through the first floor, into the kitchen, ignoring Percy, and then down into the basement. Go to pg 118 BASEMENT.

A Haunted House

Fiona is still reenacting the night her mother died in her bedroom and she goes back to the bathroom. Go to pg 111 BATHROOM.

Fiona doesn't have to go to the basement. She leaves the house. Go to pg 121 LEAVING THE HOUSE.

BASEMENT

Fiona does a lap around the basement sometimes holding her hands above her head or tight against her body so that she won't brush up against the forgotten boxes and sawhorses and piles of wood and roof shingles, and careful to not go near Dad's work area (off limits) with its bitey tools and slippery sawdust, but she has to go fast as Sam is counting and if she doesn't make it back to the stairs before he counts to twenty he kills the light (at some point he'll kill the light anyway). Fiona follows Mom to the silver, cow-sized freezer and watches her struggle to lift out a frozen block of meat. Sam places his green army men on top of the dryer and they make bets about which plastic man will stay on the longest and Fiona doesn't care if she loses because she loves smelling the warm, soft, humid dryer exhaust. Dad has been in the basement all day and they haven't eaten dinner and Sam is not there (she forgets where Sam is, but he's not in the house) and Mom has been gone for exactly one year and Fiona doesn't call out Dad's name and instead creeps down the basement stairs as quietly as she can and the only light on in the basement is the swinging bulb in Dad's work area, and a static-tinged radio plays Motown, and Fiona can't see Dad or his work area from the bottom of the stairs, only the light, so she sneaks in the dark over past the washer/dryer and the freezer, and Dad sits on his stool, his back is to her, his legs splayed out, his right arm pistons up and down like he's hammering a nail but there's no hammering a nail sound, and he's breathing heavy, and there are beer cans all over his table, and she says

A Haunted House

Dad, are we having dinner? even though she knows she should not say anything and just go back up the stairs and find something to eat, and he jumps up from off the chair (back still turned to her), beer cans fall and a magazine flutters to the dirty floor (and if it's not the exact same magazine, it's like one of the naked-girl magazines she found in Sam's room) and so do photos of Mom, and they are black and white photos of her and she is by herself and she is young and laughing and she is on the beach, running toward the camera with her arms over her head, and Fiona has always loved those pictures of her Mom on the beach, and Dad's shirt is untucked and hanging over his unbuckled pants and instead of getting mad or yelling he talks like Sam might talk when he's in trouble, a little boy voice, asking what she's doing down here, and he picks up the magazine and the pictures and he doesn't turn around to face her, and then she asks what was he doing, and he slumps back onto his stool and cries, and then he starts throwing the beer cans (empty and full) off of the wall, and Fiona runs out of the basement in less than twenty seconds. Sam says that the ghost of every person who ever lived in the house eventually goes to the basement and that some houses have so many ghosts in their basements that they line the walls and they're stacked like cords of wood.

Fiona has finally seen all of the ghosts and spent enough time with them, and she can now leave the house. Go to pg 122 LEAVING THE HOUSE.

Fiona goes back up all the stairs to stand in front of her parent's bedroom door. Go to pg 113 PARENTS' BEDROOM DOOR.

LEAVING THE HOUSE

It's colder now than it was when she arrived. Fiona walks to her car and won't allow herself to stop and turn and stare at the house. Even with the visit cut short, she knows the ghosts are not trapped in the house, not bound to both the permanence and impermanence of place, as she foolishly hoped. The ghosts do not follow behind her, in a polite single-file, Pied Piper line to be catalogued, and then archived and forgotten. The ghosts are with her and will be with her, always. It is not a comfort because she will not allow it to be a comfort. How can she? As always, Fiona is too hard on herself, and she remains her very own ghost that scares her the most.

Fiona does not forgive herself. Go to pg 93 THE FRONT DOOR.

Fiona returns to the house. Go to pg 93 THE FRONT DOOR.

Paul Tremblay

LEAVING THE HOUSE

It's colder now than it was when she arrived. Fiona walks to her car and won't allow herself to stop and turn and stare at the house. She knows the ghosts are not trapped in the house, not bound to both the permanence and impermanence of place, as she once foolishly hoped. The ghosts do not follow behind her, in a polite single-file Pied Piper line to be catalogued, and then archived and forgotten. The ghosts are with her, have always been with her, and continue to be with her, and maybe that can be a comfort, a confirmation, if she'll just let it. Fiona was ten-years-old when Mom died from colon cancer. Her father died of cystic fibrosis thirty-seven years later. Dad never remarried and moved to Florida when he got sick and Fiona wrote him letters (he wrote back until he became too weak to do so) and she talked to him every other day on the phone and she spent three of her four weeks of vacation visiting him, and her lovely brother Sam cared for Dad during the last two years of his life. Poor Sam died of pneumonia after suffering a series of strokes five years ago. She doesn't know what to do so she starts talking. She says to her father (who she knew for much longer and so much more intimately than her mother, yet somehow it feels like she didn't know him as well, as though the glut of father-data confuses and contradicts) I'm sorry that we let every day be more awkward and formal than they should've been and I'm sorry I never told you that I don't blame you for anything you did or said in grief, I never did, and I want to say, having out-lived my Marcie, that I understand. Then she says to Mom (who she only knew for ten years, less, really, in terms of her ever-shrinking timeline of memory, and of course, somehow, more) I'm sorry I didn't stay, I wish I stayed with you, and I can stay with you now if you want me to. Fiona cries old tears, the ones drudged from a bottomless well of a child's never ending grief. And she cries at the horror and beauty of passed time. And she chides herself for being a sentimental old fool despite having given herself permission to be one. As always, Fiona is too hard on herself, and she remains her very own ghost that scares her the most.

Fiona is still turned away from the house and she feels fingers pulling on the back of her coat, trying to drag her back into the house to go through it all again. Fiona still cannot forgive herself for not staying in her parents' bedroom with her mother until the end. She fears her mother's end (all ends for that matter) are cruelly eternal and that her mother is still there alone and waiting for Fiona to finally and forever come back.
Go to pg 93 THE FRONT DOOR.

Fiona is still turned away from the house and she feels fingers pulling on the back of her coat, trying to drag her back into the house to go through it all again, or maybe pull her away from everything, pull her away, finally, until she's hopelessly lost. But she doesn't want to be lost either. Fiona walks around the car, tracing the cold, metal frame with one hand, to the driver's side door, and gets in the car and starts the engine which turns over in its tired mechanical way, and she shifts into first gear. The tires turn slowly, but they do turn. Go to pg 125 THE END.

A Haunted House

THE END

On the Other Side of the Door, Everything Changes

DAMIEN ANGELICA WALTERS

Hannah opens her bedroom window, wincing at the low creak it makes, and pauses with one leg over the sill. A pile of dirty laundry sits at the foot of her bed, One Direction posters hang on the walls, and her laptop is open, but turned off, on her desk. She hasn't dared turn it on for days; the messages coming in on her phone are more than enough.

Dark smudges, the shadows of her mom's feet, creep along the floor beneath the door. They linger, and Hannah pulls her leg back inside, worrying an already ragged cuticle between her teeth. Part of her wants to open the door and let her mom in, wants to let the truth spill from her lips like vomit, wants to tell her everything, no matter what she says, no matter what happens after, but she can't make her legs or mouth move because the other part of her knows it's too late.

Her phone vibrates and tears burn in her eyes. The monsters are relentless. No need to look at the message; she knows what it says. She deleted a lot of them when it started, but now she doesn't even bother. Her phone vibrates again and she pinches the inside of her cheek between her teeth. It's Friday night, almost ten o'clock, and weekends are the worst.

The shadow feet beneath her door move, pause, and move again, moving away. Hannah takes a deep breath, shoves her phone in the pocket of her hoodie, and gives her room one last look.

Leanne paces in the living room, fingertips to temple, as though she can hold back the ache nestling there. Hannah's upstairs in her bedroom, and while Leanne wants to go and apologize, she knows her daughter well enough to know it would go over as well as a fart in church. They both need time to cool down. To breathe.

This isn't the first time they've argued—life with a thirteen-year-old is anything but bucolic—but it's the worst thus far. And prompted by such a silly thing, too. Leanne squeezes her hands into fists, releases, squeezes again.

Would you please empty the dishwasher? A simple request that tornadoed into tears and stomping feet, and then the slinging of silverware into the drawer so fast and hard the clatter rattled Leanne's teeth.

"What is wrong with you?" Leanne asked, knowing her tone of voice was too sharp, but knowing too late.

Hannah turned with a fistful of spoons. "Nothing's wrong with me."

This time, Leanne kept her tone gentle. "You've been quiet for days. You haven't been hanging out with your friends or doing much of anything other than staying in your room. Did something happen?"

Hannah shrugged one shoulder.

"You can talk to me if you want."

Another shrug, then Hannah said, "I'm not hanging out with my friends because they've been calling me names."

And Leanne laughed. It wasn't that she found it funny, but Hannah's response was unexpected and petulant, the words something out of grade school. Leanne bit back the laugh a moment too late, and Hannah exploded. F5. She threw the spoons across the counter, her mouth twisted, her face turned bright red, and she yelled, "You wouldn't understand. You're too old."

Silence hovered in the air and as Leanne opened her mouth to say *I'm sorry*, a spoon balanced on the edge of the counter fell to the floor. Hannah's words came out into a rush too fast for Leanne to follow, drowning her apology in chaos. She heard *everyone hates me* and *I hate it here* and *I want to go home*.

Leanne stood immobile, desperately wishing David were home and hating herself a bit for it. But he'd be able to turn things around. With Hannah, he's always been able to. When she was small and afraid of monsters hiding in her closet, he'd open the closet with one hand while brandishing a toy lightsaber in the other. He'd stab and swing the lightsaber at the shoes and hanging clothes—while making a reasonable facsimile of the distinctive lightsaber sound—until the hangers were dancing on the bar and Hannah's fear gave way to laughter.

At a lull in Hannah's tirade, Leanne said, "Stop

being so dramatic. Whatever happened will all blow over and they'll stop. Act like it doesn't matter and it will stop even faster. In a few years, you'll barely remember it. It isn't the end of the world."

Hannah burst into tears and ran to her room, stomping her feet and slamming her bedroom door, and Leanne sagged against the kitchen counter.

Now, she pours a glass of wine but leaves it untasted on the coffee table. She regrets what she said to Hannah, regretted it as soon as the words were in the air, but everything will be okay once they've both calmed down. Everything will be fine.

Hannah climbs from her window onto the porch roof and shimmies down one of the support columns. Luckily, the porch light isn't on—it burned out a few nights ago and no one's replaced it yet—and it's late enough that none of the neighbors, all old people, are outside. Once across the lawn, she doesn't look back.

Invisible hands in her chest squeeze tight as she reaches the end of the street, and she wipes tears from her cheeks with a sleeve. All the tears in the world won't change things, and the monsters like it when she cries; they feed off the salt and the sorrow.

The neighborhood is a series of culs-de-sac jutting off a main road like a series of tumors. She shoves her hands in her pockets and hunches her shoulders. It's early March and still chilly, colder than she thought it would be.

When she passes the cul-de-sac where Larissa lives, she pulls up her hood, hunches even more. Even though Larissa lives at the top, she doesn't want to take the risk of being seen. Her phone vibrates and she jumps and walks faster, a bitter taste in the back of her throat.

She follows the road to another and makes a left, pausing to glance over her shoulder. From here, she can't see her house, but she can see the curve in the road right before the turn off. Larissa's house, with the big flagpole in the middle of the front yard, is clear as day. Larissa, the first person she met when they moved here right before Thanksgiving five months ago. Larissa, who she thought was her friend. Larissa, one of the monsters, never mind that the human mask she wears isn't nearly tight enough to hold in the darkness it tries to conceal.

But it fooled Hannah.

"I didn't know," she says, the thump of her soles on the pavement swallowing up the sound.

Her phone vibrates yet again.

"Fuck you," she says, but the words fall like deflated balloons.

She isn't sure how far away the interstate is. A mile? Two? It never seems that far in the car, but it's still walking distance. Even if it really isn't, it will be tonight.

An SUV drives by, going too fast, the way everyone seems to drive around here. Too many cars, too many people, and all of them rude, nasty, or dismissive. The air always reeks of exhaust, cat piss, and charred meat, the latter from a nearby diner open twenty-four-seven.

She hates it here, hates everything about it. This place will never be home. It's a bad dream and when she wakes up, it's a nightmare. She misses her old house, misses her room and her friends, but most of all, she misses the water.

Their old house, on the South River in Edgewater, had a dock and a small beach. In the summer she liked to run the length of the dock and jump into the water, savoring that moment of weightlessness, hovering over the water and waiting to fall. That was always the best part. That moment that always felt longer than it truly was, that moment when you weren't part of the world at all, but floating above it.

Even when it was cold, she liked to sit on the sand and run her fingers through the coarse grains. Her dad always said you could never be sad or angry sitting by the water. If she were home, by the water, maybe she'd feel better. Then again, if she were home, none of this would've happened. No Larissa, no Jeremy, no pictures.

She traces the outline of the phone in her pocket, thinks for the hundredth time of calling Mira, her best friend back home, but she doesn't want her to know. Besides, Mira is sort of pissed at her anyway for making new friends so fast and spending time with them. She was so stupid. She should've known better.

At the first major street she has to cross, she waits for the light to change, scuffing the toe of one shoe against the pavement. Her phone vibrates again. She doesn't need to look but she does.

Dirty little whore.

She doesn't cry. Doesn't delete the message.

When Hannah told Larissa what Jeremy had asked for, Larissa said it was no big deal, said they all did it, said Hannah was special because Jeremy never asked anyone. A lie, but one that Hannah couldn't see at the time because she still thought they were friends.

Hannah didn't even want to take the picture, but

Larissa kept talking about it and talking about it. Funny how after Jeremy sent her picture to *everyone*, Larissa was the first person to send an email. *Slut*, it read. Hannah thought she was joking, until the other emails and text messages started coming in.

She was such an idiot.

And the absolute worst part? The part she doesn't even like to think about? She *liked* taking the picture, liked the way it made her feel, liked the way she looked—older, different. It made her feel pretty and powerful. Did that make her a terrible person? Did it make her a slut?

She almost didn't hit *send*, wanted to keep that sense of awe to herself, and the moment she did, the power fizzled away, leaving an empty hollow in its place.

All weekend long the messages came in, a barrage of ugliness and mockery and hate, and on Monday, she walked into school with a dry mouth and shaking hands. At first, she thought everything would be okay. They had their fun, they made her weekend miserable, time to pick on someone else. Then she saw their faces, their true faces, with their masks off. Everyone had vampire smiles and glitter-dark eyes, fingers hooked into cruel talons. Hateful and predatory. Monstrous. So sharp and clear, she wondered how she didn't see it before.

Every time tears burned in her eyes, their faces brightened, drool ran from the corners of their mouths, and their cheeks plumped. They hid laughter and the names behind palms, smothering them in coughs that served only to amplify.

Slut was scratched into the paint on her locker;

Hannah is a whore written on a bathroom stall in bright pink lipstick; *Show us your tits* on a piece of paper left on her desk. When she found the note, Mrs. Langan asked if everything was okay, and Hannah's cheeks grew warm, then hot, and the truth pressed against her lips, but she said instead that yes, everything was okay, even though a small voice was screaming. Long after Mrs. Langan nodded and walked away, that small voice continued to scream.

If she could talk to her mom, she'd tell her that she's tried to ignore it, hoping they would stop, she's tried so hard, but inside, she's all broken glass and she can't put her pieces back together. There's no way anyone can. And real monsters don't hide under the bed or in the closet; real monsters aren't afraid of sunlight.

If her parents knew, they'd hate her. They'd be ashamed and would never look at her the same way. Mostly, though, she doesn't know how to try anymore. She's tired, and all she wants is the water, the weightlessness before the cold.

Just past a gas station and a half-constructed fast food restaurant, she drops her phone into the gutter. Steps on it until she hears the screen crack and rocks her foot back and forth to make sure. The light changes and she moves on.

Leanne tiptoes upstairs and perches on the top step, the way she did when Hannah was a baby, resting her elbows on her knees and chin atop linked fingers.

Girls can be cruel, she thinks. It's always been that way, even when she was in school. The surge of hormones brought something dark and primal to the surface, a savage sort of competition that, sadly, never went away for some. Even when the cruelties were relatively minor, the hormones brought sensitivity that affected perception. Maybe it wasn't the end of the world, but it felt that way to Hannah, and Leanne knows she belittled her feelings.

She wants to go in Hannah's room, sit at the foot of her bed, and read her a story or sing a song. Would that such devices would work for a teenager. At best, she'll get a roll of the eyes and an impassioned *Mother*; at worst, she'll make it two steps into the room before Hannah yells *Leave me alone!*

Silly, maybe, sitting here, stressing about a fight that in a few days will fade into memory, and in a few years to nothing at all. She allows herself a smile. All the angst and the chaos. Her memories of her own early teen years are threaded with band names, pining for cute boys in the neighborhood, and yes, fights with her own mother, for reasons unremembered.

Leanne heads downstairs, makes it to the bottom, and turns around, wincing when one of the steps creaks. If her mother were still alive, she'd call and ask her for advice. God, how many times did she do that when Hannah was an infant? Far too many to count. Cancer took her when Hannah was three, and the thought that she won't see her grandchild grow up still sends thorns twisting in Leanne's heart.

She passes Hannah's room on the way into hers, making enough noise so Hannah knows she's there. Maybe she'll come out and decide she wants to talk. Leanne opens her closet, pulls out the half-full hamper. In their old house, they'd moved the washer and dryer upstairs; here, though, she has to go down to the basement. As she walks by Hannah's room again, she lifts her hand to knock, but instead, clears her throat and says, "I'm doing laundry if you have something you want me to run through."

There's no answer, not that she truly expected one, but at least now Hannah knows Leanne isn't angry with her. A subtle olive branch, of which she thinks her own mother would approve.

She adjusts the laundry basket balancing on her hip. Once this blows over, she'll explain that her reaction had nothing to do with Hannah and had everything to do with the move, with her dad's job, and the hours he's spending at the office.

That's partly true, but most of all, what she's upset about and can't mention to Hannah yet, is what David told her last night. He said he regretted taking the job, that he didn't think the money was worth it, that his old boss had already indicated, strongly, that they'd love for him to come back, and that he's seriously considering it.

Leanne said nothing, too shocked to speak. They'd uprooted their entire lives to move here. A good career step, David said. Unlimited potential. No more worrying about money for Hannah's college fund. Over and over again, and now she wonders if he was trying to convince himself as much as he was trying to convince her.

They spent weeks hashing out the options, the downsides, the changes, and, once they decided the benefits outweighed the risks, several more weeks setting everything in motion. And now he wants to undo everything and move them back? Without even considering how this will affect Hannah or Leanne? Not to mention the logistical hassle. They signed a year's lease for this house and rented out their old— thank god they hadn't sold it, though it was a near thing. Breaking the lease will cost them money, and then they'll have to find somewhere else to live in Edgewater until the tenants' lease is up.

Leanne's been doing remote paralegal work for the firm she worked for in Edgewater, so in theory, that won't present a problem, but once they move back, her boss will expect her to come into the office and she likes working remotely, likes knowing she's there when Hannah gets home from school.

She can't even imagine how Hannah will react to the news. She took the move harder than any of them, and it was a huge relief when she made friends so quickly. Nice girls, all of them, especially Larissa. If they do decide to move back, will that only make things doubly hard for Hannah or will she be too happy to see Mira again to care?

Leanne pinches the bridge of her nose between finger and thumb. Readjusts the laundry basket. Maybe she should mention the possibility to Hannah and feel her out; then again, it might only upset her even more.

Beneath the overpass, through Hannah's tears, trucks rush past in a blur. She wonders if her mom's already figured out that she isn't home. If so, she probably thinks she's with one of the monsters. She touches a hand to her chest. In a way, she'd be right. If she peeled back the skin of her chest, she thinks there'd be claw marks in the chambers of her heart.

It isn't the end of the world; that's what her mother said. Hannah lets out a sharp sound halfway between laugh and sob. Her mom has no idea.

Her dad probably isn't even home yet. He never worked so much at his old job. She told him that in the beginning, told him she missed him, and he said he missed her too and he wouldn't have to work like that forever. She thinks maybe he lied and wishes he'd liked his old job a little more.

At least they won't ever find out what she did.

She peeks over her shoulder, half-expecting to see the monsters standing there, smiling and waiting. No one's there, of course, but she feels their presence, their hot breath on the back of her neck, their claws tracing the length of her spine.

For a brief moment, she wonders what it would've been like to talk to her mom. Then she shakes off the thought and checks over her shoulder again, this time to make sure no cars are driving past.

She climbs over the railing and stares down at the trucks, listening to the rumble of their tires on the asphalt. Inside, she's cold and still and unafraid, but she hopes it's fast. She hopes it doesn't hurt.

Leanne stands outside Hannah's room, arms crossed and elbows cupped in her palms. She fidgets in place, lifts one hand to knock, lets it fall. It's almost ten o'clock; Hannah might be getting ready for bed.

At the low creak of Hannah's window, she gives a wry smile. Hannah is so like her father that way, always wanting a window open at night, even when it's chilly. Leanne prefers a downy pile of blankets, regardless of the weather.

She reaches for the door again and again hesitates. Take a deep breath before making a decision. A bit of advice from her mom, one Leanne's passed down to Hannah. Silly, perhaps, to think a lungful of air caught then expelled could help so much, but it always does. Leanne knows it from years of practice.

If she goes in now, will they be able to talk without it turning into another argument? Maybe it's better to wait until the morning. Everything looks better after a good night's sleep, and tomorrow *is* Saturday. No rushing in the morning, no watching the clock. She can make waffles with raspberries and powdered sugar—Hannah's favorite—and help her work through whatever's upset her. She'll listen, no matter how silly everything seems; she'll let Hannah cry or yell, whatever she needs.

Leanne stares down at the shadows her feet have made on the floor and takes a deep breath. With a shake of her head, she heads back downstairs and texts David: *Hannah and I had a big fight tonight.* His reply comes a few minutes later: *On my way home. I'll talk to her when I get there. Everything will be OK. Love you.*

She paces in the living room, scrubs her face with her hands, and takes to the stairs. Maybe letting David swoop in and take care of everything isn't the best decision. Maybe this time it's on her to fix things. Standing outside Hannah's room, she says, "I'd like us to talk now, babygirl. Or I can talk and you can just listen, but if you tell me to go away, I will."

There's no answer and Leanne sighs in relief, picturing Hannah lying in bed with her one hand under her cheek, listening. She sits with her back against the wall next to Hannah's door, pulls her knees to her chest and rests her chin atop folded arms. "Okay, then, here goes."

She closes her eyes.

"When you were little, I told your dad I wanted to roll you in bubble wrap. He thought it was because you were clumsy, but it wasn't. I just wanted to protect you from everything, from the world. Sounds so silly, doesn't it?"

Hannah doesn't answer, but she doesn't need to because it *does* sound silly. You can baby-proof a house; you can't life-proof a child. A tiny breathless laugh slips from Leanne's lips. "You know, the last time I did this, sitting outside your door like this, you were six, almost seven. We got home from your cousin Felicity's birthday party, and it was late and you were tired and said you wanted ice cream.

"We said no. For one thing, it was way past your bedtime and for another, we didn't have any ice cream. We didn't remind you that at the party, you said you didn't like it, even though we knew you did. You shrieked at the top of your lungs that we were the meanest parents ever, and you stomped into your room and threw yourself down on your bed, crying like nobody's business. I sat outside your room talking for a long time until you calmed down.

"The funniest part was that we offered you ice cream the next day and you said no, you didn't like it anymore. That lasted about a week, I think. Such a goofball you were."

Leanne shakes her head. Blinks away tears.

"I'm so sorry for tonight, babygirl. I'm sorry I didn't listen better and let you talk. I'm sorry if I made you feel like I was making light of what you said. I didn't mean to. The last thing in the world I want is to hurt your feelings or make you feel like they're not important, because they are, and I want you to be able to talk to me about anything. Like the way you can talk to your dad.

"It was hard for me to talk to my mom, too. She always told me not to worry about things so much, instead of just listening to what I had to say. I made the same mistake tonight, and I promise I won't do that anymore. I'll just zip my lips and listen.

"I love you, no matter what, and I always will."

She rakes her front teeth over her lower lip, listens for movement.

"Hannah?"

Slowly, she gets to her feet, curls one hand around the doorknob and knocks lightly with her knuckles.

"Babygirl, can I come in?"

Repent

RICHARD THOMAS

In the beginning, there was no pattern to the sacrifice, merely one more thing to clean up after a long, hard day—no reason to believe that I'd brought this upon myself. No, it was just another violent moment in a series of violent moments—so many mornings waking up in the city, the Chicago skyline vibrating in the distance, my knuckles tacky with dried blood, gently running my fingers over my bare skin looking for bruises, indentations, and soggy bandages. In the kitchen, the sound of laughter, my son and wife crisping some bacon, a million miles away. The decapitated squirrel on my front stoop, I stepped right over it, hardly seeing the fuzzy offering, heading out into the snow, boots on, leather coat pulled tight, the bourbon still warm on my tongue, my belly filled with fire. The blue feathers tied into a bouquet, lashed to the wrought iron fence, they fluttered in the wind, and I hardly noticed.

I should have paid more attention.

I huddle around a metal trashcan, the flames licking the rim, hands covered in dirt and grime, a black hooded sweatshirt around my head like a praying monk, my legs shivering under torn jeans, my skin covered in tiny bite marks, slices up and down my arms, eyes bloodshot, as I hide in the darkness, wondering how much time I have left. I stand at the end of the alley, three walls of faded red brick, eyes darting to the opening down by the street, waiting for something to lurch out of the snow that spills across the sky, the world around me oblivious to my suffering.

I threw it all away.

Perhaps we should start at the beginning.

It's finally time to repent.

⚉

As a boy I liked to work with my hands, helping my old man repair a variety of cars—the '66 Mustang in Candy Apple Red, the '67 Camaro in that shimmering deep Marina Blue. Many a day and night were spent under a car, skinning my hands and arms while trying to wrench off a nut or bolt, oil and cigarettes the only scent. When my father would backhand me over the wrong tool, I'd laugh and grab the right one, as my blood slowly began to boil. It started there, I imagine— the anger, the resentment, the need to transfer that rage. Did I drop a wrench between his fingers, watch it smack him in the face—let the car door bang his hand, step on an outstretched ankle, as I walked around the garage? Sure I did. But I never lowered the jack all the way down, letting the weight of the car settle on top of him, crushing him slowly as our black lab ran around the yard barking at cardinals and newborn baby rabbits. No, I never let the sledgehammer descend onto whatever limb stuck out from under the cars—I placed it back on the shelf and handed him a screwdriver, a hammer, a socket wrench, and grinned into the darkness.

144

Repent

But the seed had been planted. Yes, it had.

I played baseball all through high school, outfield mostly, and on the days that we took batting practice inside, claustrophobic in a slim netted cage as the rain fell on the ball fields, I'd watch one of the boys pitch me closer and closer, edging me off the plate, laughing to his friend outside the cage, as I started to sweat. I'd squint and tighten my grip, ripping line drives back up the middle, as he kept getting closer and closer until he finally beamed me in the shoulder. The coach watched from a bench on the near wall, chewing his dip, spitting into a plastic cup, a slow grin easing over his face. He loved this kind of shit. They all did. The boy pitched again, and I smashed the ball right back at him, the netting in front of him catching the line drive, a sneer pulling at his upper lip. He pitched me inside, clipping my elbow this time, and I dropped the bat, cursing under my breath. As I slowly walked toward him, massaging my elbow, my arm a jumble of nerves, trying to get the feeling back, the coach said, "That's enough," and my time in the cage was over, the pitcher smirking as he tossed a ball gently into the air, then catching it again, muttering an insincere, "Sorry, man," under his breath.

The garden slowly grew.

And the girl—I can't forget the girl. The most stunning blonde I'd ever held in my arms, part of my church group, delicate and pale, and as mean as they came. She knew the power she held over young men, and she wielded it like a sword. I did anything she asked—writing her paper for English class, driving her to the mall, giving her money for a movie or clothes, never asking for much in return. She'd laugh as she walked away, but I was oblivious. All I needed was her pressed up against me, a wash of flowery perfume, her lips glossy on mine, her soft wet tongue sliding inside my mouth as her hand rested on the bulge in my jeans, her blue eyes sparkling as she pulled away. I was hypnotized. Which is why I didn't see them, the others, the phone chirping, constantly distracted, as she kept things relatively chaste between us, while spending nights with other young men. All it took was one party, an event she didn't tell me about, walking around the house with a beer in my hand, searching for her, excited, only to head out onto the back porch, her mouth on his, tongues intertwined, his meaty paws all over her ass, my heart in my throat.

The weeds and flowers commingled, until they slowly became one.

It seems petty now, looking back, the ways I boiled over, the ways I was betrayed. Screws slowly turned into one wheel after another, until the car blew a tire, my father in the hospital—a broken arm and two black eyes, as I stood beside his bed while he slept, shadows in the corner of the room. Funny how a baseball player always seems to carry a bat, one in the trunk, for a quick round at the batting cage, nothing more, of course. I guess that pitcher shouldn't have been trying to buy weed in a sketchy part of town, right? High as a kite, leaning against his shit-brown Nova, a quick rap to the back of the skull, my swing improved, busted kneecap, and his hands now useless for holding much of anything, let alone a baseball, trying to work his curve or slider. Spirits danced in the pooling blood. And the girl—I should have left her alone, I know, but her pretty mouth just set me afire. She liked her drink—it was easy to drop a little something extra in her cup, and later, to undress her so gently, leaving her in the bedroom of that frat house, so perfect in every way. I never touched her, and neither did the other boys. We didn't have to. The rumors were enough. Gibbering words haunted the hallways of our school, ruining her for anyone else.

Up in a corner of my garage there was a bundle of twigs wrapped around a dead mouse—a dull red ribbon and metal wire wringing the wad of hair and fur, holding it tight. At the ball field, up under the dugout, was a wasp's nest, filled with birdseed and glass shards, a beetle at the center, a singular red hourglass painted on its back. Tucked into my wallet, behind a bent and faded picture of the girl, was a piece of yellowing paper, covered in hieroglyphics, a tree of life in dried blood at the center, my name etched into it with a razor blade. I brought this all to me, but I never saw it coming.

Being a cop meant I could channel my rage into official business, and I was good at it, for a very long time. And then I took one shot too many, the kid blending into the darkness, his hands full of something, pointing my way, a gun fired, and then we fired back. In those moments I was never a father, forgetting the face of my son. It was all a mistake, the kid never held anything but his cell phone, his hands out the window showing surrender, the pop in the night merely firecrackers down the street, my partner and I flying high on cocaine, eager to dispense justice, when none was needed—our offerings hollow and filled with hate.

Richard Thomas

It was over before it began, both of us on the street, and I would have been bitter if it hadn't been a long time coming. It was merely the straw that broke the camel's back—running heads into the door frame of our cruiser, planting drugs on people we didn't like, broken taillights, speeding tickets, young women frisked and violated in so many different ways, backroom deals over packets of white powder, promises made, seething eyes set back into black skulls, curled lips made of brown skin, the glimmer of a badge, the feeling of immortality, and none of it was anything good. I turned a blind eye to pyramids of broken sticks, smoldering leaves and smoking sage, barbed wire and antlers fused to skulls, flesh turned to sinew, bone to dust—evil incarnate, the deeds I'd done manifesting, coming home to roost.

How quickly I fell, the lies I told to cover up my losses, growing bolder and broader every day.

I had a new job now, fixing the problems of whoever would come to my new office. I'd taken over a crack house down the block from where I used to live, the doors boarded over, the windows too, squatting on the property because the daylight offered me no solutions. I'd sit in the living room, surrounded by torn and beaten down couches, ashtrays overflowing with cigarette butts, candles burning down to nubs. There was no heat, no electricity, and no water. I had my gun, and a thin layer of filth over my skin, taking what I needed from those that were too weak to fight back, hired out by men and women, drug dealers and cops, tracking me down to my rotting homestead, or catching me out at whatever dive bar I could walk to. Around me the ghosts of my family flickered like a television set on its last legs, snow roughing up the faded screen, their voices haunting my every choice.

I'd stay sober long enough to take the pictures, showing the hubby diddling the babysitter, the wife turned to stone, lips tight, a few folded bills tucked into my swollen hands, her mouth opening and closing, chirping like a bird, hesitating, and then asking what it would take for that thing, that finality, not wanting to say it out loud. I'd nod my head, and say I could make it happen, but there was no turning back, she'd have to be sure. She'd sip her red wine or her gin or her espresso and I'd watch the gears turn, the innocence slip out of her flesh, pale skin turning slightly green, her eyes sparking, flecks of flame, the buzzing getting ever louder, her head engulfed in a dark ring of flies, until she'd open her mouth and the snakes would spill out, the deed done, as my heart smoldered black inside my chest. I never said no.

I'd sit inside the back seat of a white Crown Victoria, radio crackling, the men in the front seat wrinkling their noses, the back of the car reeking of vomit, urine and death. We knew each other once, I imagine, my descent into madness one slow step at a time, so gradual and inevitable, that I hardly noticed the noose slipping over my neck, the poisoning so subtle that the bitter taste on my tongue never overtook the lust and hunger, my mouth filled with blood and bourbon, cigarette tar coating it all, as I rotted from the inside out. They'd hand me various things—ammunition, directions, names, addresses, knives, wire, rope, tasers, and envelopes stuffed with cash. Sometimes they would say he was guilty, off on a technicality, a botched Miranda, or nothing but circumstantial evidence. Sometimes they'd talk about witnesses that disappeared, the case ready to go to trial, suddenly the courthouse filled with ghosts—all charges dismissed. And sometimes their silence would fill the car, their dark blue uniforms a color I'd come to hate, nothing said but the place and time, the need for something they couldn't do themselves, telling me to be careful, as they remembered what I used to be, the envelopes thick, telling me to take a shower, Jesus Christ, eyes watering, as they tried to look away, tried to pretend I didn't exist.

I felt the same way.

I'd sit in a dark tavern surrounded by other shadows, glassware around me filled with various liquids, amber poured down my throat, one bar as good as the next, the seats on either side of me filled with the shapes of dark acts come to life, filling the space so that no mortal flesh would get anywhere near me, the fumes coming off of me like gasoline on a black stretch of tar, shimmering and pungent, not quite solid in my existence. When a hand finally did come to rest on my sleeve, I'd turn to see black beady eyes imbedded in a shrinking skull, a red beard flowing off of pock-marked flesh, yellowing teeth uttering threats then demanding answers then asking for help before finally devolving into a long string of begging for something violent. The truth didn't matter much anymore, so I'd take that job, too, sometimes only needing to take a few steps, a pool cue cracked over a head, a knife slid in-between ribs while the leather-clad behemoth pissed into the urinal, baring his teeth as he slid to the floor. Sometimes it was a ride into the endless night, the lights of the city sparkling like a distant galaxy, deeper into the concrete jungle, or perhaps out into the communities that ring the city, thirty miles north to never-ending cornfields, just to run a blade across a throat, a hole dug in haste, a fire burning late into the night, clothes tossed in, standing naked amongst the sharp stalks, blood collecting in a pool at my feet.

And yet, I still turned away from it all, smiling like a Cheshire cat, laughing at whatever demons lurked inside my melted brain, shadows at the periphery, a flock of birds shooting up into the sky, writhing snakes at my feet, and shattered mirrors whenever I paused to stare too long. Waiting to take my photos, as the windows filled with fog, spiral graphics emerged in the mist, wrapping around the interior of some car I'd stolen, a language I chose to ignore. The cackling radio spat out nonsense as the distracted officers tried to get the case right, hissing and popping noises coming from the interior of the cab, dispatch turning to distant tongues, biblical verse spinning out into the air, whoever utters the name of the Lord must be put to death. A cairn of stones was stacked at the end of a dirt road, lost in the suburbs, out past the farms, oak trees ringing the green fields, dusty paths between bulging harvests, and in the middle of the rocks a singular tree branch, forking in all directions, gnarled digits reaching into the sky.

For a man with no faith, it was easy not to believe.

Richard Thomas

The things we say when we are desperate, I imagine I said them all. Somewhere between the angst of my youth and the desolation of my last days on this planet, I had a life that mattered. I was in love, and she was able to see beyond the mask I wore, able to lay her hands on mine and calm the savage beast, bring me down off my high that prowling the city streets required. It shimmers like a ripple in the water, my memories of what once was, the boy in his quiet innocence, the ways we used to be a family. It was as plain as can be, a house in the suburbs, with all of the essentials—hardwood floors, fireplace for surviving the harsh Chicago winters, bedrooms and baths, a back yard with trees and flowers, a two-car garage, a dog that licked my hand no matter how many times I struck it, a basement unfinished in gray concrete where I'd disappear to in order to shed my skin. We would sit down to dinners of meatloaf, mashed potatoes, and peas, a glass of cold milk, and smiles all around the table, no questions about my day because she knew it had been anything but nice. The first thing she'd do when I got home was to drop whatever she was doing—making dinner, playing with the boy, feeding the dog, working on the computer—just to show me that I mattered, wrapping my weary head in her small, soft hands, kissing my face, hugging me, pressing up against me, to remind me why I worked so hard, her feminine lightness fluttering around me like a butterfly, bringing me down to earth, pulling my head up out of the ground, as my arms went limp, and I tried to shake it all off.

But the death came anyway.

I could lie and say that I'd become a different man,

that the wife and son had changed me, made me better, erased my past actions, and the violent acts I'd committed. The mannequin I'd become out here walked these streets with a profound selflessness, a sense of charity, and hope. And maybe I believed it all at first, that I could repent, that I could ask for forgiveness, and find absolution. But deep down I knew it wasn't true. So much had been buried, gunshots in the dead of night, open wounds spilling blood and life onto warehouse floors, back alleys swallowing naked flesh and hungry mouths—no, I knew nothing had been forgiven.

Or forgotten.

My memories of fatherhood were fleeting, and scattered, but true. It was like coming up out of an ice-cold lake, skin shimmering, numb yet awake, my heart pounding in my tight ribcage as if it might explode. I could see my son with such clarity, the way he'd wrinkle up his nose, or hitch up his shorts as we ran around the back yard kicking a soccer ball, his eyes on me as if spying a dinosaur—something he thought had been extinct, wonder wrapped around disbelief. And then the darkness would come swooping back in, and I'd disappear, my base desires overriding the logic. It wasn't that I didn't see him, I did—but for some reason he felt eternal, the time I needed, I wanted, grains of sand in a never-ending hourglass.

When he first got sick, the boy, she took him to one doctor after another, his cough filling the upstairs of our house, his tissues dotted with yellow phlegm and splotches of red, his skin going translucent as we thought cold, then flu, then pneumonia. Then cancer. I saw how it drained her, how it sucked all of the life out of her, her hair no longer golden, merely straw. Her eyes dimmed to dull metal, the oceans I used to get lost in, shallow and dirty—polluted with worry and exhaustion. She wouldn't even get up from the kitchen table when I came home, merely shifted the wine glass from one hand to the other, her lipstick rimming the glass in a pattern that wanted to be kisses, but ended up turning into bites.

And in that moment, I made a deal.

It was a warehouse on the south side of Chicago, a friend of a friend of a friend, or more like the enemy of a junkie who dealt to some whore, the information sketchy at best, the ways I'd pushed out into the world so vulnerable—a walking, gaping wound, grasping at straws, lighting candles in churches as I stumbled across the city, uttering words that I didn't believe.

Rumors.

Speculation.

The blood moon was a rare occurrence—our planet directly between the sun and moon, Earth's shadow falling on the moon in a total lunar eclipse.

It was a last resort, my time spent praying falling on distant deaf ears—knees sore from time spent groveling, fingertips singed from one long matchstick after another, holy water dousing my flesh, as my boy turned slowly into a paper-thin ghost. I told her I might not be back, and she hardly moved, almost as hollowed out as I was, smoking again, standing in our back yard, her gaze settling on me, finally seeing me for what I was. She didn't have to say that I'd brought this sickness down upon us, for she'd known I was a carrier for as long as we'd been close. She had just chosen to see me now.

I stood over the boy, as he slept, and thought of all of the things we'd never done together, and never would. The posters on the walls were of Batman and Superman, and I longed to tell him they didn't exist, to beg him to see the world as I did, which only reminded me of why I had to leave. Even this innocent soul, my son, was just another canvas upon which I needed to splatter my darkness and deceit. Whatever magic and illusion surrounded him, in his youth, why couldn't I just leave it alone? Was I so damaged that the cracks in my armor let all the light out, unable to hold dear to a single memory, or loving gesture, or gentle way?

In the corner of his room there was a large stuffed animal, a black-and-white-striped tiger, which I'd won him at Great America, one of the few times we'd spent the day together alone. We rode the rollercoasters, ate cotton candy and hot dogs, and then spent whatever money I had on a series of games I told him were certainly rigged. He looked at me with suspicious eyes—unable to believe such a thing could be true. I pointed to the ladder climb, the way it was balanced, nearly impossible to stay on top. A young boy about his age was working his way forward, getting so very close, the guy running the game easing over to the edge of the structure, leaning up against it, and when nobody was looking he nudged the frame, shaking the metal of the game, so the kid spilled onto the cushion below. I nodded my head, but the boy had missed it, squinting his eyes, and shaking his head. When we got to the ring toss, I was down to my last ten dollars.

"Nobody ever wins these things, do they?" I asked the chubby girl running the game, her cheeks rosy in the summer heat.

"Sure they do, all the time," she beamed.

"Really?" I asked. "When was the last time somebody won?"

She looked away from me, scrunching up her face, eyes glazing over as she stared off into the distance, searching for a memory that didn't exist.

"See, son," I told him. "Never happens."

He eyeballed me and exhaled.

"Can we try anyway?" he asked.

"Last week," the girl said, "I wasn't here, but Amanda was, she told me . . . "

"Save it for somebody that cares, sister," I said handing her the bill. She gave us each a bucket of plastic rings, frowning slightly, stepping back out of the way. She swallowed and tried to smile, wishing us good luck, as I glared at her from where I stood.

The boy went through his rings pretty quickly, as I tried to develop a plan, a way to surprise us both, and win one of the damn prizes for once in my life. I was working on a backward flip, the rings seeming to clang around the middle of the glass bottles, and shoot up into the air. The spin seemed important, not like a Frisbee, spinning round and round, from side to side, but like a coin flip—the motion backward, some new way of beating the system, I thought.

The boy watched me as my bucket emptied, quickly running out of chances.

"See, I said," as he looked on, the day having sapped our energy, the sun starting to set, "this thing is . . . "

156

And the plastic clinked off of the glass bottles, flipped into the air, the revolutions slowing as the voices around us drifted on the hot summer air, the smell of popcorn, my boy smiling, the ring settling over the top of a bottle, rattling back and forth before sitting down for good, staying on the top. It was a winner. We'd won.

The girl looked at the bottle, back to us, and set off the siren, cranking the handle, yelling, "We have a winner, big winner over here—winner winner chicken dinner," her smile so wide it ate her face, the kid jumping up and down, and against all logic, a grin seeping across my face as well. She asked my son which one he wanted, and he selected the tiger, almost as big as him, and he took it from the girl, soon to hand it off to me, the day almost gone, the spark of our victory pushing us onward.

"Thanks," I said, as we walked away, the counter crowded with new suckers trying to capture a bit of our luck, the magic we'd had for just a moment.

I stood over the boy and held his hand, a wave of grief washing over me, sitting down, as the tears leaked out of me, sobbing into the darkness, asking the boy for forgiveness, asking my wife for forgiveness, asking God for forgiveness, knowing that none would be coming from any of them—but asking anyway. I'd be gone soon, and it was better this way, if they let me go easy, if they just thought of me as some dark presence that would settle over some other tract of land, a mass of clouds and cold rain, waiting to erupt with lightning and thunder.

I told the kid I loved him, and then I left. I told her the same thing, my wife, and for a moment she was there again, as I whispered in her ear my secret. If I never came back, it meant that I'd won, we'd won, and that the boy might possibly be spared. Her eyes lit up for a moment, piercing the darkness.

It was all I had left to offer.

The warehouse. It's nothing special, but I'm drawn to it like a moth to the flame, and from blocks away I can tell this is either the worst mistake I've ever made, or the best thing I've ever done. Nobody stands outside the door, a cold rain falling—bits of sleet nipping at my flesh, the possibility of snow. The double doors hang open like a mouth, and inside I see a red glow, an altar in the middle of the room, a pentagram drawn on the floor in white chalk.

I take the three black candles I've brought and bring them to the pile that surrounds the altar, and light one of them from another, noticing for the first time that the ring of people surrounding the structure are entirely naked. Some are coated in blood, and some are actively violating their flesh, in a variety of ways, a bell ringing from the edge of the structure, a whispering of foreign words filling my ears. A few others at the edge of the room are wearing black robes, the hoods pulled up, no faces to be seen.

I was told to bathe, which goes against all instinct, but I'm clean as a whistle, sweat running in rivulets down my back, the room oddly hot for such a cold day. I undress and stand in the circle, not saying a word. I am not here to question, to cause trouble, I am here to absorb, to pray to dark spirits since the light ones don't seem to care. Incense burns in silver bowls, one on each corner of the altar, the scent of pine and cedar drifting to me, mixed with patchouli and musk, something sweet cutting through it, a hint of something foul underneath.

A silver chalice is being passed round, something red inside, I'm hoping wine, so I drink from it, the liquid warm and tacky, thinking of the prayers I've come to say, my boy at home, my wife lost to the night, every life I've ever taken dancing in front of me, spirits in a loping chain running circles around the candles. In my hand are slips of paper with the names of my family, my name, too, and my wishes for the evening, asking for the disease, asking for the demons to shift, to come to me in my hour of need, to let me become whatever they need me to be, if only they'll spare my wife and child. I've brought this down upon us all, the sickness in me spreading to them. When others step forward to place their prayer scrolls into their candle flames, I do the same.

There is a vibration in the room, as our various mantras are uttered from behind clenched lips and bared teeth, my eyes closed as I repeat the same phrase over and over again: come to me, spare the boy; come to me, spare the boy; come to me, spare the boy; come to me, spare the boy.

A bell rings again in the distance, and three robed men move toward the center of the ring, pulling back their hoods, as they look around the room—bald heads and black eyes, nubs pushing out of their foreheads. When they settle on me, I nod, and they walk toward me, leading me to the altar. I lie down as the room hums, the names of various demons filling the air, and I am reminded of gunshots, the screams of the fallen filling abandoned houses, back alleys, metal wrenching against metal as a car careens off the street into a wall, the sound of feet slapping the pavement, my breath increasing, until it fills my ears, the men with their hands on me, oil coating my flesh, as my skin numbs, coins placed on my eyes as I close them, the tip of a blade placed at my sternum and run down to my navel, my flesh parting, blood seeping over my ribcage, and onto the table. I moan, and they are at my ears, whispering, asking, other hands pulling back my flesh, pushing something inside me, and I pass out.

When I wake, I'm sitting behind the wheel of an unmarked sedan, the heater running full blast, the engine rumbling as my partner nudges my shoulder, handing me a cup of coffee.. I blink and take it from him, sitting up, as we stare at a set of concrete buildings, Section-8 housing, three men standing out front huffing breath into their hands—a skinny white kid with dreads, a fat black man in sweats, and a skinny Hispanic girl with a skirt so short her ass is hanging out. My partner says we're waiting for somebody to show up, and he goes on about what we'll do later once we bust these punks, some dive bar over in Wicker Park he knows about, cans of Schlitz and a decent pool table, offering me a bump of cocaine on a tiny spoon, which I take, my eyes going wide, a rush over my skin, him mumbling, thank God neither of us is married. A car pulls up, radio blasting, fat tires on a little car, the bass bumping, and he says it's time to go, so we pull out our pistols, clicking off the safeties, and open the doors, the light inside turned off, slinking in

Repent

the darkness toward the housing, a whistle and a shout, the skinny kid off like lightning, the girl tripping and falling off to the side of the house, the fat man not moving, just grinning as we rush him, the car speeding off, shots into the wheels, it skidding to the side, stopping, two kids popping out, one taking a shot to the back, the other lost in the night, the big guy raising his hands and whispering don't shoot, but I do anyway.

Somewhere far north of me a boy coughs and spits and then sits up, able to breathe. His mother sits next to him, patting him on the back, and his color comes back, his eyes bright white, a smile slipping over his face, asking for a glass of water. She sees in him something different, and she relaxes for the first time in weeks, months, running her hand over his bald head, holding him to her, the chemo, she says, maybe it's working, a gnawing at the base of her skull, something she forgot to do, somebody she meant to call back, but she can't quite place it, so she lets it go, a phantom of a shape drifting down the hallway, gone forever, a hollow pang in her chest quickly replaced by her boy hugging her, asking about a sandwich now, as the wind and cold whips around the house, a candle downstairs snuffing out, a wisp of smoke curling into the air.

I stand at the end of the alley, and warm my hands. I'm sick. The heat from the trashcan barely warms my flesh, the rats running up and down behind the garbage cans, nipping at my skin, and they'll never stop, they'll never go away now, I'm too far gone, a rotten apple bruised and dented, a cockroach at my neck, and I slap it away, eyes forever glued to the end of the brick walls, down toward the light where I can no longer go, no longer any good to anyone, including myself; especially myself. My eyes have become pools of black liquid, running down my sallow cheeks, and I shake my head, trying to focus, but it's no good, I'm blurring now, ready to let go. It will be over soon.

I forgot their names, all of the people, all of the friends, the world around me but especially the boy, his hair was brown, I know that much, his eyes the same, and she was, she was . . . no, I can't remember, she was there, she used to kiss me when I came home, she would hold my face in her hands and try to take my pain. And there were times I let her.

The end of the alleyway fills with bright light, a car passing by, the snow swirling around, and when the shadows drift over the opening, it finally steps into the space I've been watching for weeks, waiting my whole life for, elongated skull and a crown of horns, antlers above its head, lumbering toward me, sinew and muscle, hooved feet clacking on the concrete, great gusts of exhale out of its snout, a flicker of flame, eyes glowing red and there is no pleading now, nothing left to ask for, nothing to forgive.

It shifts its shape as it walks, goat head one moment, minotaur the next, a deep vibration rumbling the walls, the earth, as it laughs a guttural moaning, and before I can say anything, ask anything, it is there, my neck in its hands, as a great wingspan unfolds behind it, black as oil, a fluttering as other creatures emerge from under its leathery feathers, a pain in my chest as the cancer spreads, filling my chest with a scurry of beetles, my fingernails turning black, my mouth opening as maggots and worms spill out of my gaping last gasp and I embrace what I have been—the clanking of iron chains, gates slamming shut with a rush of foul wind and a blast of heat. As my eyes close, I see the sculptures, the piles of sticks, the pyramids, the twine and rope, the vines and metal, running up and down the alleyway, these structures I'd been making my whole life, these quiet moments of meditation, sending out into the world a stream of evil that finally added up to something. My pain and pleasure, my suffering and vengeance, a rippling in a dark pond that would infect so many for so long, the waters settling, calming down to a sheet of black ice, the last moments of my rotten life filled with the sound of my son coughing, sitting up, my wife holding him, crying, my name never to be uttered aloud again, by them, or anyone else.

Coming to Grief

CLIVE BARKER

Miriam had not taken the shortcut along the rim of the quarry for almost eighteen years. Eighteen years of another life, quite unlike the life she'd lived in this all-but-forgotten city. She'd left Liverpool to taste the world: to grow; to prosper; to learn to live; and, by God, hadn't she done just that? From the naive and frightened nineteen-year-old she had been when she had last set foot on the quarry path, she had blossomed into a wholly sophisticated woman of the world. Her husband idolized her; her daughter grew more like her with every year; she was universally adored.

Yet now, as she stepped onto the ill-bred gravel path that skirted the chasm of the quarry, she felt as though a wound had opened in her heel and that hard-won poise and self-reliance were draining out of her and running away into the dark; as though she'd never left her native city, never grown wiser with experience. She felt no more prepared to face this hundred-yard stretch of walled walkway than she had been at nineteen. The same doubts, the same imagined horrors that had always haunted her on this spot, clung now to the inside of her brainpan and whispered about the certainty of secrets. They still lay in wait here, idiot fears concocted of street-corner gossip and childish superstition. Even now the old myths came running back to embrace her. Tales of hook-handed men, and secret lovers slaughtered in the act of love; a dozen rumored atrocities that, to her burgeoning and overheated imagination, had always had their source, their epicenter, here: on the Bogey-Walk.

That's what they'd called it; and that was what it would always be to her: the Bogey-Walk. Instead of losing its potency with the passage of the years, it had grown gross. It had prospered as she had prospered; it had found its vocation as she had done. Of course, she had grown into contentment, and perhaps that weakened her. But it, oh, *it* had merely fed on its own frustration and become encrusted with desire to take her for itself. Maybe, as time had passed, it had fed a little to keep its strength up: but it needed, in its immutable heart, only the certainty of its final victory to stay alive. Of this she was suddenly and incontestably certain: that the battles she had fought with her own weakness were not over. They had scarcely begun.

She attempted to advance a few yards along the Walk but faltered and stopped, the so-familiar panic turning her feet to lead weights. The night was not soundless. A jet droned over, a longing roar in the darkness; a mother called her child in from the street. But here, on the Walk itself, signs of life were a world away and could not comfort her. Cursing her own vulnerability, she turned back the way she'd come and traipsed home through the warm drizzle by a more roundabout route.

Coming to Grief

Grief, she half reasoned, had battened upon her and sapped her will to fight. In two days' time perhaps, when her mother's funeral was over and the sudden loss was more manageable, then she would see the future plainly and that pathway would fall into its proper perspective. She'd recognize the Bogey-Walk as the excrement-ridden, weed-lined gravel path that it was. Meanwhile she'd get wetter than she needed taking the safe road home.

The quarry was not in itself such a terrifying spot; nor, to any but there was the path along its rim. There'd been no murders there that she knew of, no rapes or muggings committed along that sordid little track. It was a public footpath, no less and no more: a poorly kept, poorly illuminated walkway around the edge of what had once been a productive quarry and was now the communal rubbish-tip. The wall that kept the walkers from falling a hundred feet to their deaths below was built of plain red brick. It was eight feet high, so that nobody could even see the depth on the other side, and was lined with pieces of broken milk bottles set in concrete, to dissuade anyone from scrambling up onto it. The path itself had once been tarmac, but subsidence had opened cracks in it, and the Council, instead of resurfacing, had seen fit simply to dust it with loose gravel. It was seldom, if ever, weeded. Stinging nettles grew to child-height in the meager dirt at the bottom of the wall, as did a sickly scented flower whose name she did not know but which, at the height of summer, was a Mecca to wasps. And that—wall, gravel, and weeds—was the sum of the place.

In dreams, however, she'd scaled that wall—her palms magically immune to the pricking glass—and in those vertiginous adventures she'd peer down and down the black, sheer cliff of the quarry into its dark heart. It was impenetrable, the gloom at the bottom, but she knew that there was a lake of green and brackish water somewhere below. It could be seen, that choked pool of filth, from the other side of the quarry; from the safe side. That's how she knew it was there, in her dreams. And she knew, too, walking on the unpiercing glass, tempting gravity and providence alike, that the prodigy of malice that lived on the cliff face would have seen her and would be climbing, even now, hand over clawed hand, up the steep side toward her. But in those dreams she always woke up before the nameless beast caught hold of her dancing feet, and the exhilaration of her escape would heal the fear, at least until the next time she dreamed.

The opposite end of the quarry, far from the sheer wall and the pool, had always been safe. Abandoned diggings and blastings had left a litter of boulders of Piranesian magnitude, in whose crevices she had often played as a child. There was no danger here: just a playground of tunnels. It seemed miles and miles (at least to her child's eye) across the wasteland to the rainwater lake and the tiny line of red brick wall that beetled along the top of the cliff. Though there had been days, she remembered, even in the safety of the sun, when she would catch sight of something the color of the rock itself stretching its back on the warm face of the quarry, clinging to the cliff in a tireless and predatory pose not a dozen yards beneath the wall. Then, as her child's eyes narrowed to try to make sense of its anatomy, it would sense her gaze and freeze itself into a perfect copy of the stone.

Stone. Cold stone. Thinking about absence, about the disguise required by a thing that wished not to be seen, she turned into her mother's road. As she selected the house key, it occurred to her, absurdly, that perhaps Veronica was not dead: simply perfectly camouflaged in the house somewhere, pressed against the wall or at the mantelpiece; unseen but seeing. Perhaps then visible ghosts were simply inept chameleons: the rest had the trick of concealment down pat. It was a foolish, fruitless train of thought, and she chided herself for entertaining it. Tomorrow, or the day after, such thoughts would again seem as alien as the lost world in which she was presently stranded. So thinking, she stepped indoors.

The house did not distress her; it simply reawakened a sense of tedium her busy, clever life had put aside. The task of dividing, discarding, and packing the remnants of her mother's life was slow and repetitive. The rest—the loss, the remorse, the bitterness—were so many thoughts for another day. There was sufficient to do as it was, without mourning. Certainly the empty rooms held memories; but they were all pleasant enough to be happily recalled, yet not so exquisite as to be wished into being again. Her feelings, moving around the deserted house, could only be defined by what she no longer saw or felt: not her mother's face; not the chiding voice, the preventing hand; just an unknowable nothing that was the space where life used to be.

In Hong Kong, she thought, Boyd would be on duty, and the sun would be blazing hot, the streets thronged with people. Though she hated to go out at midday, when the city was so crowded, today she would have welcomed the discomfort. It was tiresome sitting in the dusty bedroom, carefully sorting and folding the scented linen from the chest of drawers. She wanted life, even if it was insistent and oppressive. She longed for the smell of the streets to be piercing her nostrils, and the heat to be beating on her head. No matter, she thought, soon done.

Soon done. Ah, there was a guilt there: the ticking off of the days until the funeral, the pacing out of her mother's ritual removal from the world. Another seventy-two hours and the whole business would be done with, and she would be flying back to life.

As she went about her daughterly duties, she left every light burning in the house. It was more convenient to do so, she told herself, with all the to-ing and fro-ing the job required. Besides, the late November days were short and dismal, and the work was dispiriting enough without having to labor in a perpetual dusk.

Organizing the disposal of personal items was taking the longest time. Her mother had acquired a sizable wardrobe, all of which had to be sorted through: the pockets emptied, the jewelry removed from the collars. She sealed up the bulk of the clothes in black plastic bags, to be collected by a local charity shop the following day, keeping only a fur wrap and a gown for herself. Then she selected a few of her mother's favorite possessions to give to close friends after the funeral: a leather handbag; some china cups and saucers; a herd of ivory elephants that had belonged . . . she had forgotten who they had belonged to. Some relative, long gone.

Coming to Grief

Once the clothes and bric-a-brac had been organized, she turned her attention to the mail, sorting the outstanding bills into one pile and the personal correspondence, whether recent or remote, into another. Each letter, however old or difficult to follow, she read carefully. Most she dispatched to the small fire she had lit in the living-room grate. It was soon a cave of bat-wing ashes; black and veined with burned words. Once only, a letter found tears in her: a note, written in her father's gossamer hand, which awakened agonies of regret for the wasted years of antagonism between them. There were photographs among the leaves, too; most as frozen as Alaska: arid, fruitless territory. Some, however, catching a true moment between the poses, were as fresh as yesterday, and a din of voices spilled from the aged image:

—*Wait! Not yet! I'm not ready!*

—*Daddy! Where's Daddy? We must have Daddy in this one!*

—*He's tickling me!*

Laughter pealed off these images; their fixed joy parodied the truth of deterioration and annihilation whose proof was borne by the empty house.

—*Wait!*

—*Not yet!*

—*Daddy!*

She could hardly bear to look at some of them. She burned first the ones that hurt the most.

—*Wait!* someone shouted. Herself, perhaps, a child in the arms of the past. *Wait!*

But the pictures cracked in the heart of the fire, then browned and burst with blue flame, and the moment—*Wait!*—the moment went the way of all the moments that had surrounded the instant that the camera had fixed, gone away forever like fathers and mothers and, in time, daughters too.

She retired to bed at three-fifteen a.m., the bulk of her self-assigned chores done for the day. Her mother would have applauded her efficiency, she suspected. How ironic that Miriam, the daughter who had never been daughterly enough, who had always wanted the world instead of being content to stay at home, was now being as meticulous as any parent could have possibly wished. Here she was, cleaning away a whole history; consigning the leavings of a life to the fire, scouring the house more thoroughly than her mother had ever done.

A little after three-thirty, having mentally arranged the business of the following day, she drained the last of the half tumbler of whiskey she'd been sipping all evening and sank, almost immediately, into sleep.

She dreamed nothing. Her mind was clear. As clear as darkness is clear, as emptiness is clear; not even Boyd's face, or his body (she often dreamed of his chest, of the fine pattern of hair on his stomach) crept into her head to pollute the featureless bliss.

It was raining when she awoke. Her first thought was: Where am I? Her second thought was: Is today the funeral, or tomorrow?

Her third thought was: In two days I'll be back with Boyd. The sun will be shining. I'll forget all of this.

For today, however, there was more unappetizing work ahead. The funeral was not until tomorrow, which was Wednesday. Today the business was mundane: checking the cremation arrangements with

Beckett and Dawes, writing notes of thanks for the many letters of condolence she'd received, a dozen other minor duties. In the afternoon she would visit Mrs. Furness, a friend of her mother's who was now too crippled with arthritis to attend the funeral. She would give the old lady that leather handbag, as a keepsake. In the evening it would be again the same, sorry business of sorting through her mother's belongings and organizing their redistribution. There was so much to give to the needy—or the greedy— whichever asked first. She didn't care who took the stuff, as long as the job was finished soon.

About mid-morning, the telephone rang. It was the first noise she'd heard in the house since waking that she hadn't made herself, and it startled her. She lifted the receiver, and a warm word was spoken in her ear: her name.

"Miriam?"

"Yes. Who is this?"

"Oh, love, you sound absolutely washed out. It's Judy, sweetheart; Judy Cusack."

"Judy?"

The very name was a smile.

"Don't you remember?"

"Of course I remember. How lovely to hear your voice."

"I didn't ring any earlier. I thought you'd have so much on your hands. I'm so sorry, pet, about your mother. It must have been a blow. My dad died the year before last. It really knocked me sideways."

Vaguely Miriam could picture Judy's father, a slender, elegant man who'd smiled once in a while and had said very little.

"He'd been very ill. It was a blessing, really. God, I never thought I'd hear myself say that. Funny, isn't it?"

Judy's voice had scarcely changed at all; she frothed with pleasure the way she always had, the body Miriam saw in her mind's eye was still rounded, with a lingering puppy fat. Eighteen years ago they had been the best of friends, soul mates; and for a moment, exchanging pleasantries with that breezy voice, it was as though the time between this conversation and their last had shrunk to hours.

"It's so good to hear your voice," said Miriam.

It was good. It was the past speaking, but it was a good past, a sunlit past. She had almost forgotten, in the toil of this autopsy she was busy with, how fine some memories could be.

"I heard from the people next door about your coming home," Judy said, "but I was of two minds whether to call. I know it must be a very difficult time for you. So sad and all."

"Not really," Miriam said.

The plain truth sneaked out without her meaning to say it; but there it was now, said. It wasn't a sad time. It was a drudge, it was a limbo, but she wasn't holding a flood of sorrows in abeyance. She saw that now, and her heart lightened with the simplicity of the confession. Judy offered no reproof, only an invitation.

"Are you feeling well enough to come over for a drink?"

"I've still got a lot of sorting to do."

"I promise we won't talk about old times," Judy said.

"Not one word. I couldn't bear it; it makes me feel antiquated." She laughed. Miriam laughed with her.

"Yes," she said. "I'd love to come . . . "

"Good. It's a bind, isn't it, when you're an only child, and it's all your responsibility. Sometimes you really think there's no end to it."

"It's crossed my mind," Miriam replied.

"When it's all over, you'll wonder what the fuss was about," Judy said. "I coped with Dad's funeral, though at the time I thought I was going to fall apart."

"You didn't have to handle it alone, did you?" Miriam asked.

"What about . . . " She wanted to name Judy's husband; she recalled her mother writing to her about Judy's late—and if she remembered correctly, scandalous—marriage. But she couldn't remember the groom's name.

"Donald?" Judy prompted her.

"Donald."

"Separated, pet. We've been separated two and a half years."

"Oh, I'm sorry."

"I'm not." The answer came back in a flash.

"It's a long story. I'll tell you about it this evening. About seven?"

"Could we make it a little later? I've got so much to do. Is eight all right?"

"Anytime, love, don't rush yourself. I'll expect you when I see you; we'll leave it at that."

"Fine. And thanks for ringing."

"I've been itching to call since I heard you were back. It's not often you get a chance to see old friends, is it?"

A few minutes shy of noon, Miriam faced what she

expected to be the most debilitating of her duties. Though she wouldn't confess it to herself, she felt a tremor of disgust as she parked outside the funeral home. There was a dull, stale taste at the back of her throat, and her eyes seemed spoiled with grit. She frankly had no wish to see her mother again, not now that they couldn't talk, and yet when the urbane Mr. Beckett had said to her on the phone, "You will want to view the deceased?" she had replied, "Of course," as though the request had been on the tip of her tongue all along.

And what was there to fear?

Veronica Blessed was dead; she'd died peacefully in her sleep. But Miriam found that a phrase, a random phrase that she remembered from school, had crept into the back of her head that morning and she couldn't rid herself of it:

"Everyone dies because they run out of breath."

That thought was there now, as she looked at Mr. Beckett, and the paper lilies and the scuffed corner of his desk. To run out of breath, to choke on a tongue, to suffocate under a blanket. She had known all those fears when she was young, and now they came back to her in Mr. Beckett's office and held her hand. One of them leaned over and whispered maliciously in her ear: Suppose one day you simply forget to breathe? Black face, tongue bitten off.

Was that what made her throat so dry? The thought that Mama, Veronica, Mrs. Blessed, widow of Harold Blessed, now deceased, would be lying on silk with her face as black as the Earl of Hell's riding boots? Vile notion: vile, ridiculous notion.

But they kept coming, these unwelcome ideas, one

quick upon the heels of another. Most she could trace back to childhood; absurd, irrelevant images floating up from her past like squid to the sun.

The Levitation Game, a favorite school pastime, came to mind: six girls ranged around a seventh, trying to lift her up with one finger apiece. And the accompanying ceremony:

"She looks pale," says the girl at the head. "She is pale."

"She is pale."

"She is pale."

"She is pale."

"She is pale," the attendants answer by rote, counterclockwise.

"She looks ill," the high priestess announces.

"She is ill."

"She is ill."

"She is ill."

"She is ill."

"She is ill," the others reply.

"She looks dead—"

She is—

There'd been a murder, too, when she was only six, two streets down from where they'd lived. The body had been wedged behind the front door—she'd heard Mrs. Furness tell all to her mother—and it was so softened by putrefaction that when the police forced the door open it had concertinaed into a bundle that proved impossible to unglue. Sitting now beside the scentless lilies, Miriam could smell the day she'd stood, hand in her mother's hand, listening to the women talk of murder. Crime, come to think of it, had been a favorite subject of Mrs. Furness. Had it been through her good offices that Miriam had first learned that her nightmares of the Bogey-Walk had their counterpart in the adult world?

Miriam smiled, thinking of the women casually debating slaughter as they stood in the sun. Mr. Beckett seemed not to notice her smile; or, more likely, was well prepared for any manifestation of grief, however bizarre. Perhaps mourners came in here and threw off all their clothes in their anguish or wet their pants. She looked at him more closely, this young man who had made a profession of bereavement. He was not unattractive, she thought. He was an inch or two shorter than she, but height didn't matter in bed; and moving coffins around would put some muscle on a body, wouldn't it?

Listen to yourself, she thought, pulling herself up short. *What are you contemplating?*

Mr. Beckett plucked at his pale ginger mustache and offered a look of practiced condolence to Miriam. She saw his charm—what meager supply there was— vanish in that one look.

He seemed to be waiting for some cue from her; she wondered what. At last he said:

"Shall we go through to the Chapel of Rest, or shall we discuss the business first?"

Ah, that was it. *Better to get the farewells over with*, she thought. He could wait a while longer for his money. "I'd like to see my mother," she said.

"Of course you would," he replied, nodding as though he'd known all along that she wanted to view the body; as if he were somehow completely conversant with her most intimate workings. She resented his fake familiarity but made no sign of it.

He stood up and ushered her through the glass-paneled door and into a corridor flanked by vases of flowers. They, like the lilies on his desk, were artificial. The scent she could smell was that of floor polish, not blossoms; no bee had hope of succor here, unless there was nectar to be taken from the dead.

Mr. Beckett halted at one of the doors, turned the handle, and ushered Miriam ahead of him. This was it, then: face-to-face at last. *Smile, Mother, Miriam's home.* She entered the room. Two candles burned on a small table against the far wall, and there was a further abundance of artificial flowers, their fake fecundity more distasteful here than ever.

The room was small. Space enough for a coffin, a chair, a table bearing the candles, and one or two living souls.

"Shall I leave you with your mother?" Mr. Beckett asked.

"No," she said with more urgency and more volume than the tiny room could accommodate. The candles coughed lightly at her indiscretion. More softly she said, "I would prefer you to stay, if you don't mind."

"Of course," Mr. Beckett dutifully replied.

She wondered briefly how many people, at this juncture, chose to keep their vigil unaccompanied. It would be an interesting statistic, she thought, her mind dividing into disinterested observer and frightened participant. How many mourners, faced with the dear dead, asked for company, however anonymous, rather than be left alone with a face they had known a lifetime?

Taking a deep breath, she stepped toward the coffin, and there, snoozing on a sheet of pale cream cloth in this narrow, high-sided bed, was her mother. *What a foolish and neglectful place to fall asleep in*, she thought; *and in your favorite dress. So unlike you, Mother, to be so impractical.* Her face had been tastefully rouged, and her hair recently brushed, although not in a style she had favored. Miriam felt no horror at seeing her like this; just a sharp thrill of recognition and the instinct, barely suppressed, to reach into the coffin and shake her mother awake.

Mother, I'm here. It's Miriam.

Wake up.

At the thought of that, Miriam felt her cheeks flush, and hot tears well up in her eyes.

The tiny room was abruptly a single sheet of watery light; the candles two bright eyes."Mama," she said once.

Mr. Beckett, clearly long inured to such spectacles, said nothing, but Miriam was acutely aware of his presence behind her and wished she'd asked him to leave. She took hold of the side of the coffin to steady herself, while the tears dripped off her cheeks and fell into the folds of her mother's dress.

So this was death's house; this was its shape and nature. Its etiquette was perfect. At its visitation there had been no violence; only a profound and changeless calm that denied the need for further show of affection.

Her mother, she realized, didn't require her any longer; it was as simple as that. Her first and final rejection. *Thank you*, said that cold, discrete body, *but I have no further need of you. Thank you for your concern, but you may go.*

Coming to Grief

She stared at Veronica's well-dressed corpse through a haze of unhappiness, not hoping to wake her mother now, not hoping even to make sense of the sight.

Then she said, "Thank you," very quietly.

The words were for her mother; but Mr. Beckett, taking Miriam's arm as she turned to go, took it for himself.

"It's no trouble," he replied. "Really."

Miriam blew her nose and tasted the tears. The duty was done. Time now for business. She drank weak tea with Beckett and finalized the financial arrangements, watching for him to smile once, to break his covenant with sympathy. He didn't. The interview was conducted with indecent reverence, and by the time he ushered her out into the cold afternoon, she had grown to despise him.

She drove home without thinking, her mind not blank with the loss but with the exhaustion of having wept. It was not a conscious decision that made her choose the route back to the house that led alongside the quarry. But as she turned into the street that ran past her old playground, she realized that some part of her wanted—perhaps even needed—a confrontation with the Bogey-Walk.

She parked the car at the safe end of the quarry, a short walk from the path itself, and got out. The wire gates she'd scrambled through as a child were locked, but a hole had been torn in the wire, as ever. Doubtless the quarry was still a playground. New wire, new gates; but the same games. She couldn't resist ducking through the gap, though her coat snagged on a hook of wire as she did so. Inside, little seemed to have changed. The same chaos of boulders, steps and plateaus, litter, weeds and puddles, lost and broken toys, bicycle parts. She thrust her fists into her coat pockets and ambled through the rubble of childhood, keeping her eyes fixed on her feet, easily finding again the familiar routes between the stones.

She would never get lost here. In the dark—in death, even, as a ghost—she would be certain of her steps. Finally she located the spot she'd always loved the best and, standing in the lee of a great stone, raised her head to look at the cliff across the quarry. From this distance the Walk was barely visible, but she scanned its length meticulously. The quarry face looked less imposing than she'd remembered; less majestic. The intervening years had shown her more perilous heights, more tremendous depths. And yet she still felt her bowels contracting as though an octopus had been sewn up at the crux of her body, and she knew that the child in her, insusceptible to reason, was searching the cliff for a sign, however negligible, of the Walk's haunter. The twitch of a stone-colored limb, perhaps, as it kept its relentless vigil; the flicker of a terrible eye.

But she could see nothing.

Almost ashamed of her fears, she retraced her steps through the canyon of stones, slipped through the gate like an errant child, and returned to the car.

The Bogey-Walk was safe. Of course it was safe. It held no horrors, and never had. The sun was valiantly trying to share her exhilaration now, forcing wan and heatless beams through the rain clouds. The wind was at her side, smelling of the river. Grief was a memory.

She would go to the Walk now, she decided, and give herself time to savor each fearless step she took along it, jubilating in her victory over history. She drove around the side of the quarry and slammed the car door with a smile on her face as she climbed the three steps that led off the pavement onto the footpath itself.

The shadow of the brick wall fell across the Walk, of course; and its length was darker than the street behind her. But nothing could sour her confidence. She walked from one end of the weed-clogged corridor to the other without incident, her whole body high with the sheer ease of it. *How could I ever have feared this?* she asked herself as she turned and began the journey to the waiting car.

This time, as she walked, she allowed herself to think back on the specifics of her childhood nightmares. There had been a place—halfway along the Walk and therefore at the greatest distance from help—that had been the high-water mark of her terror. That particular spot—that forbidden few yards that, to the unseeing eye, were no different from every other yard along the Walk—was the place the thing in the quarry would choose to pounce when her last moments came. That was its killing ground, its sacrificial grove, marked, she had fervently believed, with blood of countless other children.

Even as the taste of that memory returned to her, she approached the point. The signs that had marked the place were still to be seen: an arrangement of five discolored bricks; a crack in the cement that had been minuscule eighteen years ago and had grown larger. The spot was as recognizable as ever; but it had lost its potency. It was just another few of a hundred identical yards, and she bypassed the spot without the contentment on her face faltering for more than an instant. She didn't even glance behind her.

The wall of the Bogey-Walk was old. It had been built a decade before Miriam was born, by men who had known their craft indifferently well. Erosion had eaten at the quarry face beneath the teetering brick, unseen by Council inspectors and safety officials from the Department of the Environment; in places the rain-sodden sandstone had crumbled and fallen away. Here and there, the bricks were unsupported across as much as half their breadth. They hung over the abyss of the quarry while rain and wind and gravity ate at the crumbling mortar that kept them united.

Miriam saw none of this. She would have had to have waited a while before she heard the uneasy grinding of the bricks as they leaned out against the air, waiting, aching, begging to fall. As it was, she went away, elated, certain that she'd sloughed off her terrors forever.

That evening she saw Judy.

Judy had never been beautiful; there had always been an excess in her features: her eyes too big, her mouth too broad. Yet now, in her mid-thirties, she was radiant. It was a sexual bloom, certainly, and one that might wither and die prematurely, but the woman who met Miriam at the front door was in her prime.

They talked through the evening about the years they'd been apart—despite their contract not to discuss the past—exchanging tales of their defeats and their successes. Miriam found Judy's company enchanting; she was immediately comfortable with this bright, happy woman. Even the subject of her separation from Donald didn't inhibit her flow.

"It's not verboten to talk about old husbands, pet; it's just a bit boring. I mean, he wasn't a bad sort."

"Are you divorcing him?"

"I suppose so; if I have a moment. These things take months, you know. Besides, I'm a Libra; I can never make up my mind what I want." She paused. "Well," she said with a half-secret smile, "That's not altogether true."

"Was he unfaithful?"

"Unfaithful?" She laughed. "That's a word I haven't heard in a long time."

Miriam blushed a little. Was life really so backward in the colonies, where adultery was not yet compulsory?

"He screwed around," said Judy. "That's the simple truth of it. But then, so did I."

She laughed again, and this time Miriam joined in with the laughter, not quite certain of the joke. "How did you find out?"

"I found out when he found out."

"I don't understand."

"It was all so obvious, it sounds like a farce when I tell it; but he found a letter, you see, from someone I'd been with. Nobody particularly important to me—just a casual friend, really. Anyway, he was triumphant; I mean, he really crowed about it, said he'd had more affairs than I had. Treated it all like some sort of competition—who could cheat the most often and with whom." She paused; the same mischievous smile appeared again. "As it was, when we put our cards on the table, I was doing rather better than he was. That really pissed him off."

"So you separated?"

"There didn't seem to be much point in staying together; we didn't have any kids. And there wasn't any love lost between us. There never really had been. The house was in his name, but he let me have it."

"So you won the competition?"

"I suppose I did. But then, I had a hidden advantage."

"What?"

"The other man in my life was a woman," Judy said, "and poor Donald couldn't handle that at all. He more or less threw in the towel as soon as he found out. Told me he realized he'd never understood me and that we were better apart." She looked up at Miriam and only now saw the effect her statement had had. "Oh," she said, "I'm sorry. I just opened my mouth and put my foot in it."

"No," said Miriam, "It's me. I'd never thought of you . . ."

" . . . as a lesbian? Oh, I think I've always known it, right back to school days. Writing love letters to the games mistress."

"We all did that," Miriam reminded her.

"Some of us meant it more seriously than others." Judy smiled.

"And where's Donald now?"

"Oh, somewhere in the Middle East, last I heard. I'd like him to write to me, just to tell me he's well. But he won't. His pride wouldn't let him. It's a pity. We might have been good friends if we hadn't been husband and wife."

That seemed to be all there was to say on the subject; or all Judy wanted to say.

"Shall I go and make some coffee?" she suggested, and went through to the kitchen, leaving Miriam to toy with the cat and her thoughts. Neither were particularly fleet-footed that night.

"I'd like to go to your mum's funeral," Judy called through from the kitchen.

"Would you mind?"

"Of course not."

"I didn't know her well, but I used to see her out shopping. She always looked so smart."

"She was," Miriam said. Then: "Why don't you come in the lead car with me?"

"I'm not a relative."

"I'd like you to." The cat turned over in its sleep and presented its winter-furred belly to Miriam's comforting fingers. "Please."

"Then thank you. I will."

They spent the remaining hour and a half drinking coffee, and then whiskey, and then more whiskey, and talking about Hong Kong and their parents, and finally about memory. Or rather, about the irrational nature of memory; how their minds had selected such odd details to fix events while neglecting others more apparently significant: the smell in the air when the words of affection were spoken, not the words themselves; the color of a lover's shoes, but not of their eyes.

At last, way after midnight, they parted.

"Come to the house about eleven," Miriam said. "The cars are leaving at about a quarter past."

"Right. I'll see you tomorrow, then."

"Today," Miriam pointed out.

"That's right, today. Take care driving, love. It's a foul night."

The night was breezy; the car radio reported gale-force winds in the Irish Sea. She drove home cautiously through the empty streets, the same gusts that buffeted the car raising leaves from the dead and whirling them up into the glare of the headlamps. *In Hong Kong*, she thought, *there would still be plenty of life in the streets this time of night.* Here? Just sleep-darkened houses, closed curtains, locked doors. As she drove, she mentally followed her footsteps through the day and the three encounters that had marked it out. With her mother, with Judy, and with the Bogey-Walk. By the time she'd done her thinking, she was home.

Sleep came fitfully through the blustery night, punctuated by dustbin lids whipped off by vicious licks of wind, the rain, and the scratching of sycamore branches against the windows.

The next day was Wednesday, December 1, and the rain had turned to sleet by dawn.

The funeral was not insufferable. It was at best a functional farewell to someone Miriam had once known and now had lost sight of; at worst, its passionless solemnity and well-oiled ritual smacked of frigidity, ending as a conveyor belt took the coffin through a pair of lilac curtains to the furnace and the chimney beyond. Miriam could not help but imagine the interior of the coffin as it shuddered through the theatrical divide of the curtains; could not help but visualize the way her mother's body shook with each tiny jerk of her box toward the incinerator. The thought, though self-inflicted, was all but unbearable. She had to dig her fingernails into the flesh of her palm simply to prevent herself from standing up and demanding a halt to the proceedings: to have the lid pried off the coffin, to fumble in the shroud, and to pluck that blank body up in her arms one more time; lovingly, adoringly thanking her. That moment was the worst; she held herself in check until the curtains closed, and then it was over.

As partings went, it was perfunctory, but it clung, in its plain way, to a measure of dignity. The wind was biting as they left the tiny red brick chapel of the crematorium, the mourners already dividing to their cars with murmurs of thanks and faint looks of embarrassment. There were flakes of snow in the wind: too large and too wet to amount to much as they flopped to the ground, but rendering the glum surroundings yet more inhospitable. Miriam's teeth ached in her head; and the ache was spreading up her nose to her eyes.

Judy hooked her arm.

"We must get together again, love, before you leave."

Miriam nodded. Leaving was less than twenty-four hours away, and tonight, as a foretaste of liberty, Boyd would ring. He'd promised to do so, and he was sweetly reliable. She knew she'd be able to smell the heat of the street down the telephone wire.

"Tonight . . . " Miriam suggested to Judy. "Come round to the house tonight."

"Are you sure? Isn't it a bit of a trial being there?"

"Not really. Not now."

Not now. Veronica had gone, once and for all. The house was not a home any longer.

"I've still got a lot of cleaning up to do," Miriam said. "I want to hand it over to the agents with all Mother's belongings dealt with. I don't like the thought of strangers going through her stuff."

Judy murmured her agreement.

"I'll help, then," she said. "If you don't think I'll get in the way."

"A working evening?"

"Fine."

"Seven?"

"Seven."

A sudden, vehement gust of wind caught Miriam's breath, dispersing a few lingering mourners to the warmth of their cars. One of her mother's neighbors— Miriam could never remember the woman's name—lost her hat. It blew off and bowled across the Lawn of Remembrance, her pop-eyed husband clumsily pursuing it across the ash-enriched grass.

At the height of the quarry, the wind was even stronger. It came up from the sea and down the river, funneling its fury into a snow-specked fist; then it scoured the city for victims.

The wall of the Bogey-Walk was ideal material. Weak from the flux of years, it needed little bullying to persuade it to surrender. In the late afternoon, a particularly ambitious gust took three or four glass-crowned bricks off the top of the wall and pitched them into the quarry lake. The structure was weakest there, in the middle of its length, and once the wind had started the demolition, gravity lent its elbow to the work.

A young man, cycling home, was just about to reach the middle of the footpath when he heard a roar of capitulation and saw a section of the wall buckle outward in a cloud of mortar fragments. There was a diminishing percussion of bricks against rock as the ruins danced their way down to the foot of the cliff. A gap, fully six feet across, had opened up in the wall, and the wind, triumphant, roared through it, tugging at the exposed edges of the wall and coaxing them to follow. The young man got off his bicycle and wheeled it to the spot, grinning at the spectacle.

It was a long way down, he thought as he stepped toward the breach and cautiously peered over the edge. The wind was at his heels and at the small of his back, curling around him, begging him to step a little farther. He did. The vertigo he felt excited him, and the idiot urge to fling himself over, though resistible, was strong. Leaning over, he was able to see the bottom of the quarry; but the face of the stone directly beneath the hole in the wall was out of sight. A small overhang obscured the place.

The young man leaned farther out, the icy wind hot for him. *Come on*, it said. *Come on, look closer, look deeper.*

Something, not a yard below the yawning gap in the wall, moved. The young man saw, or thought he saw, a form—whose bulk was hidden by the overhang—move. Then, sensing that it was observed, freeze against the cliff wall.

Get on with it, said the wind. *Give in to your curiosity.*

The young man thought better of it. The thrill of the test was souring. He was cold; the fun was over. Home time. He stepped back from the hole and began to wheel his bicycle away, a whistle coming to his lips that was part in celebration of escape and part to keep whatever he felt at his back at bay.

At seven, Miriam was sorting through the last of her mother's jewelry. There was very little of value in the small perfumed boxes, but there were one or two pretty brooches nesting in beds of greying cotton wool that she had decided to take home with her, for remembrance. Boyd had rung a little after six, as he had promised, his voice watery on a bad line, but full of reassurance and affection. Miriam was still high from his conversation. Now the telephone rang again. It was Judy.

"Lovey, I don't think I ought to come over this evening. I'm feeling pretty bad at the moment. It came on at the funeral, and the pains are always bad when it's cold."

"Oh, dear."

"I'd be lousy company, I'm afraid. Sorry to let you down."

"Don't worry; if you're not well . . . "

"Pity is, I might not get to see you again before you go back." She sounded genuinely distressed at the thought.

"Listen," Miriam said, "if I get this work finished before it gets too late, I'll wander round your way. I hate telephone farewells."

"Me too."

"I can't promise."

Coming to Grief

"Well, if I see you, I see you; we'll leave it at that, eh? If I don't, take care, love, and drop me a line to tell me you got home safely."

By the time she stepped out of the house at nine-fifty, the gale had long since blown itself out, only to be followed by a stillness so profound, it was almost more unnerving than the preceding din. Miriam locked the door and took a step back to look at the front of the house. The next time she set foot here (if, indeed, she ever did), the house would be re-occupied and, no doubt, repainted. She would have no right-of-way here; the pains of remembrance she had experienced in the last few days would themselves be memories.

She walked to the car, keys in hand, but decided on the spur of the moment that she would walk to Judy's house. The gale-cleansed air was invigorating, and she would take the opportunity to wander around the old neighborhood one final time.

She would even take the Bogey-Walk, she thought; she'd be at Judy's in five or ten minutes.

There was a long, deceptive curve in the Walk as it followed the rim of the quarry. From one end, it was not possible to see the other, or even the middle. So Miriam was almost upon the gap in the wall before she saw it. Her confident step faltered. In her lower belly something uncoiled its arms in welcome.

The hole gaped in front of her, vast and inviting. Beyond the edge, where the meager light from the street had no strength to go, the darkness of the quarry was apparently infinite. She could have been standing on the edge of the world; there was neither depth nor distance beyond the lip of the path, just a blackness that hummed with anticipation.

Even as she stared, morsels of cement crumbled into space. She heard them patter away from her; she could even hear their distant splashes.

But now, entranced by her sudden dread, she heard another noise, close by, a noise she had prayed never to hear in the waking world, the grit of nails on the stone face of the quarry, the rush of caustic breath from a creature that had waited oh, so patiently for this moment and was now slowly and purposefully dragging its way up the last few feet of the cliff toward her. And why should it hurry? It knew she was frozen to the spot.

It was coming; there was no help to be had. Its arms were splayed over the stone, and its head, dark with grime and depravity, was almost at the rim of the Walk. Even now, with its victim almost in view, it didn't hasten its steady climb but took its awful time.

The little girl Miriam had been wanted to die now, before it saw her, but the woman she was wanted to see the face of her ageless tormentor. Just to see, for the horrid instant before it took her, what the thing was like. After all, it had been here so long, waiting. It had its reasons for such patient malice, surely; maybe the face would show them.

How could she have thought there could ever be escape from this? In sunlight she'd laughed off her fears, but that had been a sham. The sweat of childhood, the night tears (hot, and running straight from the corners of her eyes into her hair), the unspeakable terrors, were here. They had come out of the dark, and she was, at the last, alone. Alone as only children are alone: sealed in with feelings beyond articulation, in private hells of ignorance whose corridors run, unseen, into adulthood.

Now she was crying, loudly, bawling like a ten-year-old, her crumpled face red and shining with tears. Her nose ran, her eyes burned.

In front of her, the Bogey-Walk was weakening, and she felt the irrevocable pull of the dark. One of her steps toward the gap in the wall was matched by another hauling of the flat black belly over the quarry's face. Another step, and now she was a foot from the crumbling edge of the Bogey-Walk, and in a matter of moments it would take her by the hair and split her apart.

She stood by the dizzying edge, and the face of her dread swam up from the bottomless night to look at her. It was her mother's face. Horribly bloated to twice or three times its true size, her jaundiced eyelids flickering to reveal whites without irises, as though she were hanging in the last moment between life and death.

Her mouth opened; her lips blackened and stretched to thin lines around a toothless hole, which worked the air uselessly, trying to speak Miriam's name. So even now there was to be no moment of recognition; the thing had cheated her, offering that dead, beloved face in place of its own.

Her mother's mouth chewed on, her rasping tongue trying vainly to shape the three syllables. The beast wanted to summon her, and it knew, with its age-old cunning, which face to use to make the call. Miriam looked down through her tears at the flickering eyes; she could half see the deathbed pillow beneath her mother's head, half smell her last, sour breath.

The name was almost said. Miriam closed her eyes, knowing that when the word was spoken, that would be the end. She was without will. The Bogey had her; this brilliant mimicry was the final, triumphant turn of the screw. It would speak with her mother's voice, and she would go to it.

"Miriam," it said.

The voice was lovelier than she'd anticipated.

"Miriam." It called in her ear, its claws now on her shoulder. "Miriam, for God's sake," it demanded.

"What are you doing?"

The voice was familiar, but it was not her mother's voice, nor that of the beast. It was Judy's voice, Judy's hands. They dragged her back from the gap and all but threw her against the opposite wall. She felt the security of cold brick at her back, against the cushion of her palms. The tears cleared a little.

"What are you doing?"

Yes, no doubt of it. Judy, plain as day.

"Are you all right, love?"

Behind Judy, the dark was deep, but from it there came only a pattering of stones as the Bogey retreated down the quarry face. Miriam felt Judy's arms around her, tight; more possessive of her life than she had been.

"I didn't mean to give you such a heave," she said, "I just thought you were going to jump."

Miriam shook her head in disbelief.

"It hasn't taken me," she said.

"What hasn't, sweetheart?"

She couldn't bring herself to talk in earshot of it. She just wanted to be away from the wall; and the Walk.

"I thought you weren't coming," said Judy, "so I thought—bugger it—I'll go round and see you. It's a good thing I took the shortcut. What in heaven's name possessed you to go peering over the edge like that? It's not safe."

"Can you take me home?"

"Of course, love."

Judy put her arm around her and led her away from the gap in the wall. Behind them, silence and darkness. The lamp flickered. The mortar crumbled a little more.

They stayed together through the night at the house, and they shared the big bed in Miriam's room innocently, as they had as children.

Miriam told the story from beginning to end: the whole history of the Bogey-Walk. Judy took it all in, nodded, smiled, and let it be. At last, in the hour before dawn, the confessions over, they slept.

At that same hour, the ashes of Miriam's mother were cooling, mingled with the ashes of thirteen others who had gone to the incinerator that Wednesday, December 1. In the morning, the remaining bones would be ground up and the dust would be divided into fourteen equal parts, then shoveled scrupulously into fourteen urns bearing the names of the loved ones. Some of the ashes would be scattered; some sealed in the Wall of Remembrance; some would go to the bereaved, as a focus for their grief. At that same hour, Mr. Beckett dreamed of his father and half woke, sobbing, only to be soothed back to sleep by the girl at his side.

And, at that same hour, the husband of the late

Marjorie Elliot took a shortcut along the Bogey-Walk. His feet crunched on the gravel, the only sound in the world at that weary hour before dawn. He had come this way every day of his working life, exhausted from the night shift at the bakery. His fingernails were lined with dough, and under his arm he carried a large white loaf and a bag of six crusty rolls. These he had carried home, fresh each morning, for almost twenty-three years. He still repeated the ritual, though since Marjorie's premature death, most of the bread was uneaten and went to the birds.

Toward the middle of the Bogey-Walk, his steps slowed. There was a fluttering in his belly; a scent in the air had awakened a memory. Was it not his wife's scent? Five yards farther on and the lamp flickered. He looked down at the gap in the wall and from out of the quarry rose his long-mourned Marjorie, her face huge.

It spoke his name once, and without bothering to reply to her call, he stepped off the Walk and was gone.

The loaf he had been carrying was left behind on the gravel.

Loosened from its tissue wrapping, it cooled, slowly forfeiting the warmth of its birth to the night.

Cards for His Spokes, Coins for His Fare

JOHN F.D. TAFF

Can I ask you a question, the most important one I can think of?

Sure. I might not know the answer. Or I might not be able to tell you, but you can ask me anything.

Can you tell me how to let go of something? Something precious?

Simple. Don't hold onto it for too long.

The Schwinn was brand new, gleaming, pale white.

The color of clouds, of bones, of ghosts.

"Wow," Scott said, still too stunned to smile.

He ran his hand unbelievingly down the ten-speed, from its rubbery seat down its smooth center bar to the ram's curls of its handlebars. His fingers flitted over the gear levers, squeezed the brakes.

A real ten-speed, he thought. *A grown-up bike.*

And not a birthday or even a Christmas present.

He turned to his parents, both standing nearby, quiet, expectant smiles hovering on their faces.

"So, what do you think, kiddo?" his father asked. "You don't seem too happy about . . . *oof!*"

Scott's sudden embrace knocked the air out of his father.

"It's cool . . . it's dy-no-mite!" he shouted.

Laughing, his father hugged him back. "Well, that's better."

Scott released his dad, threw his arms around his mother. "Thank you! Thank you! Thank you!"

His mother, who appeared happy but a little more dubious about the gift, placed one hand on his shoulder, ruffled his hair with the other, bent to kiss the top of his head.

"You're welcome," she said, putting her lips to his ear. "You just be careful, mister."

"Honey . . . ," his father chided.

"Mom . . . ," Scott moaned at the same time, pulling away and regarding her with an exasperated look.

She smiled again, and it hung there in the air over her face, as if scrawled over a sketch of an anxious mother.

"Hey, a mom can be worried," she said, ruffling his hair again. Scott saw her flash her eyes quickly at his father, who gave a little shrug in response. Scott knew that he was not supposed to see this, that it wasn't supposed to register with him. But since he'd gotten older—12 years old this past February!—they were all coming to an accommodation about what was registering with Scott these days . . . what he noticed, what he understood.

"Well, I'm sure you and your dad have some things

to go over before you take off, so I'll let you go to it," his mother said. "But first . . . "

She held out her closed right hand to Scott, who stood there for a moment as if he didn't know what to do. So she waggled the hand at him, and he finally put out his own, palm up, underneath it.

His mother opened her hand, and two coins fell out.

Scott saw two quarters cupped in his hand, looked at his mother quizzically.

"One for a phone, if you need to reach us. And one for the bus, if you need to get home."

Scott heard this as mom-speak for, *One for a phone, if there's a problem. And one for the bus, if there's a problem.*

"Put them in your pocket, and promise me, *swear* to me, Scott Phillips, that every time you go out on this bike—I don't care when, I don't care how far, I don't care for how long—that you'll always have these two quarters in your pocket."

If there's a problem . . .

"Yes, mom."

"I mean it. Don't spend it on comics or candy. It's for emergencies only, young man. Swear it."

Smiling, Scott jammed his pinky finger out to her, and it was her turn to look at him in confusion.

"Okay, pinky swear!" he said, laughing.

His mom stuck her own pinky out, hooked it around his, and they shook.

"Pinky swear," she said, then smiled at him again—that same, rueful smile—and drifted back into the house.

Scott watched her go. "What's wrong with mom?"

"Oh, it's nothing kiddo. She just doesn't want you to grow up, that's all."

His father sighed heavily. "OK, so before you get the dreaded safety lecture, let me give you a little something from me."

He passed a small packet to his son.

Baseball cards. Topps, of course, with the requisite slab of chalky, pink bubblegum.

For a moment he thought of this as a strange gift for his father to give him right then. He thought about the players he'd like to have—George Brett with the Royals, Tug McGraw with the Mets, Nolan Ryan with the Angels. Maybe Hank Aaron with the Brewers or Johnny Bench with the Reds. And, of course, the card that always seemed to elude him, Lou Brock with the Cardinals.

As he took the single packet, though, it finally struck him.

Cards. Baseball cards for the spokes of his new bike.

"Wow . . . thanks, Dad!"

Scott turned the pack over in his hands. It was the cello-pack, slightly more expensive at a quarter, with 18 cards inside.

"You know what to do with it, don't you?" his father chided, looking on as Scott ripped the package open, absently jammed the gum into his mouth, chewing automatically.

Rifling through the cards, he quickly took inventory. A few names he didn't recognize immediately—Skip Pitlock with the White Sox, Mike Wallace with the Yankees. A Ron Santo from the much-hated Cubs. Four cards from the Giants—

Gary Lavelle, Dave Heaverlo, Jim Barr and Glenn Adams.

And a double play that made his heart stop . . . Bob Gibson and Lou Brock from the St. Louis Cardinals—his home team!

"Dad . . . wow . . . oh wow!" he said, showing his father the two cards.

"Wow is right! Two redbirds in one pack!"

"Not gonna use these two, that's for sure," Scott said, ogling the two cards like unearthed treasure and sliding them carefully into the middle of the pack, where they'd be protected by the other, lesser cards.

"Which ones are you going to use?" his father asked.

Scott fanned the cards out, surveying the names and slices of faces.

Four cards, two on each bike tire.

"Well, there are four Giants," he said, sliding them from the deck. "Perfect."

So, Dave Heaverlo, Glenn Adams, Jim Barr and Gary Lavelle were all pulled from the deck. The rest were neatly squared, wrapped in the cellophane sleeve, and slid into the front pocket of Scott's jeans.

The bike . . . oh, the bike was a thing of beauty.

Taken from the Schwinn catalog—which had arrived three months back in a manila envelope that his mother had placed on his dinner plate before supper—the bike was exactly as pictured.

A 24-inch Schwinn Varsity Sport.

To answer the needs of thousands who have been asking for a lightweight style 10-speed bike, began the catalog description, *here is the new 1975 Schwinn 24-inch-wheel Varsity Sport. Scaled to fit the smaller rider. Every safety feature, every high-performance component found on the full-size Varsity is here. Choice of colors: Bone, Chestnut, Lime Green or Yellow. Wt. 36 1/2 lbs.*

A ten-speed bike . . . a grown-up bike.

No more banana seats for Scott. No more ape-hangers or sissy bars.

Now, he had gear shifts and dual brake calipers and ram's horn handlebars.

Now, he had a bike like the older kids' bikes, one that could take him out of his subdivision and into the larger world.

Now, he had freedom.

His dad gave him the safety lecture. He showed him how to shift, how to brake, how to signal, how to do just about everything. He told him how to cross streets, how to ride on the side of roads, even how to tuck his jeans cuffs into his socks to prevent them from being snagged in the chain.

But he also saw Scott getting antsy, Scott not paying attention, Scott just wanting to ride the thing.

"OK, let's get these cards on and you can be on your way," his dad said, reaching into his pocket and producing four wooden clothespins.

"I don't think your mother will mind."

Scott took the pins, knelt before the bike. For a moment, he stroked the smooth metal. It was cool though the air was warm and heavy, as St. Louis air almost always was.

Cards for His Spokes

He started to clip the first card to the spokes of the bike, but his father *tsked*, kneeled beside him. Taking the clothespin from Scott, he clipped it to the right side of the front fork, slid the first card, Glenn Adams, into its pincers, so that the card stuck into the spokes.

"Do it that way, Scotty, and they'll stay on longer."

"Daaad!" Scott responded. Just as he graduated to this new, bigger bike, Scott had also begun demanding to be known by his name, not by the diminutive *Scotty*. That name had gone the way of kid's meals at McDonald's and Underoos.

"Okay, okay," his dad chuckled, standing. "The last time, I promise."

Scott stood, too, disengaged the kick stand and mounted his new Varsity Sport.

"One more thing," his father said, holding something more out.

Three crisp, new one-dollar bills, folded neatly in thirds.

"You know, for stuff," he said, winking. "Mom doesn't need to know about it."

"Thanks, Dad," Scott said, stuffing the money into the pocket with the rest of the baseball cards.

"Enjoy your gift, Scott. Be careful and be back before dinner, if you know what's good for you . . . and me," his father said.

"I will!" Scott said, standing on the pedals and taking off down the driveway, wobbling slightly and not looking back.

Not looking back.

⊂∞⊃

Scott raced from home, feeling the air cool as it rushed

past him, ruffled his t-shirt, his hair. He wasn't going *too* fast, though. No, he wanted people to see him, see his new bike.

He wanted to show off.

But there weren't many people out early on this summer weekday morning, which was too bad since it was still cool outside and that wouldn't last long. It never did in St. Louis. Already the air had the implicit edge of heat on it, hinting at the inevitable assault of the climbing sun and the relentless humidity. Soon, it would be hot and dank, and the air would no longer be cool and kind, but as smothering as a damp blanket just out of the dryer.

Now, though, the sun was out in the bright blue, cotton-streaked sky, and the air was soft as he slipped through it. A few adults acknowledged him as he sped by—old Mr. Trank, as always bent over his enormous garden, Mrs. Garrison, Todd's mother, sweeping her front porch, Mr. and Mrs. Jenkins climbing into their car, waving jauntily.

But none of his friends were out yet to see him, not even any of the kids he didn't particularly like.

Too bad because they might have seen a suddenly more grown-up Scott Phillips pedal by on his new bike, his spare, lithe form working the pedals, curled over the handlebars, his tanned arms flexed, his hair, already sun bleached, blowing out behind him. His smile like the beam of a headlamp, aimed forward, aimed past the limits of his old bike—the boundary of his subdivision—toward the outer world, the *whole* world.

They might have seen Scott Phillips transported.

Cards for His Spokes

Scott did as his father had told him, stopping at the traffic light, waiting for the "Walk" sign to light up, then walking his bike across the busy two-lane road that had been the border of his old world.

His parents had never let him leave the subdivision on his old bike—what he increasingly thought of as his "baby" bike. But now, with a whole $3.50 in his pocket and the permission of his parents to take the bike to the local strip shopping center, well . . . the sky was the limit.

As he pedaled down Howdershell Road, he mentally charted the path he'd take: past St. Dominic's (which he and his friends called St. Pringle's because of its modern, curved and sloping roof) to the IGA, turn left onto Lynne Road, then about 10 blocks to his ultimate goal, Village Square.

This was the sprawling, open-air mall that housed most everything Scott thought important—a Dairy Queen, a candy shop, and a record store. But mostly it was the cramped little bookstore that was his goal; a bookstore selling comic books and the science fiction paperbacks he was increasingly becoming addicted to.

Before, he had to beg his mother to take him there . . . and that was only when she had the car. Now, with his new 10-speed, he could practically go whenever he wanted.

In his mind, he saw how the day would unfold. Parking his bike at Village Square, flipping through the new comic titles, buying three or four issues (all at one time!), grabbing some candy and a soda, then heading over to McMillan Park, where he'd lean up under the shade of a tree, read his purchases, eat his candy and cool off with a Coke. Then back home in plenty of time for dinner, to prove to his mother that this bike, this freedom wasn't a bad idea.

With all that running through his mind, he pedaled harder, launching the bike down sun-dappled Lynne Road, lined on either side by ranch house after ranch house. Sprinklers were on now, fanning lawns with water. A few kids were out jumping through these sprays, running and giggling. A dog ran after him for the length of three houses, before giving him a desultory bark and turning reluctantly back for home.

As he neared the end of the street, he stopped the bike, turned back to where he'd come from. The entire, ruler-straight length of Lynne Road was a narrow green-gold tunnel of houses and trees, receding into the distance. At its far end, obscured by distance and sunlight, was Howdershell Road.

As he stood there with his bike, marveling at how far he'd come, he noticed a clump of shadows, backlit by the powerful late morning sun.

It looked like kids . . . four kids on bicycles, unmoving, silhouetted against the golden smear of light at the end of the street.

Their dark shapes didn't move at all as he watched, and that seemed odd. It was as if they were looking at him, directly, *specifically* at him. Their lack of movement struck him as so odd, in fact, that it gave him a funny, ticklish feeling in the pit of his stomach, like he sometimes got when he rode in the car with his dad and they went over a particularly sudden drop in the pavement.

Scott watched the shadows for a moment longer,

then, shrugging, he remounted his bike, set off for Village Square.

∞

Later, in the other place, Flattop told him it was the orange sherbet that had done it, that had changed everything that day.

At first, Scott found this hard to believe, but, having nothing else that made sense, he shrugged it off.

Orange sherbet? Well, okay . . .

∞

Scott visited the candy shop first, almost as a way to delay the gratification of heading to the book store. Comic books had just gone up to 25 cents from their price of just 20 cents a year before, and that had put a real crimp in Scott's budget. His usual allowance of 50 cents a week used to buy him two books and a candy bar. Now he had to either buy two books and forgo the candy or buy one book and two candies, which was generally more candy than he wanted, or buy one book and one candy, leaving him with the strangely useless amount of 15 cents.

But today, he'd received not just the nifty new 10-speed, but three whole dollars from his dad. Scott's head spun . . . he could buy eight comic books and a Coke and some candy . . . or maybe just a buck's worth of comics—still four issues!—a Coke and a slew of candy. Pocket the change and add it to his allowance next week.

Or maybe a paperback sci-fi novel. As Scott had moved from children's underpants and his childish nickname, so, too, was he starting to drift away from comics. The racks of fantastically covered science fiction and fantasy novels (usually by artist Darrell K. Sweet) had begun to grab his attention—Silverberg, Foster, Clarke, and Asimov, Bradbury, Sturgeon, and Heinlein. But these books were generally about a buck apiece, which meant buying even one forced him to save for at least two weeks. And as any kid could attest, two weeks without candy or a comic book was like withdrawal for a heroin addict.

The choices that were unlocked by his father's unexpected gift of three dollars were overwhelming, confronting Scott with so many possibilities that he almost couldn't decide.

So he darted into the candy shop first, to spend a carefully budgeted amount of money before heading over to the vastly more tempting book store. He devoted a great deal of time poring over the shop's wares—eventually drawing the attention of the shopkeeper, who, Scott realized, probably thought he was preparing to rip him off.

Scott grabbed two packs of Lik-m-Aid, a Hershey bar and two sticks of Laffy Taffy—banana and grape. That set him back just 45 cents, leaving him with more than enough for a Coke and a few comics . . . and perhaps a paperback.

Scott walked past his bike, still parked at the bike rack, and headed toward the book store, the paper bag with his candy swinging happily at his side.

The shopping center was shaped like a horseshoe, and the bookstore was at its center. He passed by the department store his mother took him to every year to buy his school clothes, the sporting goods dealer with its mannequins of men in soccer outfits and women in tennis skirts, a knick-knack store, the record store with albums by Queen, Elton John, the Eagles, KC & the Sunshine Band, and The Captain & Tenille. Like paperback books, music was beginning to exert a powerful gravitational pull on him. Soon his little 45 rpm turntable and pocket AM/FM radio wouldn't be enough, and he'd need a stereo and some records to go with it.

Perhaps later, though. Maybe his next birthday.

Not today.

The little bell jingled as he entered, and Scott took a deep breath as the door closed behind him, sealing him off from the outside world. Here in the bookstore, the air was cool, crisp and smelled of paper and ink and the glue binding it all together. The shop was plain, just five aisles of low shelves filled mostly with paperbacks and gigantic racks of magazines and newspapers covering the far wall.

Near the front, close by so the cashier could glare at the audience of mostly kids who pawed over them, were the spinners filled with comic books—two for Marvel, two for DC. Scott rarely, if ever, bothered looking at the DC titles.

Today, though, he drifted past them, went by without even looking, and went to the aisle with the science fiction books. And as he stood there looking at the covers and trying to decide which single book he'd plunk his money down for and take home, a curious thought came into his head.

Orange sherbet.

He picked up a copy of a book called *Sign of the Unicorn* by Roger Zelazny and stared at its cover blankly for a few moments.

All the while, he could think of nothing but orange sherbet, the cold of it against his lips, his tongue; the taste of it, tangy and creamy down his throat.

The only ice cream place in the shopping center was a Dairy Queen. But Scott knew that no amount of plain, white soft-serve would be enough.

He suddenly, and quite forcefully, wanted . . . *needed* . . . a scoop or two (What the heck? He had the money!) of orange sherbet.

And, he realized just as forcefully, he could get it himself.

That thought was so liberating, so freeing that his head literally spun.

But the only other ice cream shop he knew of was the Velvet Freeze, about a mile up the road. The problem with this was that road, Lindbergh, was the major thoroughfare in the area, a four-lane behemoth lined with strip shopping centers and fast-food restaurants and grocery stores. And while his parents hadn't exactly forbidden him to take his bike on this road, he knew that it was only because the very idea of doing that was so patently absurd that it didn't bear discussion.

Surely, he would never even think about doing *that*.

Scott knew that they wouldn't approve, that they'd be furious if they found out, that they'd most likely ground him from the bike for some period of time.

But it was those four simple, little words that took root in his mind, grew until they overshadowed everything else.

If they found out . . .

Nearly vibrating with the dual excitement of his

revelation and his decision, he walked the Zelazny paperback up to the cashier and paid for it, 97 cents with tax, pocketed the change and left with another bag.

Heading toward his bike, he saw something out of the corner of his eye . . . a clump of shadows at the far end of one of the U-shaped shopping center's arms.

He shielded his eyes with one hand, squinted.

Kids on bikes, four of them, silhouetted against the light. Looked to be one older kid and three younger ones. The larger one was definitely a guy, but he couldn't see if the others were boys or girls or some mix of the two.

Were they kids he knew? Kids from his neighborhood or school?

Because one thing seemed certain. They definitely appeared to be looking at him . . . *watching* him.

And now, they seemed to be following him.

A little self-conscious now, Scott looped the handles of his bags through the handlebars, climbed onto his bike, backed it from the rack.

For some reason he didn't understand, seeing those kids made his stomach twitch.

He cast one look behind as he set off for Lindbergh, but they didn't seem to follow him. As before, they didn't even move. People moved around them, like water flowing around rocks in a stream. But they took no more notice of this than the rocks might the water.

Scott pedaled fast, trying to shrug them off.

Thinking only of orange sherbet.

As Scott came to the end of the shopping center's main

entrance, he began to have second and even third thoughts.

Lindbergh was a real road, not one of the gentle two-laners that meandered through his subdivision or past his school. It was two lanes in each direction, and the speed limit was not the gentle, unrushed 20 or 25 miles per hour, with a few cars going by, but a heady 45 miles per hour and packed with cars.

Scott stood with his bike for a few seconds, weighing his options as vehicles whizzed past. He could feel the air of their passing buffeting him, pushing him as if trying to shake some sense into him.

Each side of Lindbergh had a wide, gravel shoulder, more than enough room for a bike, to be sure. In fact, several kids on bikes went by as he sat there.

All of them, he noted sourly, visibly older than him.

As he sat there, another thought crept in, one that carried considerably more weight.

None of them had a bike cooler than his.

That one thought effectively drowning out all others, Scott stood on the pedals, steered his Varsity Sport onto the shoulder, and made his way to the Velvet Freeze.

Riding against traffic on the shoulder of the road was exhilarating and terrifying at the same time. The cars came right for him, or so it seemed, brushing by so close that he could, literally, reach out and touch them had he wanted to.

Scott rode beside the highway and felt more alive than he'd ever felt before. He felt every muscle in his body working in its prime—his legs pumping, his arms keeping the bike on course. His heart thrummed blood through his veins, and everything, every little mysterious thing inside his body seemed to be working together gloriously.

It was probably a mile or so up Lindbergh to the strip mall that housed the Velvet Freeze. He'd have to pass through a couple of intersections—some of them major—but that didn't worry him. This was going so well, it seemed so easy, he wondered that he hadn't tried this before, even with his baby bike, though the thought of that sent a chill through him.

And that chill made him think of the strange, shadowy figures he thought might be following him.

As before, he started to turn behind, to see if they still followed. But he realized that, this near the fast-moving traffic, it would be crazy to just turn around . . . or even stop and turn around.

Just ahead, there was a cut-out into a small parking lot of a free-standing store. There were no cars there at the moment, so he decided to pull in there, take a breather and look back.

It happened, as they say, so fast . . .

He leaned into the left-hand turn, and his bike leaned with him, slipping deftly into the parking lot.

He heard a horn, but it sounded distant, as if coming from the nearby traffic.

He felt a tremendous shove from behind, as if a giant hand had reach out and swatted him.

The bike skittered on the gravel parking lot, then simply smashed against whatever had shoved it.

Scott was thrown over the handlebars, felt himself sailing through the air for one giddy, heart-stopping moment.

All was light.
Then all was dark.

◯◯◯

Scott opened his eyes onto two things.

First, the blue, blue sky. It stretched unbroken from one horizon to the other, and for a moment, this time more queasy than giddy, he felt like he was flying again.

But then he felt the gravel under his back, the aches and pains of a thousand hurts, from his head to his legs.

And screaming . . . that was the other thing that surrounded him . . . *screaming.*

He shook his head, sat up.

He was in the parking lot, and at his feet was his bike. It lay in the gravel, its front wheel twisted, its shiny white metal dusty and scraped, its seat knocked askew. All of the other hurts faded at that instant, and his heart hurt most now.

My bike! My brand-new bike! Not even a day, and it's already ruined!

And hurting almost as much . . .

Mom and dad are never going to let me ride anywhere now.

Scott looked at his arms and legs. Surprisingly, they seemed uninjured. He didn't see any cuts or scrapes or even any rips in his jeans. His head hurt, and he swiped his hand across his face and forehead, looked at his palm for blood.

None.

But, boy, his head sure hurt, something that wasn't helped by the screaming.

Cards for His Spokes

Just past the twisted metal of his bike, he saw the shiny bumper of a car. The front end was caved in just a bit, and the hood was pushed up. Near the front of this car, he saw two legs—bare woman's legs—and he blinked, raised his head.

It was a young woman in a short black skirt, and she was screaming at him. She was loud enough to hurt his ears, but he couldn't make much sense of what she was saying.

She seemed upset, angry even, but she made no attempt to go to him or help him up.

She just . . . *screamed.*

And in that, Scott saw a way out of all this, out of explaining everything to his parents, out of being grounded, out of possibly losing his new bike.

He'd simply leave—ride away, *flee* . . .

He looked down at his limbs again, checking one more time to make sure there were no broken bones jutting out or blood spurting from anywhere. When he was satisfied, he climbed gingerly to his feet.

A little sore, but everything seemed okay . . . and, bonus, the woman wasn't paying all that much attention to him.

He went to his bike, lifted it up. The front wheel seemed bent out of true, but other than being dusty and a little scraped here and there, it didn't seem badly damaged at all.

He would tell his parents that he'd had a little spill, that's all . . . happened all the time, no need to worry.

"I'm all right, really, ma'am," he said, sliding the front wheel between his legs and clamping it between them. Then, he twisted the handlebars until the wheel came back in line with the body of the bike.

"So," he said, coming around and sitting on the seat, which was still crooked. "I'll just . . . ummm . . . head on home . . . and you can just . . . ummm . . . go on with your shopping."

He veered around the car, shot out of the parking lot and back onto the shoulder of Lindbergh, her screams following him.

He hated to look back, because he was sure she was screaming at him to stop, screaming at him to come back and take responsibility for her car, come back until the police arrived to sort it all out.

But he did look back.

He looked back because he'd never run from anything this big in his life, never fled from an adult, never even contemplated a situation where he'd be running from the police.

What he saw nearly made him run off the road.

He'd almost forgotten the kids on the bikes, but there they were now, close by, right in the parking lot he'd just left.

He kept pedaling the bike, pedaling furiously, but he twisted in the seat to look behind, to get a good look at them this time.

Four of them.

The oldest of them was a big, bluff blonde boy with a buzz cut wearing a muscle shirt. He looked maybe 14 or 15. Flanking him on either side were a younger boy and girl, maybe 12 years old. They both looked scrawny. The boy was emaciated, and the girl looked filthy.

Just ahead of them, on a smaller bike, was a boy of about eight. This boy glared at Scott, and his whole body radiated malice and anger that shimmered around his form like a heat haze.

Their eyes met, and the little boy scrunched his face into a horrible grimace, lurched his bike out of the parking lot.

He was followed in quick succession by the other three, all of them riding pell-mell along the side of the road, their bikes swaying back and forth with the force of their pedaling.

Scott gulped his heart up into his throat, and he flung himself back around in the seat, worked his legs furiously. Over the sounds of the traffic, over the sounds of his bike and his own racing heart, he heard the reassuring *clickety-clackety* of the baseball cards in his spokes, and he thought of his dad, his mom.

He thought of the two quarters in his pocket.

If there's a problem . . .

How he might just have to use them.

This made him angry, gave him a spectacular burst of adrenalized energy.

The bike shot down Lindbergh, and Scott realized that he didn't know exactly where he was going.

But he knew he had to get away from her.

Away from *them*.

Halfway to Velvet Freeze, the fear, the electric exhilaration began to ebb, and Scott's muscles felt flabby and exhausted. His lungs ached, his thighs burned, and his arms were sore from clenching the handlebars so hard.

The cool morning had given way to a relentless summer day. The sun, hanging directly overhead now, was unshaded by cloud or tree, and its heat was sapping. Scott could feel it in the air, radiating up from the asphalt of the road, reflected back at him from the silver-stream of cars whooshing by.

He had to stop, had to take a breather.

Veering farther off the road, the bike left the narrow margin of the shoulder onto a scraggly verge of weeds and trash that declined shallowly into a gulley. This, in turn, emptied into a concrete drainage ditch that disappeared into a corrugated metal pipe under the road.

From this vantage, a little safer distance from the road and its relentless traffic, Scott looked for the kids, the woman, the police; he wasn't precisely sure which.

No one followed him.

He could barely make out the sign of the store in whose parking lot he'd been hit, far in the distance, lost in the gleaming heat.

But there was no one following him, no police sirens, no screaming women.

Just hot asphalt and a gleaming snake of cars curling away in both directions.

He took a deep breath, let out a sigh, collapsed atop his bike. His legs felt rubbery and he really, really wanted to go home.

He leaned his head against the handlebars, and the cool metal felt good against his pounding skull, his hair sweat-plastered to it.

When he opened his eyes, he saw immediately that he was missing something.

Somethings.

His bags. The one with the candy and the one with his paperback.

Gone.

He'd looped them through the handlebars before

he left Village Square, but they must have been knocked loose when the lady hit him.

If he wanted them, he'd have to go back.

Shit!

The curse came from his lips so quickly, so unexpectedly that he actually slapped a hand over his mouth in surprise.

With that, he started to giggle.

He couldn't go back. If he went back for his stuff, he'd surely be stopped by the lady . . . or even the police.

Or even, he thought, *those kids . . .*

And that stopped the giggling cold.

No, he couldn't go back.

He'd simply lost his purchases for the day. He was out about a buck-fifty, but that was that. He'd just have to eat it. He hoped his father wouldn't ask him what he'd done with the money, because he'd have nothing to show for it.

As he contemplated this, he raised his face to the sun, felt like crying.

He rode it out, though, until it passed.

He simply would not cry. He was too old for Underoos and "Scotty," and he was far too old for crying.

When he opened his eyes again, he saw it, across the street.

Velvet Freeze.

Orange Sherbet, he thought. *At least I can get some orange sherbet, then head home.*

Just up ahead was an intersection, so he walked the bike up to the traffic light, pushed the button, feeling a little light headed.

The traffic slowed to a stop, and the *Walk* sign across the street lit up. Scott still looked both ways, as he'd been taught, rode the bike across the first two lanes, paused to make sure the sign was still illuminated, moved quickly across the remaining two lanes to the other side of the highway.

There, just a few buildings up, was the Velvet Freeze.

They were there, too.

Scott's foot slipped off the pedal, and the bike skewed to the side, stopped.

All four of them, the flattop kid, the scrawny one, the filthy little girl.

And the small, angry one.

Scott could see them clearly from this distance, could see their eyes, how they followed him.

He reacted instinctively.

The bike was already partially turned back toward the light, so Scott stepped on the pedals, made a hard turn into the intersection.

Just as his bike jumped down off the curb, the *Walk* sign winked out, and the orange hand lit up.

Don't Walk.

Scott ignored it, lowered his head, pushed hard on the pedals, launched across the road.

As he did, he heard "Scott! Wait . . . *don't!*"

It was the older kid, the flattop, he knew it without looking. The boy's voice rose above the idling traffic, the sound of the wind in Scott's ears.

How does he know my name?

But Scott didn't stop.

He was barely across the second two lanes when the light changed, and the cars nosed forward.

Cards for His Spokes

Pulling up on the handlebars, he brought the bike's front tires up, jumped the curb, gained the shoulder on the side he'd just come from moments ago.

His breath was harsh in his ears, and sweat trickled the length of his back, dripped into his eyes. He swiped a hand absently across his brow, turned to look across the road.

There, through the whirr of the passing cars, he could see them, clustered at the other side, glaring at him fiercely, so anxious to get to him they seemed to vibrate in the seats of their bikes.

Scott didn't wait, he pushed off down the side of the road, but this time followed the ditch into the drainage culvert, carefully navigating the steep hill with his feet on the ground rather than in the pedals.

"Scott!" he heard the boy cry again, but he didn't wait, didn't look back.

At the bottom, a thin trickle of water snaked across the cracked and jumbled surface of the culvert, and he had to dodge all sorts of debris—bricks, tumbled shopping carts, and old tires.

He was fairly sure where this channel went, surfacing in some common ground in a neighborhood just a few blocks away from his own. He'd simply follow it out, then head home.

Forget the book, forget the candy, forget the god-damn orange sherbet, he thought. *At least I still have my bike.*

As this thought settled over him, he steered the bike through a gentle turn, came around the bend . . .

. . . and saw the four riders, spread out across the ditch there before him.

How? was all he could think, and he jerked the bike hard to the left, went partially up the inclined concrete banks, then turned completely around, back down the wall, and retreated. The *clickety-clack* of the baseball cards in his spokes echoed across the walls of the ravine.

"Stop! *Please!*" came the voice, but Scott was operating purely on fear now. It had been a helluva day, with the high of getting his new bike and the low of getting hit by a car.

And in between, this . . . whatever *this* was.

Being followed around by four kids he didn't know, yet somehow knew him.

It was too much, so Scott simply fled.

Darting in and out between debris, returned to where the drainage ditch passed under the highway. A wide, angular concrete apron led up to the mouth of the metal pipe that opened there; a mouth filled with shadows and dribbling spilth.

He'd have to go in there, *through* there to escape them.

Scott slid to a stop.

Somehow, impossibly, the four were there ahead of him, grouped across the apron, blocking him from racing into that terrifying maw.

Not knowing what else to do, where else to go, he simply stood, one foot on the ground, the other on a pedal, the bike leaning.

He breathed heavily, and fear wrapped icy arms around his stomach, squeezed.

"Scott," said the flattop boy. "Finally."

"What do you want?" Scott yelled, his voice cracking in exhaustion and dread.

Cards for His Spokes

The older boy rode his bike off the lip of the drainage pipe, came to a stop right beside Scott. The other three followed, slowly, forming a semi-circle around him, as much to be near him as to block him from fleeing.

"We're here to help, Scott," Flattop said. "We're here to take you home."

From this close, Flattop's face looked smooth and kind, and Scott found some of his fear sloughing away, dissipating.

"Who are you? Did my parents send you?"

"No, your parents didn't send us," Flattop smiled. "We just knew to be here. It's kind of like our job."

"Our job, yeah," the angry little one sneered in agreement.

"Shh," Flattop said, without anger. "He still doesn't know."

Scott frowned in confusion. "I don't know what?"

Flattop's eyes shaded momentarily.

"That you're dead, kid."

Scott stiffened, his fingers tightened on the handlebars. "You mean you're gonna . . . "

"No, we're not gonna *do* anything to you, Scott," Flattop said. "You're already dead. You got hit by a car, remember?"

"Yeah . . . so?" he said. "How can I be dead? I'm right here."

"No," Flattop said, and his tone was firm but sad. "You're back there."

And suddenly, they were.

There was no *pop!,* no flash of light or gaudy theatrics.

In that instant, they were not in the culvert

anymore, but under the bright, hot sun in the parking lot of the store.

The young lady in the short, black skirt was there, too, still screaming.

The car was there, with its crumpled hood.

As was the twisted wreck of his bike. Scott stared at the baseball cards his father had helped him clip to the bike earlier. One was missing altogether, and the other three were crumpled and torn, splashed with red.

And there, laid out in front of them—in front of *him*—was the twisted wreck of Scott.

His body lay curled on the pavement near the bike, one hand tucked beneath, one hand with bloody knuckles extended over his head. His legs were thrust out, and he noticed one of his shoes was gone, exposing his striped tube sock.

His shirt was rucked up, and his white, white belly was cut and scraped.

A pool of glistening ink spread from beneath his body, as if the asphalt beneath it were melting in the overbearing sun. He saw the glint of dark red, the strange dent in the curve of his head from which it flowed.

All of this was confusing and distressing. He could plainly see the body there—*his body!*—yet, here he was, standing with his bike, neither of them damaged.

Still the woman screamed and screamed.

"Is that . . . *me?*" he croaked.

Flattop's smile was thin and severe. "Yes."

Tears filled Scott's eyes. "I don't believe you. I can't be dead. I'm right here. That's not me!"

As if on cue, the small, angry kid moved his bike

forward, nearer to Scott. He was smiling, ferocious and determined. He stopped right beside Scott, reached out and touched him, gently, with one finger.

That one, small touch—the boy's tiny finger tapping against Scott's chest—exploded through Scott's consciousness like a detonation. Hundreds of sensations scoured over him, a formication like a million stinging ants crawling over his skin.

A constellation of pain illuminated every nerve in his body. He felt bones within his arms and legs shattering, the pain like supernovas bursting inside him.

He experienced the curious sensation of his skull quite literally splitting, and felt something vital leaking out. Liquid pattered across his shoulders, rained to the ground, spattered the tops of his sneakers.

Scott collapsed, fell to his knees.

As he did so, he looked up, saw that the younger two riders—the girl and the other boy—had dismounted and had come to stand before him.

The boy was emaciated, an articulated skeleton. His hair was wispy, no-colored. His skin was the unhealthy yellow of jaundice, and his eyes were sunken into bruised hollows that fell deeper than his collapsed cheeks.

He reached one bony hand out, touched Scott's sternum, just where the angry boy had touched him.

Scott's stomach twisted on itself, and he vomited a slurry of nearly colorless liquid, splashing onto the pavement and mixing with the spreading pool of blood coming from the body.

More disturbingly, he let loose his bladder, his bowels, felt the warmth of this soak into his underwear, trickle down his pants legs. Its smell rose to his nostrils, already clogged with the flat, metallic smell of his own blood, and he was momentarily embarrassed.

The boy stepped back, and his sister, a twin perhaps, stepped forward, reached out with a filthy, scabby hand to also touch him.

As the slight pressure of her finger faded, Scott felt his body swell, his gut expanding, his limbs puffing. He looked at his hand, propping him up against the pavement, and watched it inflate, the fingers splitting like sausages, the flesh beneath rising, then putrefying, bubbling, running like soft butter.

He felt the sudden urge to cough then, as something pushed its way from his stomach, up his esophagus; something with mass, something writhing.

His lips parted almost on their own, and he belched up a great bubble of foul-smelling gas and a cloud of insects—tiny flies that flew out from between his clenched teeth and a squirming tangle of worms and maggots that plopped to the asphalt in a pool of mucilaginous slime.

Scott tried to draw in a breath. He desperately needed to scream. But he couldn't. Nothing in his body seemed to be under his control anymore, and he remained frozen, bent over the pavement, looking at his body there before him, his *other* body.

His *real* body, he knew.

Just then a hand appeared in his field of view, and he looked up.

It was Flattop, reaching to him.

Scott shakily lifted his own hand, clasped the boy's.

And it was over, as quickly as it had begun.

Cards for His Spokes

Scott was standing there, whole again, not leaking any fluids, not feeling any of the overwhelming pain he'd felt moments ago.

He gasped in a breath, felt his knees buckle in overwhelming relief.

And the kids, all of them, rushed to him, kept him on his feet. When they felt sure he was able to stand on his own again, they stepped away, slowly.

Except for Flattop. He kept hold of Scott's hand, but gently.

"Sorry for that, but you sorta had to know," he said.

"I'm . . . *dead*," Scott said, more to hear it spoken from his own mouth than for any other reason.

The four kids looked at him with a stern sadness in their eyes, even the angry little kid.

"So now what?" Scott said, noticing that things had gone quiet around them. The car, the screaming lady, his own dead body were gone. The road was still there, as were the store and the parking lot, but the rest of it faded the farther away from this little tableau it got, obscured by what looked like a heavy fog.

What was left had the feel of an empty stage, the audience gone, the props put away, the actors taking one last look.

"Now we leave," Flattop said, gesturing off into the grey void.

"To go . . . *where*?" Scott asked, suddenly realizing what this all truly meant.

Realizing where he *wasn't* going, where he'd never go again.

"To the other side, kid, the other world . . . the larger world."

Scott panicked for a second.

He wasn't ready. This wasn't right.

He needed . . . he needed to go home, *his* home, if only for a moment.

If only to see . . .

He remembered something, dug into his pockets to find it.

The baseball cards he'd stuffed in there earlier that morning fell from his pocket, scattered across the fading asphalt.

He dug deeper, pulled one out, held it up to Flattop.

If there's a problem . . .

"My mom gave this to me. I want to see her before I go," he said, holding one of the two quarters up before Flattop.

The boy eyed the quarter somberly, his eyes narrowing.

"Your mother is wise," he said, and his voice held a tone, an edge that didn't sound as if it belonged to any boy, 15 years old or otherwise. It had the weight of ages behind it, and for a moment, Scott was afraid the older boy would simply snatch the coin from his hand, leave him there alone in that dwindling oasis of reality.

Flattop sighed, and did reach out to take the coin, gently, sliding it into the front pocket of his jeans.

He turned to the other children. "Go on ahead and prepare the way. I'll be along presently."

The three kids mounted their bikes and sped away without a word, disappearing into the mist like horsemen in a western.

Flattop turned back to Scott. "This will hurt more than the three touches you endured. Do you understand this?"

Scott bit his lip.

"I wanna see my mom."

"You are here," Flattop said, and the mist receded, revealing the front lawn of Scott's house, the porch, the front door. But nothing else emerged from the fog, and the whole scene had a weird, twilight aura about it.

Flattop nodded toward the house, and Scott climbed off the bike, let it fall silently to the grey grass. He bounded from it, pushed through the front door, slid into the hallway, his sneakers squeaking on the floor.

"Mom!" he yelled, and his voice seemed to echo through long, invisible corridors, fading slowly. "Mom!"

He found he was breathing hard, could feel the beat of his anxious heart tremble through his body. It seemed so strange to have these feelings in death, but he pushed that aside.

It didn't matter . . . not right now.

"Scotty?" he heard a small voice. "Is that you?"

"Mom!"

"I'm here, baby."

Scott dashed down the hallway into the family room. It looked dim here, colorless and unreal. He could see the carpet, the texture of the couch, the pictures on the mantel, on the walls, but they seemed fake, almost like illustrations of the real thing.

And there she was, curled atop the couch—one hand tucked beneath, one hand extended over her head—sleeping.

He went to her, knelt beside her, took her hand in his.

Scott could feel her, feel the muscles of her hand,

the bones, feel the warmth of her blood and the beat of her heart and her slow, easy respiration.

"Mom," he said, burying his head in her shoulder. He could smell her—the clean scent of her shampoo, the familiar cachet of her soap, her perfume. She ran her hands through his hair, and he closed his eyes, felt them well up.

"I was so worried," she murmured, kissing his head. "You and that bike."

"I'm here now, Mom," he said, raising his head. "But I've got to go."

Scott saw her frown, but also noticed that she hadn't opened her eyes, hadn't really awakened.

"Go? Where do you need to go, honey?" she asked, and he felt her hands tighten on him.

"I need to go . . . away. Sorry. I'm sorry . . . but I've got to go."

"When will you be back?" she said, her voice sounding small.

Scott opened his mouth to say something . . . but could not find the words.

So, he leaned in and kissed his mother on the cheek, rested his forehead on hers.

"Why do you have to go?" she whispered in his ear.

"It's time, I guess. My time. But don't worry. I'm okay, it's just that . . . well . . . it's okay, I guess."

"I don't want you to leave honey."

"And I don't want to leave, Mom. But it's not as bad as I thought . . . I mean . . . I'll miss you and everything, but . . . "

"But what, sweetheart?" she asked, her voice breaking.

Scott pulled away from her, looked at her sleeping face and smiled though she couldn't see it.

Cards for His Spokes

"It seems easy, Mom, really. I mean, easy to give it up."

"Easy? Scotty, how is it easy?"

"I didn't have it for very long, Mom."

Scott kissed her again, each cheek, her forehead. As he rose, he felt her hands slip from his hair, caress his face as they fell away.

That memory, more than anything else, was the one he'd carry with him.

"I love you, Mom," he said, and he wasn't sure if the fog had crept into the house or if his eyes were clouded with tears.

Both, really.

"I love you, too Scotty. I always will," his mother breathed, snuggling back down into the couch. "I always will."

Scott stepped away slowly, made his way to the front door.

Turning, he looked back at the curl of his mother on the couch.

"Mom?"

"Yes, Scotty?" she murmured, sinking slowly into the dream world he'd roused her from.

"Don't be too hard on Dad . . . about the bike. I loved it . . . every minute of it. Please tell him that I love him, too."

With that, he stepped through the front door and out onto the lawn.

Flattop was there, waiting.

Scott scrubbed the heel of his hand across his eyes, cleared the tears there.

"Now, we need to go," Flattop said, holding out his hand to Scott.

For a moment, Scott was confused. Then, he knew.

He slid his hand into his pocket, fished out the remaining quarter his mother had given him.

He dropped it into Flattop's outstretched palm, lifted his bike from the grass.

Looking down, he was surprised to see the baseball cards were back, pristine and whole, clipped so that they clacked against the spokes.

Can I ask you a question, here at the end?

Sure. At this point, though, you might know the answer better than me.

Can you tell me how to let go of something? Something precious?

Simple. You don't . . . not really. You take it with you, hold it in your heart, in your memories.

Forever.

The flattop kid mounted his bike, and led them away.

Scott followed him into the grey nothingness.

Into everything.

Cellar's Dog

AMANDA GOWIN

If only the Internet hadn't gone out and sent her tapping her boyfriend's number, if only she and Will hadn't stopped at Logan and Chrissy's for a dime bag, if only Douglas and Irving Cellar hadn't been planted in the middle of that sagging sofa like two jagged teeth in a brown microfiber grin, if only Doug Cellar hadn't been ripe for a larger audience and flashing baggies—a magician rolling temptation over and under his knuckles with winks and taunts at Will— Laticia Deal wouldn't be shackled into the loose circle of a makeshift Friday night party. She could tick ifs on her fingers until dawn, but it didn't bring her any closer to the door or make time pass faster.

Far as she could tell, the clock had been sitting at quarter to midnight since she fell into the circle and the cluttered coffee table snapped a bracelet on her ankle.

"Fucking monster, is what he is," Douglas Cellar wrapped his thick fingers around the pipe and coughed around a cloud of smoke. "Black as one of them moviestar coloreds." He laughed and Logan laughed with him. Laticia twisted away from Will's snaking Don't

Say Nothing grip, and she tried not to look at Doug's son, Irving. "Me and the boy was up huntin' offa the Ball farm—back where they was logging—and caught it in a old bear trap. We just took it up there 'cause we found it in Pap's shed, think he used it to trap beaver," Doug looked at Laticia and grinned. "Didn't expect nothing to come of it."

A box fan pointing outward rattled in the window, sucking a little of the smoke and static electricity from the living room, but not enough to breathe easy or see clearly.

"Took what up where?" Chrissy was stretched like a lizard over the recliner, and opened her eyes a slit to take the pipe as it came her way.

"The trap, whatcha think?" Logan snapped, and reached past the boy to turn on the flat screen. He punched up the game on the PlayStation and tossed the second controller to Will. War filled the room, the canned sound of killing, the speaker so close to the boy's head Laticia wondered if he could hold a thought but the sound of guns. Laticia came close to eye contact, but spun her head when she caught herself drifting below his pale eyebrows. She hit the pipe and clanged it, cashed, on the glass coffee table.

"Daddy—"

"Hush. But we caught him, alright. Damn near skinned his back paw like a glove, but I had a grain sack over his head before he could pull loose. I tied him and tossed him in the back and we lit out—nothin' we done wrong, just wanted to get that beast home."

"Why? Whatcha gonna do with some wild dog? Besides get rabies," Chrissy tittered laughter over the sound of the guns, and stretched further, Chester

Cheetah's faded ears and sunglasses peeking over the edge of her top.

Doug raised his grey eyebrows and laid a look on Chrissy like she was a pitiful creature indeed. "Why go into space? Why grow an ear on a rat's back?"

"What the fuck—"

"He means 'cause he can, Chrissy," Logan said, eyes never leaving the screen, fingers working the controller like a master pianist. "Whatcha reckon, Doug? Fightin' him, or trainin' him to hunt?"

"Fuck if I know," Doug grinned with the glee of a mad scientist. "We trimmed him up nice, like they do them pit bulls. Took a chunk outta me," He spread his palm toward them. Around the punctures of few-day-old teeth marks, Laticia looked to see if his lifeline ended anytime soon. Looked for some sign of Children's Services, DEA, DUI in his future.

Saw only the invincibility of the very mad.

"Fuck your dog."

Logan opened his mouth to snap at Chrissy but shifted his eyes enough to see she was crinkling powder straight onto the coffee table and that was alright; he kept with the game.

She pushed herself back into the cushions of the dirty futon and concentrated on not looking at the kid. Elbowing Will, she screamed with the bone she shoved in his ribs *We gotta get outta here*, but he took it for play and elbowed her back.

Laticia looked from the lines Chrissy was cutting and straight into the eyes of the boy, who read her plainly. His eyes were like saucers, blue as a pilot light, and with one slow, accepting blink he told her, *There ain't no getting out*. Laticia dropped her gaze to his laced fingers, and saw how white the knuckles were. Against his knee rested the knee of his daddy, and Douglas Cellar laced his own hands.

"He thought he was tough before," Doug muttered, somehow louder than the gunfire, "But I'll learn him his place. Everything learns its place in the end."

Doug locked eyes with Laticia, his as blue as the boy's but deep with forty more years' tinkering and malevolence. He held her there, through the smoke that hung in the room, and she clenched her teeth, didn't dare shudder.

"Where you keepin' him?" Will asked, when Logan paused the game to roll a dollar bill.

"The wolf?"

"Since when was he a wolf?"

"Shut your cunt," Logan yelled at Chrissy, but Doug was content to stay the center of conversation.

"Had him in the shed but he 'bout tore a hole through the back. I chained him up to the old Chevy 'fore we left."

"He's gonna tear the bumper up," piped Irving Cellar.

"He does I'll kick the shit outta him."

With a slow blink the boy's eyes matched the blankness of his daddy's, pupils narrowing to pinpricks as he asked, "Can I kick it, too, Daddy?"

The laugh came up deep from Doug's belly and he ruffled Irving's hair with a mechanic's hand, greasy nail-beds buried in that straw blond. "Yeah, boy," he said with not a little pride, "You can kick it, too."

Laticia reached for her purse and bumped the empty pipe on the table; it spun like a compass needle, pointing to her and the faded furniture and the coke and the weed and the PlayStation, the statue of the Indian chief in the middle of the coffee table, and finally eight-year-old Irving Cellar and his saucer-sized eyes.

"I'm goin' on home, Will, you can walk it from here, cantcha?" Laticia stood, willed her knees not to knock and her hand to move slow and steady putting her pocketbook strap on her shoulder. All eyes on her, but she just had to make it out of the room, that was all, outside the circle. Just out of the room and all would be well.

"We're just getting started, Tish," Will half-whined, but she eluded his grip and in two steps made it to Chrissy's chair. Four more and she'd make the door.

Four more steps. She leaned in to Chrissy and murmured loud enough for all to hear, "I got my time something fierce, girl. I don't get home soon this place is gonna look like *Bloodsport*."

Chrissy laughed, Chester Cheetah's glasses rising and falling on her tit, and suddenly no eyes were on Laticia; they were anywhere else.

"I'll see y'all later," she made her voice steady and counted the four steps to the door, watched her fingers close around the handle, felt the invisible tether snap. She didn't exhale, not while they called out goodbyes, didn't exhale until the screen door shut behind her and she was down the trailer steps, until she could see the moon.

The June air smelled like honeysuckle and gasoline. Laticia breathed deep, over and over enough to make herself dizzy, cleaning her lungs of their exhaled breath and the stench of sweat and pot and Lysol. She stood at the car long enough for someone to flip on the porch light across the street, but when Laticia raised her hand the light blinked back off.

The street was a blur, she took the turns too fast and barely tapped the brakes at stop signs, widening the gap between herself and that place. She was out of the trailer court and had clipped a mirror before she slowed, cranking down both windows.

Half a mile out she passed Will's apartment building and was on Dickason, laying on the brake to avoid a cat when she saw another set of eyes, two points of light reflected in her headlamps on the opposite side of the street the cat had run. Back on the gas, eyes forward, she passed the Cellar house.

"We trimmed him up nice," she said softly. At the stop sign she gripped the wheel until her knuckles were white as the little boy's, and couldn't bring herself to say out loud, *Can I kick him too, Daddy?*

She looped the block, headlights off, before she could change her mind and let the car creep, a gravel at a time, back down the Cellars' block on Dickason Street.

The house to the right of Douglas Cellar's was boarded up, and the house to the left flashed a For Sale by Owner sign canted to one side in high grass. Across the street, Laticia couldn't say, only that there was a light on, but whoever might be home at midnight on a Saturday night, would they sic Douglas Cellar on anyone? *Twenty-five and you never done one good thing. Tell yourself you're better than all this trash, but you smoke their weed and fuck their boys and keep your goddamn mouth shut.*

"Hypocrite."

The word stung, even coming from her own mouth.

Cellar's Dog

When she saw eyes again she dropped the car into park and slipped out as quick as she could to cut the interior light.

Crunching up the driveway toward the truck, she held her left hand out, low. Still no dog in sight, but she could make out the chain around the bumper. If it was loose, and the beast they said it was, it would tear her to pieces, eat her up, nothing left in the driveway but eyes and the palms of her hands.

Movement beneath the truck, the shifting of gravel. She stopped. "Hey, boy," she whispered. "Just wanna turn you loose. Just wanna let you . . . "

What emerged from beneath the pick-up was too large to be a dog. In the almost-pitch she could only see its shape, and her heart thumped *A bear, A bear, A bear*. Little by little it manifested a dog-shape after all, and she whispered large breeds: "St Bernard. Sheep dog. Great Dane. That whatchamacallit from *Turner and Hooch*," in the softest voice she could and willed her feet move forward. Her other hand went out, and with ten feet between herself and the mass she braced for a growl. "Cujo was a St. Bernard. But you're not Cujo. You're a wolf, aren't you? A big, black wolf . . . with no tail. Oh Christ." The chain could've been fifteen feet or two, but Laticia's horror trumped fear and she left it behind, shuffling forward and dropping to her knees as the dog inched forward.

Pennies and Blu-Cote, and pine needles and the earth after it rained, her nose was full of its scent. She released a whine from between her teeth as the monster, half-slain, limped into the light.

"Trimmed you up good," she heard herself whisper, and the dog released a rolling growl, then raised its wolf-snout into the air and howled. From their kennels, the hounds joined the cry.

The plan had been to turn the dog loose, to fuck over Douglas Cellar good and proper, to give whatever they'd trapped an honest shot. When she parked there'd been no intention to dig for bolt cutters in the bed of the truck, to let the dog smell her legs and feet, smearing her with blood as she worked the chain loose, tears streaming down her face, the Cellars' hounds continuing to howl from the pens in the backyard, careful not to touch its ears or feet or—or the place its tail had been. She'd had no intention to crouch beside it, beside this thing almost as big as she was, spread her beach towel in the backseat and coax it into her car with a piece of leftover cheeseburger from a fast food bag on the floor.

Laticia stood at her refrigerator at one in the morning, the dog silent at her feet with glassy brown eyes cautious, and fed it leftover fried chicken. It ate from her hands, crunching the bones with huge white teeth, licking the floor for grease with a tongue nearly the size of her hand. She sang to it, cooed to it, all the while mindless of the tacky brown mess on the linoleum and the size of its jaws. When the chicken was gone she opened cans of ravioli and dumped them in an empty Tupperware dish, singing under the fluorescents in her little house as the dog lapped at the sauce, its coat shining black with blood.

When the food was gone it lowered itself to the floor, nose between its paws. "What do I do now?" Laticia whispered, and far off a dog bayed. The monster pricked jagged ears at the sound, its lip sliding back like the lid over piano keys. She took a quilt from the closet and spread it on the screen porch. "Safe," she whispered. "We're both safe." It followed her out, eyes on her as she locked the outer door, then the porch door between them.

Wet hair masked her face in the shower. *It's over. All of it.* She could end it with Will in the morning. If she had her way, their whatever-it-had-been would die a quick and quiet death in the quicksand of the inevitable, but it wasn't his way. She dreaded the begging, and crying and conversations about love that were rooted less in reality than Will's inner stock of Things to Say When a Girl Leaves You that had come with her first two break-up attempts in the short few months they'd shared a bed and a pipe. But she'd bear it this time, and it would pass—and with what lay quiet on the screen porch, if the betrayal and the severed ties were laid open in tomorrow's light, maybe it would go quicker than she dared hope. Maybe Will wouldn't hump the dead horse until he was sore and limp. Maybe he'd slink away to the next girl, knowing when the screen door shut behind her she was shutting it on all of them.

She dressed and strained to hear, but the dog didn't make a sound as far as she could tell. Laticia climbed into her mother's old bed and began to outline the next day's possible scenarios, tracing their paths in the ceiling tiles.

The clock on the nightstand read 5 a.m. when she threw off the covers and padded through the house, through the smeared blood, and peered out the door. On the quilt, under the half-moon light, the beast slept.

Dawn crept up grey and foggy; she added the smells of Pine-sol and coffee to the stink of cigarette smoke when she put on a pot and mopped the dried blood off the kitchen floor with a dishrag. Sun picked at the gold flecks in the pink Formica table, drew a bright line on the glass Las Vegas ashtray, too full to reveal its Flamingo bottom. She scrubbed her hands and lit another cigarette, poured another cup of coffee, flicked through the phonebook's marked pages one more time. At seven on the dot she called Ben Miller, three houses down, catching him before he left for work. When he walked over it was in uniform.

"No, no, I got coffee on, don't stand out there." Coffee on, but no bra under her tank top. Baby blue terry cloth shorts and long legs in the doorway, she flipped her robe wide open before closing and tying it in a prim bow. Every little bit helped.

"Will in there?" Ben took off his hat like a good boy, and took two steps forward.

"No, and not likely to be, ever again," she sniffed at the air, turning, and Deputy Miller made the kitchen before gravity caught the door.

"Something bad happen? That why you called?"

Laticia clattered a clean mug from the dish rack, her back to him. "Yes and no. No—not with Will—I—that's just done. Sugar? And sit down. Please."

"Okay. And yes, yes to sugar. Laticia, are you okay? You never called—"

"It's fine—just keep your voice down," she looked sideways, but heard no movement. She was beginning to think it was dead. "Just sit with me for a minute. It's been a long night." Dropping into the chair opposite him, she pushed the mug to him across the table with the tips of her fingers. "Long night," she repeated, and was back on her feet. She dumped the ashtray, lit a cigarette, pushed up the kitchen window and stood with her hip bones against the counter, looking out over the sink, over the town.

"I haven't been inside since your mom passed," Ben said, too lightly, too carefully. "What's it been, five years? You haven't changed much, around the house I mean. Or you—you don't look any different, either, I just meant—well, all the pink. I remember the . . . but you took the pictures all down, didn't you?"

"I stole Douglas Cellar's dog." She took a long drag off her cigarette, exhaling out the window and casting clouds across the town. With a careful puff, she sent a smoke ring that hung in a perfect circle around the steeple of the Baptist church. "I have to get it to the vet, Ben. He tried to clip it—cut its ears, tail. It's disgusting. He might never of knew I did it, but I gotta take it to the vet. Its leg is all fucked up, he caught it in a bear trap up in the woods."

Discarding his optimistic ease, police posture crept up his spine, straightening him in the chair. "Jesus, Tish. When?"

"He's had it a few days, but I took it last night. I meant to let it loose, but it was all bloody, so I put it in the car and brought it home."

"It's here now?" The cigarette he'd been smoking lay forgotten in the ashtray. He rubbed the heel of his hand on his forehead.

"Yeah, it's out on the porch. Been here all night . . ." She almost added "I think," remembering the torn screen in the door, but that could've happened anytime. "Look, you got a police camera or whatever?

You gotta take crime scene pictures and stuff, right? Just take pictures of it, of what he did, so—"

"You didn't do anything illegal, Tish. I mean, no more than move a wild animal with no permit to someplace else with no permit. You think he'd go through the police? He'll be over here if he figures it out. Ah, hell."

"I know. Help me."

Beyond the door noises commenced. A low groan, weaker than a howl, and skittering noises.

"Just take the pictures, so it's like on record or whatever, in case something happens. It's not like a pet dog, it's a—part coyote or part wolf, or one of them mastiffs, that size. But wild."

"So you brought it home and put it on the back porch."

"Yes." Laticia sipped her coffee. "That's exactly what I did. Fuck that whole bunch of white trash."

"Doug's on parole, but—"

"—but he'd kill me for spite if he found out, he doesn't give a shit."

Ben was nodding slowly, his mouth pulled down at the corners, she didn't need to look at him to know that. He'd stretch his legs under the table and cross his ankles, like somehow uninterrupted blood flow would make a logical answer appear from thin air.

Laticia kept her eyes on the window. Across the valley on the other side of town the face of the hill was dotted with little houses, just like this one. Just like Ben's.

First they'd been a cluster of mining shacks, clinging to the slopes. Eventually rebuilt by the mining company, they became pretty and cheap cookie cutter tract houses with foundations of balsa wood and hope. But the mines always close. Fifteen years passed and the houses still gripped the hills that crept up behind them little by little, barnacles on a sinking ship. Eventually it would roll over them, swallow everything like one efficient and merciless typhoon wave. In the town below, the men that hadn't followed the next lode would look up from the purr of the lumber mill, glance left to right, and bend back to the saws. She curled her toes into the linoleum, hanging on.

"You know how in the movies, there's always those scenes where a guy's about to get executed, shot right in the head, and that's the moment they use to show you what he's really like? He either blubbers and begs and dies all snotty and pathetic, or finally just spits at them and says, 'Fuck you.'" Laticia looked down at her hands, the purple polish on her nails chipped from all the holes she dug. "I feel like I just said, 'Fuck you.'"

Ben sighed deep. "I'll get the camera."

When he stepped through the porch door, color drained from his face and one hand went involuntarily to his holster.

The dog's teeth appeared.

"Don't," Laticia cooed, and stroked the bloody head, its fur tacky. She squatted next to it. "If you were him would you trust a man? Don't talk. Just turn the flash off and take the pictures. I can't tell what's blood because he's so dark. But here, his back leg, and his tail—well, the nub—get all that. It's just bone." Her hands were staining pink as she petted, but she didn't care. "It's okay," she told it. "Get the ears, too. Can you imagine what he looked like before Doug got hold of him?" She took the beast's face in her hands. "You'll be fine. Then we'll set you loose, and you can go be scary again, okay?"

An hour later Ben was still at the kitchen table. "Karen's on her way. She usually just does cattle and horses, but I can't see hauling that thing across town. And it'll be quieter this way. We good?"

"Perfect." Laticia was dressed, barefoot with her hair in a knot on the back of her head. She pointed to his mug but he shook his head. "Can't you stay 'til Karen gets here?"

"Afraid to be alone with that thing?"

"No. Afraid to be alone if Cellar figures me out."

"Not much chance of that."

"Can't you stay just because?" She rubbed her palms together.

Slowly, Ben leaned forward and turned the poodle salt and pepper shakers to face each other, gilt nose to gilt nose.

Karen's big dually rumbled up, stopping the conversation before it started.

One peek at the animal, and Karen said she wasn't touching the goddamned thing until it was sedated. They crushed up the tranquilizers and stirred the powder into a can of SpaghettiOs. Karen watched over Laticia's shoulder as the dog lapped up the orange slop, rolling its eyes to follow their movements but offering no objections. Laticia's hands only shook afterward as she poured them all coffee in the kitchen. When the animal was unconscious, Karen looked it over and said, "Tailypo."

"What?"

"Tailypo," Karen folded herself cross-legged next to her tackle box of gear, holding suture needles up in the light. "Just an old story Pa used to tell when we camped out. Man traps a dog or a monster in the woods, steals its tail—sells it, eats it, depends who tells the story. Monster comes back the next few nights, tears up the man's dogs, house, eventually him, looking for the tail."

She stitched him up the best she could, cleaned and treated the parts she couldn't. "I don't know how long it'll be out, to be honest, but it'll live. I'll leave you some dog food, but it probably won't eat it. In a day or two I say drive as far as you can in any direction and turn it loose in the woods. He's no domestic, that's for sure."

"What is he?"

"Hell if I know. Some sorta crossbreed—probably mostly wolf. It's good, what you did, but get it out of here as soon as you can."

Laticia dug through her purse at the table. "What do I owe you?"

Karen shook her head, steam coming off her hands under the faucet. "Douglas Cellar is a piece of shit. His little boy . . . " she rubbed her hands on a dish towel and pressed her lips together. "My Michael is in the same class as Irving Cellar. Last night Mikey said Irving cried in class, and his grandma picked him up early. And Mikey, bless him, said Irving must be having nightmares because he drew pictures of the Big Bad Wolf all week."

Ben cleared his throat.

"Only Big Bad Wolf in that child's life is his father, and I can't think of anyone else that would do somethin' like this. But no one will hear a word from me. Y'all just be careful. And another two cents that ain't mine to give: glad to see you back together. I knew it was just a matter of time." Karen poked a clean finger into the front of Ben's uniform, and smiled at Laticia. "I was a chaperone at your Junior Prom, betcha didn't remember that. And you two looked like you stepped out of a fairy tale. Anyway."

Karen was down the steps and climbing into her truck before the flush was all the way up Laticia's cheeks, thrust halfway into the past. She blinked.

"You were my first," Ben said, "for what it's worth." His eyes were naked, face red. She heard him take a deep breath, and her fingers went numb.

Ben's belt crackled to life. Of course it did.

He was down the steps before Karen's truck was out of sight; Laticia looked out the door and saw him lean in his cruiser, talking into the radio. Head down, he returned.

"What?"

"I need my hat."

"What's going on?"

"Domestic call from Miss Annabelle across the street from the Cellars'. Doug's in the backyard with an axe, busting up his kennels. His hounds are all dead."

"Where's Irving?"

"With Miss Annabelle. My hat, Laticia."

She hung on when he reached for it.

"I gotta go."

Another engine rumbled up the hill. Chrissy's Neon.

"Shit."

Chrissy cranked down her window, lit a cigarette and waved, smiling. "Morning, Deputy Miller. Am I interrupting anything?" She was in last night's clothes, rubbing her nose with the back of her hand.

Ben stood between Laticia and the car, eyes on neither. "Not a thing. If you'll excuse me, I gotta get going. Just got a call your friend Doug butchered all his dogs and seems bent on a funeral pyre."

"He didn't kill them dogs," Chrissy called, as Ben passed her without a glance. "This what you been up to, then, Tish?"

Ben looked back, hazel eyes steady. "Take care of yourself, Laticia." He climbed in his cruiser and pointed it down the hill, disappearing without ceremony in a puff of dust.

They watched him go, then Chrissy asked again, "Seriously though, you fucking that pig?"

She shook her head.

"I would." Chrissy pushed the door open and hauled herself out like an old woman with glass bones.

"Tell Will I'm done with him. You think it'll help, tell him Ben was here. Shit, Chrissy. Don't you get tired? I'm tired," Laticia said. "And I'm bored." She shrugged and sat down on the top step.

Flicking her cigarette into the gravel and leaning against the car, Chrissy said, "I got no quarrel with you, Laticia. But Will's my cousin. He's still up, they're both still up—Logan spent the rent on another eight ball and some speed, said 'Go see if Tish really went home.' This daylight is killing me." She lit another cigarette. "Little Irving slept in our bed, snuck off and fell asleep sometime. Doug carried him out this morning in his arms like a baby." With the sun on her face and her guard down, Chrissy looked almost like a real person, like a human. "Yeah, Laticia. Yeah, I'm tired."

"He shouldn'a been there."

"He's seen worse. So have I, so have you. And we turned out just fine." Chrissy smiled at the lie, and Laticia matched it.

The late morning sun suspended time; in the yellow light pressing into the hill, Laticia unfolded two ratty lawn chairs, and Chrissy sat down in the one next to her.

"You remember in the old cartoons when the sheepdogs and wolves would go on lunchbreak or change shifts, and there was that break, where they'd stop being like they had to be and just . . . " Laticia waved her arm.

Chrissy hhmphed. "I remember."

"This feels like that. A lotta this morning has felt like a movie, or TV, or a dream. So much talk, my head's spinning. It's like trying to swim after not doing it for years. I don't think I've had any sorta real talking to people in—well, probably since Mom died."

Bachelor's buttons and daisies winked blue and white at them on the slope below.

"I never figured you'd stay."

"Forgot to leave."

"Me, too!" Chrissy grinned, and they both laughed.

Monet painted the light on the haystacks, didn't he? Laticia didn't say it out loud, but the light reminded her of those paintings. Somewhere a milkweed pod burst and exhaled; wishes blew past them and over the hill in a snow globe gust. "Make a wish," she told Chrissy.

"Can't. I gotta clock back in." Chrissy pushed herself up from the chair. "My wolves need mindin."

Laticia checked the dog; still unconscious. Kneeling beside it, she laid both hands flat on its ribcage, feeling it breathe. "I would keep you," she whispered. "If you weren't a feral, chopped-up Tailypo too sick to remember you probably want to kill everything, I think we'd be friends."

Laticia stretched out on the couch with the front door locked and the door between kitchen and porch propped open. She drifted off, watching the ocean-like patterns her mother's embroidered sheer curtains made on the shag carpet and dreamed into the past, if the past were a kaleidoscope, and the moments fell random and overlapped, vivid chaos.

Laticia Deal, she signed the visitor's log and saw her name a few lines up, from the morning before, and a few lines up from that. Took her place in the cold plastic chair to stare at the IV bag and rolled the bottle of Darvocet-pink polish between her hands. Closed her eyes, opened them, saw her hands buckling the straps on her silver heels. "It's not love," she told her reflection, and painted her lips. "He's here!" her mother called. Then from the doorway, "Tish, hurry, quick. He's dropped everything, it's adorable. Just peek, I won't go to the door 'til he gets himself straightened out." Laticia turned, but her mother wasn't in the doorway, instead it was Irving Cellar. He told her, "Daddy said I could tame him, and he'd be mine. I never had no dog before. Daddy had hounds, but them wasn't for playin' with, Daddy said." The little boy looked her up and down. "You look just like Cinderella." She put both hands over her face to hide him, and when she removed them she was back in the plastic chair, and the monitor beeped steady, ensuring visitors never reached REM sleep. Behind her were noises she could only describe as *wet*, and a tearing like fabric. Looking back, she saw the beast, the wolf, whole. Ears pointed and laid back, tail long and curved. Its coat was black, sleek, more like a raven's feathers than fur. "So that's what you look like." The animal perked up at the sound of her voice. It was beautiful, standing there on the room's other bed. White teeth shining, the tick, tick, tick of blood dripping onto the tile floor. "No, don't mind me, finish him," Laticia made a shooing motion with her hand, and the animal nosed back into its work, Douglas Cellar's trunk laid open wide, the beast straddling him, pulling the intestines free. Doug groaned, and Laticia put a finger to her lips, scowling. "Sshhh, you'll wake my mother." He nodded, eyes round as saucers, blood seeping from between his lips. The heart rate monitor began to buzz wildly and she flailed her arms, searching for the call button. Laticia's hand came up with her cellphone, and she stared. "Oh."

She'd found the phone by touch, and opened her eyes on the living room with a deep intake of breath, as if surfacing from deep underwater. Shaking, she pushed the button and said hello.

"Tish?"

"Ben? What time is it?"

"I don't know—noon, maybe? Tish, I'm at the bottom of the hill."

Her legs tingled pins and needles as she ran through the house to the porch. The quilt was blood-soaked and empty.

"You don't have to come down, but I thought you'd at least want to know—"

"I'll walk down. I'm on my way."

The sun was gone. She drowned the knot in her

throat at the kitchen sink with a can of Coke, watching the storm clouds roll in. They softened everything, there was mercy in the dark.

One blue flip-flop and one purple was all she could come up with in a hurry. She pulled the door shut behind her and watched her legs carry her through the gravel dust more than felt them. Past Ben's house, past two others and she made the turn in the road carved into the hill; it made the shape of a less-than sign.

Ambulance lights flashed; Laticia stopped in her tracks.

Past the five houses to her left, a knot of neighbors tightened and loosened, and past them were cruisers, Ben with a roll of yellow tape, EMTs talking but not doing, and Douglas Cellar's red Jimmy crumpled around the telephone pole.

She broke into a run and Ben spotted her—he handed off the tape and caught her elbow before she made the crowd.

"Tish, you don't have to—"

"Is he dead?"

"Yes." Ben folded one arm around her and when she let out a joyous squawk, he clapped a hand over her mouth.

She pawed it away. "Irving?"

"Laticia."

"What about Irving?"

"Yes."

The word rolled through her body, stole her breath. Through the people, the lights, she saw a black mound at the edge of the road. "My dog?" she whispered.

"That was not your dog."

She smacked his hands away and pushed through

the spectators, ducked the tape and stood before the SUV's bloody windshield.

"Miss Deal, it's a crime scene."

Laticia ignored him, ignored his official-sounding voice.

Between the vehicle and the dog, litter had rained from the open windows. She stepped on fast food wrappers, beer cans, and was almost to the ditch when she saw the paper stuck to her purple flip-flop. Laticia stopped to pull it free and Ben grabbed her by the elbow, dragging her away, back under the tape and through the people that paid her no mind. The EMTs were unloading the stretchers. The crowd collectively drew breath, hungry for the sight of blood.

Laticia dropped to her knees at the edge of the road, flattening the paper on her thighs. Tears dripped, or rain, and she rubbed them into the picture.

"He's ruined his last beautiful thing," she said, to herself more than Ben.

Ben knelt next to her and took her hand. She let him, which counted for something. "I'll walk you back home. Come on."

"I'm keeping this."

"Then hide it."

She folded the white paper carefully, concealing the Big Bad Wolf drawn in black crayon and the little boy with sky blue eyes, crescent moon for a smile.

When We All Meet at the Ofrenda

KEVIN LUCIA

The horizon above Hillside Cemetery was slowly bruising a crimson-purple, shading to the velvet darkness of an autumn Adirondack evening. Night birds sang. The crisp air nipped Whitey Smith's hands and face. Dry leaves rustled underfoot as he shuffled along the path leading toward the cemetery caretaker shed. His assistants, Judd and Dean, had raked leaves all week, but it hadn't mattered. Never did. When autumn came, leaves covered the ground. Was the way of things.

Flowers bloomed in Spring. Crops grew during summer. Leaves fell in autumn, and things died during winter, except Maria, who had died a month ago of pancreatic cancer, which was the way of things.

People died.

He shuffled to a stop. Grasped the knob on the shed's door, swallowing a grimace as arthritic pain arrowed glass slivers into his knuckles. Muttering "Sunnuvabitch," he turned the knob and tried to open the door but couldn't. Rained yesterday, and the door had swelled as it always did afterward, catching in the doorframe.

He tugged harder.

The door popped open, but he was rewarded for his efforts with an aching pulse in his right shoulder. It had been hurting lately. Ever since something twisted in it when he and Judd were burying the Jensen kid last spring after he rolled his car on Bassler Road.

Whitey stood before the shed's open door, right hand still on the knob (his joints still burning) left hand gently kneading the leathery meat of his right shoulder, which throbbed dully. Dr. Fitzgerald at Utica General said it was probably a torn rotator cuff. He'd recommended surgery. Or at least therapy. Whitey had waved off the recommendation, claiming he had neither the time nor the money for either, a self-fulfilling prophecy after Maria's diagnosis.

Whitey didn't enter the shed immediately. He stood there, eyes closed, rubbing his shoulder, savoring the heady scent of oil and gasoline from the lawnmower out back. It was one of his favorite smells because it reminded him of the night he first saw Maria.

He'd first seen Maria Alverez while standing outside the pit area at Five Mile Speedway, hands hooked on the chain-link fence separating him from the powerful cars tended to by mechanics wearing gray smudged overalls. Some of the cars were jacked, tires being changed or their undersides inspected by men lying under them. Others had hoods open, swallowing mechanics intently fixing either carburetors or changing spark plugs. A few cars roared as drivers tested their engines.

When We All Meet

At age ten, the world beyond the fence appeared grand. Every Saturday night men conjured strange masculine magic from gasoline-fueled beasts. After spending his childhood watching the races with his father, Whitey Smith would race himself during the early years of his tenure at Hillside Cemetery. This of course earned his modified 1940 Ford coupe (number 72) the nickname "Grave Wagon."

Those days, however, were distant dreams when he first saw Maria in the Five Mile pits. He'd only been ten, she an exotic twelve, handing her father tools as he worked under a chopped and stripped Chevy.

Whitey fell in love instantly. She hadn't been wearing anything remotely girlish, clad only in a smaller version of the gray overalls other mechanics wore, hair pulled tight into a ponytail. Face composed and serious, as she watched her father (Carlos Alverez, Whitey would later learn) work underneath the Chevy. Whitey fell in love with her intense expression, her narrowed eyes, pursed lips, (which he suddenly wanted to kiss), and the oil smudge—a beauty mark—on her cheek.

He would chase her, worship and annoy her, woo her and then win her. He'd someday race for her, and would always cherish her.

Now he mourned her.

Whitey inhaled another breath of oil and gasoline, then reached in and flicked a light switch inside the shed's door. Dim orange light spilled from a single bulb hanging from the shed's ceiling, illuminating the spartan area, which had become his living space since he'd buried Maria at Hillside.

Against the wall a simple cot, blankets tucked in.

Next to it, a wooden crate serving as a nightstand for a small lamp he'd gotten at Handy's Pawn and Thrift. At the cot's end sat an old footlocker bought at a garage sale long ago. Pushed into the far corner of the shed was a refrigerator, with his Coleman stove on top.

The tools of his trade hung neatly on the far wall. Two different sizes of shovels, several dirt and grass rakes, hand rakes, weed whacker, a pick and a pitchfork. The small riding lawnmower, push mower and snow-blower (to keep the access roads clear during winter), rested in an adjoining small garage. In the center of the shed sat a kerosene heater.

Whitey grunted as he moved slowly toward his cot. The shed offered everything he needed, regardless what his eldest Carlos thought. Carlos kept saying he'd catch his death out in the cold. Claiming he understood Whitey's pain in one breath, accusing him of "playing goddamn Huck Finn" in the next. Ungrateful snot had grown too big for his britches, partying in New York City with his writer boyfriend. Said Whitey was foolish to believe in all the old tales of Dia de los Muertos, that Maria wouldn't come back. Hell with him, anyway. When had Carlos . . .

(or was that Marcus?)

. . . valued his mother's traditions? All Hallow's Eve, Saint's Day, All Souls Day, Dia de los Muertos. Those quaint Mexican customs (of which his sons had acted increasingly ashamed) meant nothing to him, so how *could* Carlos (Marcus?) understand Whitey's need to be close to Maria tonight?

Whitey sat down on the cot, knees popping, his lower back aching. Didn't matter what they thought. He'd determined to spend October by Maria's side here at the cemetery, and he had. Only one more night left. Tonight, All Hallow's Eve. Dia de los Muertos. Day of the Dead. Technically it fell on November 2nd, but after they'd gotten married, Maria had insisted on celebrating it Halloween night. To her, it felt right to celebrate Dia de los Muertos the same night the whole town armed their porches with grinning jack-o'-lanterns while costumed youth patrolled the streets.

Some front yards on Halloween boasted haunted graveyards filled with foam headstones, skeletons and lurching zombies. Their front yard on Henry Street offered a monument to the Day of the Dead. Central to the display had always been the ofrenda, a wooden altar Whitey had built from sheets of plywood. On it, Maria always assembled an offering for their dead relatives and loved ones, to welcome their spirits on a night when the boundaries between worlds grew thin.

Sitting on his cot, Whitey recalled the days when Carlos and Marcus marveled at the ofrenda. For years it had lit their eager, drinking faces with soft electric light glowing from strings of orange and yellow bulbs, and the flickering of ceremonial candles. During those innocent years, the boys thought they had the best Halloween exhibit in town. The finest touch? The Coqueta Catrina and Elegant Catrin (two opulently clothed foam skeletons), standing silent and grinning watch on either side of the ofrenda.

Their lawn did boast foam headstones also, but they were garlanded with bright orange and yellow marigolds. Before each, Maria filled plastic bowls full of candy apples, homemade pumpkin empanadas, pumpkin spice brownies, and of course, homemade Calaveras. Sugar-candy skulls. She and Whitey—faces painted in Calaveras masks, dressed as the Coqueta Catrina and the Elegant Catrin—directed the children to these bowls.

Whitey sighed. As children, Carlos and Marcus had begged to sit before the ofrenda, long after the trick-or-treaters had gone. But it got "old," they said when teenagers. They'd even gone so far as to accuse Maria—their *mother*—of not really believing in Dia de los Muertos at all. She'd "co-opted" it, according to Marcus . . .

(or was it Carlos?)

. . . made it her "thing" to show how "Mexican" she was. Said even she thought the stories nothing but superstition. So disrespectful, it made Whitey's hands shake with barely-restrained (but still futile) rage thinking about it. He sounded just like his brother.

(but which one?)

Whitey bent and covered his face with shaking hands.

After being struck dumb by Maria's transcendent twelve-year-old beauty at Five Mile Speedway, Whitey didn't instantly pursue her. After all, she was twelve and in sixth grade. An unattainable prize for a lowly fourth grader.

However, as they progressed out of grammar school into junior high and eventually high school, a combination of happenstance and Whitey's own quiet determination kept them crossing paths. By the time Maria was a senior and Whitey was a sophomore, they were friends. They walked home from school together. They sat together at lunch. During the summers they picked blueberries at Mr. Trung's, browsed garage sales, and once they braved the first floor of old Bassler House, the dilapidated Victorian farmhouse on the edge of town. They wandered through Raedeker Park Zoo, talking about nothing and everything. They watched the Wednesday night summer movies at Raedeker Park when it was a monster movie or a western, and they endlessly searched Handy's Pawn and Thrift for the trinkets only young people found fascinating.

The tipping point occurred Maria's senior year, when Whitey asked her to the annual Halloween movie at Raedeker Park. At the time, he hadn't understood her unusually excited acceptance of his invitation. Only later did it dawn upon him: For the first time he'd asked her to go somewhere *with* him, formally.

When he knocked on her door and she opened it, he could only stare, speechless. Her usually light-brown face was a startling white. Large black ovals circled her eyes, mimicking the gaping eyeholes of a skull, but they didn't make her eerie or frightening. She appeared mysterious. Otherworldly. Likewise, her nose was painted black—a skull's empty nose cavity—her lips were also white and sectioned by black lines into two rows of skeletal teeth.

On her forehead and cheeks, faint colored lines—yellow, blue and red—swirled in delicate patterns. Looking closer, he noticed the small blue circles bordering her eyes, as if a chain of sapphires circled each. As a finishing touch, a red flower blossomed on her chin.

She stared at him for a heartbeat. Whitey opened

his mouth and closed it, still speechless, because she was unearthly and ethereal. It flitted across his mind to ask if she was practicing for Halloween, but the painted mask invoked a seriousness which transcended a mere spook mask.

Finally, he swallowed and managed, "Wow. You look amazing."

Maria smiled, transforming her face into a beautiful and disconcerting grinning skull. "Thanks!" She stepped out, shut the door behind her, and they left for Raedeker Park.

After a few steps, Whitey said, "It *is* awesome. I mean it. Is it . . . I mean . . . "

"For Halloween? Not exactly. We're doing a family heritage project in Mr. Groover's class, and I've been studying Mexican customs. Cause, you know," she jerked her head back toward her house, "Mom and Dad won't talk about Mexican stuff because they're trying so hard to be American. Which is fine. I've got no problem being American, except whenever Grandma Louisa tries to tell stories about Mexico, Mom and Dad hush her, like she's going to spill all these embarrassing secrets. Especially when she tries to tell us about Dia de los Muertos. So I decided to study it for my History project this year."

She offered Whitey a brilliant grin, which only made her more beautiful and ghastly. "My parents weren't happy. Got an 'ay dios mio' from Mom, which is impressive. But anyway, it's for a school project, and they know I hate school, so I guess they figured if it'll get me interested in schoolwork, it's okay."

They left Henry Street and crossed onto Main, heading to Raedeker Park. "Dia de los Muertos. Day of the Dead, right? Mrs. Millavich talked about it in Spanish last week, but . . . I, uh . . . "

Whitey shrugged. "I sorta wasn't paying attention."

Maria's painted-on skull smirked as she punched his shoulder. "Of course not. She was probably wearing one of her tight-knit sweaters." Whitey said nothing and kept grinning, because of course, it was true.

"I'll skip the parts about the Catholic church and All Soul's day. Day of the Dead is ancient. It recognizes death as a natural part of life. Not something to be feared. That's why the face-paint." She tapped her cheek. "This is a calavera, representing the human skull not as something scary but something beautiful, because it's a part of life. They make little sugar candies in the shape of skulls. Can't buy them around here. Next year, I'm going to learn how to make them myself."

Samara Hill, which led to Raedeker Park, lay only a few blocks away, but suddenly Whitey wanted to walk slower, and make the time last. "What else is the Day of the Dead about?"

Maria talked excitedly, gesturing with her hands, warming to the subject. "Mostly, it's about honoring those who have gone before us. You decorate loved ones' headstones, offer their favorite foods in clay bowls, maybe sing their favorite songs or hymns. Nana always mentions it every year because Grandpa is buried out on Shelby Road, and she gets upset we don't erect an ofrenda and celebrate for his spirit to return."

"What's an ofrenda?"

"An altar you place at a loved-one's gravesite. You put pictures of them on it, maybe some keepsakes they loved in real life, candles, bowls of their favorite foods . . . "

"Do you believe people's souls actually come back on the Day of the Dead?"

Maria shrugged, smiling wistfully. "I don't know. I know it's an important part of my culture . . . which my parents want to ignore. I'm not going to get all traditional or anything. I like America fine. But I want this *one* thing from my heritage, y'know? And I'm going to celebrate it from now on."

Blazing inspiration pumped Whitey's heart. "Can I . . . celebrate it with you? I mean . . . can boys have their faces painted, too?"

They'd reached the next-to-last intersection before Samara Hill. Maria turned and favored him with an earnest expression of affection which burned its way into his soul. "Of *course* boys can have their faces painted as a calavera. And of course you can celebrate it with me."

She reached out and gently took his hand. Squeezed it, and held on to it. He smiled, and, because he didn't trust himself to speak (and maybe she likewise) they turned and crossed the street, Whitey realizing he'd done something far greater than simply ask Maria Alverez to the annual Halloween movie.

A soft knock on the door pulled Whitey from his memories. His knees tired and sore (as always these days), he didn't stand. Only looked up and said, "Come in."

The door opened. Sheriff Chris Baker removed his hat and stepped in. "Evening, Whitey." He gestured at Whitey with his hat. "Your Elegant Catrin looks especially fine, this year. Wasn't sure you'd be celebrating, especially after . . . well. Happy to see you're carrying on."

Whitey smiled slightly. Sheriff Baker was young and relatively new on the job, and he still had some things to learn. But he knew how to flatter his elders. "Thank you, Sheriff. I'm not so fine, really. A tired old man wearing white face paint and a dusty old tuxedo bought forty years ago at Handy's Pawn and Thrift. Nothing more."

Sheriff Baker waved off Whitey's dismissal. "Humble as always, Whitey, but this town loves you as much as it loved Maria."

Whitey smiled fully now, blinking back an irritating wetness in his eyes. "You're too kind, Sheriff. Parents obviously taught you some manners."

"My mother didn't suffer fools, sure enough."

Whitey folded his hands in his lap, feeling mild impatience at being interrupted (something he'd felt more and more the past few years, because he was old, and tired, and interruptions wearied him, and he hated the whole feeling, which only made him feel older). "What brings you out here, Sheriff?"

Sheriff Baker shrugged. "Patrolling. Halloween and all. Wanted to stop by, make sure none of the kids were sneaking around here, getting into mischief."

Despite his irritation at the interruption, Whitey chuckled. "We haven't had any problems in the cemetery since before your time, Sheriff. Why don't you tell me the real reason you're here."

Sheriff Baker's smile faltered. He actually appeared embarrassed. "Well. Understand, Whitey . . . no one's been talking behind your back. We all imagine how you're feeling right now, this being your first Day of the Dead without Maria. But a few folks have noticed you didn't put up your ofrenda or Day of the Dead decorations this year . . . and they're worried, I guess. Hoping you're all right."

Whitey forced a smile. "Death is a part of life, Sheriff. Maria taught me that. *But*." He allowed his smile to slip a bit; he'd come to respect and like the new sheriff, and believed he could trust him with some of the truth.

Some, of course.

Not all.

"I wasn't quite up for it this year. I did answer the door for a few children, but I didn't have it in me for anything more." He offered the Sheriff a sad smile. "I'm sure you understand how much it takes out of a man to his lose his wife, regardless of the age."

Sheriff Baker nodded, distant pain glimmering in his eyes. Whitey didn't like thinking he was taking advantage of the Sheriff's recent loss—his wife had died shortly after he took office here in Clifton Heights—but a growing impatience for the sheriff's departure warred with his sense of propriety. The time was coming to welcome Maria's spirit from the Other Side. He wanted to be alone, and his desire outweighed his concerns for the sheriff's own grief. "I know you understand what it means to lose your wife. I didn't have the gumption for the whole production this year."

Sheriff Baker nodded. He glanced around the shed, gesturing with his hat. "Got things nice and fixed up. You comfortable out here? Not too cold or anything?"

Whitey sighed and leaned back against the wall, stifling a grimace at the small brace of pain in his lower back. "All right, Sheriff. Who sent you? Which of my boys called you, asked you to come out and check on me?"

Sheriff Baker frowned, confusion and also worry showing in his expression. "The boys? Whitey . . . I don't understand. The boys . . . "

⁓

" . . . *have been asking for you, Maria. They wanted to be here, but they can't come yet.*"

A weak, fluttering smile. Eyes sad and regretful, yet understanding. "*You haven't told anyone, have you? About the boys? I don't think they'd understand, and I don't want . . .* "

"No, Maria. That's nobody else's business. But they miss you. They miss their Momma."

Another sad smile, stretching tight skin over sharp cheekbones. "*I know. But it is the way of things. We live, then die. So long as you build the ofrenda, light my candles on Dia de los Muertos, if you prepare . . . I will come. I promise.*"

"I've made all the preparations. Like you've always wanted. Like you said you wanted, if . . . "

Raw emotion closed his throat. He'd tried to be strong. God, he'd tried. He'd managed to put a good face on it; he'd managed to act brave, but he couldn't do it anymore. "*Maria, please. Don't leave me.*"

A slow blink. Eyes dulling as their light receded, faint voice rasping, "*I must. It is the way of things.*"

"*But I can't. The boys. They keep nagging me. Night and day. They keep telling me what I can and can't do. I'm not a child. I don't want to move into an old folks' home, or a nursing home, but the boys, they won't . . . the boys . . .* "

On their first trip to Mexico, they saw the catacombs. They stayed in Mexico City on November 2nd because Maria wanted to see the Day of the Dead up close. They watched parades with hundreds of people dressed as the Coqueta Catrina and the Elegent Catrin, wearing Calaveras face paintings the likes of which they'd never seen. They munched on sugar candy skulls bearing their names. They listened enraptured to men playing Guitarrones on the street corners. When night fell, they visited the graveyard on the outskirts of town and watched in awe and reverence as families lit candles on ofrendas at tombstones and sang songs to their beloved dead.

Maria was inspired. She asked Whitey to build an ofrenda in their front yard, for all of Clifton Heights to see on Halloween night. And it was on that trip, the next day, when Maria told Whitey—made him swear on his solemn word—how she wanted him to celebrate Dia de los Muertos with her, should she pass first.

Whitey realized his slip soon as Sheriff Baker frowned. "The boys? I'm . . . not sure I follow, Whitey."

Whitey offered him a weak smile, hoping he appeared as baffled as Sheriff Baker no doubt imagined he was. "Pay no mind to me, Sheriff. I'm an old, sad man rambling after losing the love of his life, is all."

Whitey could see he'd inflected the right tone, as the younger man's face relaxed. "I understand. After

Liz passed, I wandered in a daze for weeks. Didn't know which end was up."

He gestured around the cabin with his hat again. "Whitey. It's none of my business. But is everything okay? You managing all right at home? You mentioned the boys, and I . . . "

Another flickering, weak-old-man-can't-blame-me-I'm-losing-my-mind grin. "Apologies, Sheriff. I'm not myself right yet. Still haven't gotten my wits about me."

Sheriff Baker nodded, sympathy glimmering in his eyes. "I understand. Certainly do." He replaced his hat on his head and moved to leave, but paused before stepping out the door. "Listen, Whitey. If you ever need anything, don't hesitate to call."

"Thank you," Whitey said sincerely, lying with his next words, "I will."

Sheriff Baker nodded, tipped his hat, said "Happy Halloween, Whitey. Feliz dia muerte," and stepped out into the night.

Whitey eased himself down the ladder, rung by rung, into the cellar he'd dug under the shed when he'd rebuilt it shortly after accepting the head caretaker's position. Back then he'd only the barest idea as to why he'd dug the cellar. The old shed he'd rebuilt because it had been a ramshackle affair. He'd wanted something better, so he'd erected a finely built shed which doubled as a surprisingly comfortable sleepover when he'd occasionally drank too much at The Stumble Inn. Maria had nothing against drinking and had never persecuted him for having a few too many, but he'd never felt comfortable coming home tipsy, worried one of the boys would see him stumbling to bed.

Oddly enough, he hadn't any booze the entire time he'd slept here since Maria passed.

He stepped off the last rung and onto the cellar's concrete floor. He put his hands on his hips and looked around, appraising his handiwork, thinking how pleased Maria would be when she saw it because, after all . . . it was what she'd asked for. The day after Dia de los Muertos, in Mecico City.

"Ay, dios mio," Maria whispered as she descended the rickety wooden ladder after Whitey and their guide, into the subterranean depths of the catacombs outside Mexico City. "I've read about it and seen pictures, but I've never . . . "

Their tour guide, a plain-faced man named Juan, glanced at her in mild surprise. "You are Mexican, si?"

Maria smiled apologetically at him. "Si. But I was raised American. My parents became citizens before I was born. But all my life, I've . . . I've felt something in *here*," she thumped her heart with a closed fist. "A wish to know who I was. To know my culture. I've studied and read for years, but this . . . " she gestured at the shadowed depths of the catacombs, lit by flickering orange light bulbs hanging by wires from the ceiling, " . . . this, and the celebrations, Dia de los Muertos . . . seeing this is a dream come true, since I was a teenager."

Juan nodded once with a small smile, as if he'd seen it before, and didn't find it strange. "Well then, *señorita*." He waved ahead. "Welcome to the catacombs."

As they followed Juan down the narrow corridor dug out of red hardpan and rock, Whitey marveled at how dry the air was, but also how cool. It didn't smell foul or rotten, as he'd feared it would. The only scent tickling his nostrils was of dust, an ancient spice he couldn't place, and the musk of old books.

They passed the corpses leaned upright against the wall. Whitey was amazed at their condition. Their desiccated skin—like dried leather—had pulled tight without rot. No maggots, rats or any of the more sensational signs of decay. Something about the dry, cool air, perhaps. Or something done special to the bodies themselves, like with Egyptian mummies.

Or, perhaps it was fortunate they hadn't descended into the catacombs after a recently interred body. In either case, the experience—especially for Maria—of walking down the softly lit dirt corridor past rows of the dead wasn't ghoulish, or ghastly, or stomach-churning in the least. It was intriguing, mysterious, enthralling . . .

And it was peaceful. Even the corpses' faces appeared composed and relaxed. Their hands folded on their midsections (Whitey had never been sure how the arms had stayed put; perhaps they'd been wired into place), their empty eyes gazing nowhere.

"Oh yes," Maria murmured, hands clasped together in eerie pantomime of the corpses leaning against the wall, her eyes shining, "Yes, Whitey. Like this someday. Promise me, all of us together, like a family."

"Of course," Whitey murmured, thinking nothing

of it, thinking it was only inspiration from the moment, nothing more.

"*Promise* me, Whitey. Please."

And he did.

Whitey stomped his boots on the cellar's cement floor. Thankfully, he'd poured several feet of sand and gravel before laying the concrete. Amazingly, after all these years, the floor was still relatively smooth, with few cracks and no heaving.

He placed a hand on the brick wall he'd mortared himself. It felt cool and dry, mostly, as did the air. Not quite as arid as the Mexican catacombs, but it was the best he could manage in the Adirondacks, and would have to suffice.

Flickering light drew his gaze to the cellar's far wall. He faced the ofrenda he'd so lovingly constructed for Maria years ago, when she'd first decided to celebrate the Day of the Dead on Halloween night. He'd had to disassemble it, bring its parts here to reassemble. It hadn't been easy. His hands shook these days, and his back hurt. Of course, he'd had since Maria's diagnosis to complete it. He'd sensed from the beginning hers was a losing battle.

For a moment, gazing upon the ofrenda, sharp grief twisted his insides. Thick white candles had been lit on all the ofrenda's shelves, firing the bouquets of red, orange and yellow marigolds. Framed pictures of Maria from when he'd started dating her to pictures from before her illness lined the top shelf. Next to them, sugar candy skulls he'd made himself, with her name written on their white crystalline foreheads.

Also, some of her favorite bits of jewelry. The floppy gardening hat she always wore when tending the flowers lining the front walk. Sheets of wax paper and the thick black sticks of wax she used for her tombstone rubbings, a hobby she'd begun ten years ago.

The ofrenda's second shelf burned with candles and was lined with marigolds also, but featured pictures of both Marcus and Carlos. Next to the pictures, toys from their youth. A football, basketball, soccer ball, and a baseball. Marcus's old Nikon camera, from before he'd discovered writing. A hammer, saw and a clutch of nails, because Carlos had fallen in love with Whitey's hobby of carpentry and had pursued it as a career. Both of them, good boys. Strong boys. Devoted boys, as unique as day and night.

Before the car accident, which had stolen Marcus, five years before. Before the unexpected heart attack claiming Carlos a year later. Suddenly, he and Maria had been rendered childless, having survived their children, which no parent should ever have to suffer.

But it was all right, now.

They were together again at last. Whitey had been worried, initially, how the boys would fare. This, after all, wasn't the cool and dry catacombs of Mexico. The cement floor and brick walls had helped, and it never got hot here, even in the summers, but there had been spring thaws to deal with. He'd a mess to clean— simply from seeping fluids and general decay—the first several springs. Also, Marcus had suffered a maggot infestation which had been . . . unpleasant. Since then, however, they'd weathered the years well.

He hadn't been able to stand them against the wall,

however, as done in the catacombs. The embalming process had made them too rigid. He'd managed to prop them, seated, backs against the ofrenda, hands folded in their laps, sightless eyes gazing at him . . . somewhat accusingly, which did bother him, when he was honest with himself. For what could they accuse him of? What had he done wrong? He was only honoring Maria's wishes, after all. Bringing them together as one family, forever.

He turned and grasped the rope hanging from the rectangle opening above, attached to a stick propping the door he'd installed into the floor when he'd dug out the cellar. With a quick tug, he pulled the stick into the cellar. The door swung shut with a *thump* and the *click* of the special latch and lock he'd recently installed. A lock which could only be opened from the outside, which he'd also fused shut with an acetylene torch. He'd fastened a throw rug onto the hatch, concealing it from passing eyes. Perhaps, when he turned up missing, someone would eventually discover them down here like this. Perhaps for them, it would be like Maria descending into the catacombs so long ago.

Regardless, Whitey made his way in the flickering candle light—which cast shadows on his family's faces, and in those shadows he saw them gazing at him—to Maria's side. He lowered himself to the dry concrete floor, gathered her stiffness into his arms, and waited for the Day of the Dead.

Uncountable hours later, candles long since extinguished, a heavy presence—an intangible weight—filled the small catacomb. Whitey smelled

Maria's perfume. Her rich chestnut hair, before it fell out. The warm baked-flour odor of fresh empanadas. Whitey sat up and stared into the darkness, heart pounding with joy as he whispered, "Maria? Is . . . is that you? Maria? It's *me*. I'm here, darling. I'm . . . "

Her head—light from decay—shifted against his neck.

Whitey cried, fear squeezing his heart (because her dry touch was so cold) as he pushed weakly off the wall to his feet, tottering away into the darkness, stiff joints screaming. Hands out, searching the blackness, he felt brick, turned and flattened back against the far wall. He frantically dug into his pocket for his lighter . . .

And heard it.

Scratching.

Dragging. Something . . . several somethings . . .

carlos

marcus

if I believe in it, it will happen

wasn't supposed to be like this

. . . shifting and crawling toward him.

Whitey's hand closed around the lighter in his pocket. Squeezed it, feeling the cool metal housing a flame that could . . .

No.

Fear drained away.

He tottered several steps toward the dragging, clicking, sliding. His legs trembled, knees buckling, and he fell to his knees. Opened his arms.

Waiting.

Maria reached him first. And she didn't smell bad at all (not like her perfume or hair or freshly baked empanadas, but not bad, either) as she nestled her withered mouth at the base of his neck. Sighing, he craned his head back and, gently holding the back of her desiccated head, pressed her to him, so her teeth could get a better grip on his jugular.

And with his other, he welcomed his sons as they came together, at last.

As he'd believed they would.

Hey, Little Sister

MARIA ALEXANDER

Childhood memories wind through my thoughts like the fire trails burned into the surrounding foothills. I marvel at the destruction of the summer blaze as I head up Highway 50. My wife Allie's getting her drink on with her fellow bridesmaids in San Francisco this weekend. Since the bride made it clear "No Boys Allowed," I said *au revoir* this morning and took off in our black Prius to see Sophia, my severely disabled sister. She lives just three hours away at the old homestead in Placerville. Or "Hickville" as I like to call it.

After texting the public guardian for permission, I pick up Sophia for her usual Saturday afternoon hair appointment. The caregiver waves to us as we pull out of the driveway, her brows scrunched together with worry. Whether she's worried because I'm wearing a black Nine Inch Nails t-shirt with equally dark jeans, or if it's because she has some other phantom fear, I can't tell. My sister's soft, crooked smile lights up my passenger's seat.

"Why don't you wave back, Sophie?"

"I'm not . . . a child . . . you know," she says in her halting speech. Not in years, anyway. She's just over forty, but mentally she's about six. Maybe seven.

"I know!" I wink at her. "So, yer gettin' yer hair did? We going to the barber?"

"Nooooo," she laughs.

"I dunno. It's cheaper. I think you should give it a consider, there," I reply.

Laughing harder, she tells me how to get to the salon. I'm shocked she remembers. Then again, before our mother died five years ago, she took Sophia to that same salon every week for twenty years to get her gorgeous sable hair washed and styled. Brain-injured folk like Sophia don't like to bathe. It was probably the only way Mom could guarantee at least Sophia's head didn't stink. Since they went regularly for so long, Sophia's injured synapses must have been able to forge a rare path to that destination.

We find the tiny island of business buildings tucked halfway up one of those charred hills. Sophia's disability placard lets us park near the door, and we enter the busy salon reeking of rummy suntan lotion and Fukushima-brewed hair products. The woman at the front desk unleashes a hundred-megawatt smile at Sophia. She's the sort of gal that would have scared me to death in high school. Bronze skin, blond highlights, pink manicure, perfectly straight teeth, v-neck tee dipping into a hint of cleavage and khaki shorts that reveal her tightly sculpted limbs. I was the nerdy goth boy in the computer lab who could barely manage to look a girl in the eye through my overgrown black bangs, much less court one of these leonine goddesses that prowled the campus in basketball uniforms or cheerleading skirts. Even at six-foot-three, I can still be that knee-knocking little boy around women.

"Hi, Sophia! Who's your friend?" the woman asks.

"Hey, I'm Barry." I shake her limp hand. "Sophia's older brother."

"Ah, yeah, I see the resemblance. I'm Carol," she replies. Did her smile just dim? "It's good to meet you. Come on back, sweetie! Lane is waiting for you."

Sophia wobbles off, her leg braces and poor balance binding her eager stride. I sink into one of the seats by a table piled with fashion magazines, checking photos on my phone from Allie's celebrations. God, I'm a lucky sonuvabitch. Amazing wife who puts up with weird-ass, mopey me and my damned obsessions. She says the glass is half-full even when I insist there's no glass at all. I chuckle at a photo of the bridesmaids lined up doing the Amy Schumer pose for the movie *Trainwreck*, beer bottles to lips, fingers wagging at the camera. It's barely lunchtime and they're already at it.

"Uh, Barry?" Carol bites her thumbnail, hip leaning against the front desk, and she glances at the front door. "Can we talk?"

Crap. Something must be up with my sister.

We step outside into the bracing heat dusted with the scent of burned grass. When the sunlight strikes her face, I notice faint lines around her mouth. Man, I suck at ages. She's older than I originally guessed.

"You look so much like Sophia," she says.

"Yeah. Too much like our dad, I'm afraid." My nerves start dancing a jumping-bean jig. Something about her look tells me this is going to be awkward. Does Dad owe them money? I can take care of that. I make plenty doing database programming for a telecommunications startup.

She crosses her arms, struggling to find my eyes. "I'm sorry you lost your father."

I shrug. "Thanks. We didn't exactly get along, so . . . "
Understatement of the year. He was an abusive
monster who'd made our childhoods nightmarish with
physical and verbal abuse, not to mention the ongoing
sexual comments he made to Sophia that perpetually
freaked her out. After Mom died, I'd tried to get the
county people to step in and take Sophia out of the
house. I failed because there wasn't enough evidence
that Dad was abusing his disabled daughter to
interfere. Dad hated me for it and cut off contact
between me and Sophia. I didn't even know if they
were safe during the fire. I had friends cast runes and
do tarot readings to reassure me when relatives didn't
respond to my calls.

"I want to apologize," she says at last.

"For what? Taking care of my sister's hair? I should
be thanking *you*. She can be a handful with her
tantrums."

She looks down. "We should have reported him."

Darkness squeezes my vision, heart kangaroo-
kicking my throat.

"After your mom passed away, he continued to
bring Sophia here. Every week, like clockwork. But
he'd make all kinds of . . . inappropriate . . . comments
to the girls working here. And to your sister. He'd . . .
kiss her. On the mouth," Carol winces. "I once saw him
put his tongue in. And his hand went —"

Rage rears up like a viper, twisting and spitting. I
turn away from her, hands balling into fists, and walk
off into the scalding parking lot.

"Barry! I'm so sorry. We talked to him, and—"

"You *talked* to him? Why the fuck didn't you *report*
him?" God, I'm shaking. Nausea spikes my throat.

"I don't know. We just didn't want to—"

"What? Interfere? FUCK YOU! YOU SHOULD HAVE FUCKING INTERFERED. Can't you see she's defenseless?"

People stare at us through the windows of the other shops. Carol scurries back inside the salon. My breakfast comes up, spattering the curb, scorching my mouth. I kneel in the weeds by the parking lot, sinking in molten grief.

I knew it. God-fucking-dammit, *I knew it.*

Since childhood, you see, I've had dreams. Not telling the future, but rather, seeing *through* people and events. If someone lies to me, does something miles away, I see the real events in a dream. It's how I found out about Dad's illegal activities. And other things. Mom called me her Superman because of my "x-ray" vision.

After Mom died, I'd had nightmares of Dad molesting Sophia. Nothing graphic, thank God, but there was no question what was happening. Unfortunately, you can't take a dream journal into a courtroom and ask the probate judge to give you conservatorship. Allie and I had even talked about kidnapping her, but decided against it. I lost weeks of sleep to anxiety.

But does Sophia remember any of it? Maybe her brain injury is a blessing for once. Twenty-five years after the car accident, her memory is still so bad that it dances a constant box step between reality and fantasy. Unless a witness like this woman had come forward, Sophia would never have brought charges against Dad. Her memory was too weak to register trauma unless it was an event that everyone around her discussed repeatedly.

He would have gotten away with it. He *did* get away with it.

Storm clouds rumble behind my eyes as I pay for Sophia's hair wash and style. I leave without saying goodbye to Carol. Before I unlock Sophia's car door, I crush her in a big brother hug, my heart breaking. "I love you, Booger."

"Don't call me that, Mary!" she says, pushing me away. Mary and Booger. She remembers childhood nicknames.

I take her home.

Sophia shows me how her caregivers have cleaned out the master bedroom and moved in her bed. I still picture the piss-stained mattress that they found Dad on when he died, but that's been tossed. We watch some TV and play a game of Scrabble, Dad's favorite game. It's amazing how good she is at it. I go through some spider-infested boxes in the garage for the caregiver and do some maintenance on Sophia's ancient computer running Windows 98. But the whole time, the storm clouds in my head keep thundering. I consider texting Allie, but I don't want to spoil her celebration.

Besides, it's all done. Past.

After the dinner I barely touch, a new caregiver arrives and starts her overnight shift. I say goodbye to Sophia, who's already dressed in her flowered cotton pajamas, and plant a big kiss on top of her misshapen head. I then make the American Sign Language symbol for "I love you"—two middle fingers bent down into my palm, fingers and thumb extended. It was how she talked to us before she got her speech back. Sophia's wide brown eyes twinkle as she returns the gesture.

Raina.

My car flies over the hilly roads as I try the last known number I have for her. Disconnected. I *have* to reach her. She's the only one who'd understand. And I have to talk to someone. *Now.* The pain feels like glass shards in my lungs. I don't want to call aunts and uncles who would then be as tormented as I am about what had happened—or, worse, disbelieve it. But my old high school friend Raina would. I haven't spoken to her since Mom died, but she'd remember Dad.

If only I could reach her.

I drive to Daffer's, the last place I hung out with Raina. Cigarette smoke lingers outside over the burly motorcycles lined up near the door. Inside, the place hadn't changed much. Rickety wooden tables are surrounded by chairs on sawdust floors. The classic rock music on the jukebox is turned up high enough to drown out the shady conversations. I plant myself on a barstool and ask for a shot of Knob Creek. And then another. And another, until my thoughts spin out like a carnival ride, the seat tethers stretching dangerously into the surrounding murk of my rage. I should have killed him. When we were kids, I could have found a way to do it and not got caught. It would have stopped the pain early. Maybe Sophia would never have gotten hurt. She'd been staying at a friend's house to get away from him. If she'd been home, she would never have gotten in her friend's car that day . . .

Eyelids heavy, I pay the bartender and stagger to

the door. To the car. I sink into the back seat of the Prius, lock the doors, doze. No idea how long. I awake in fits, sobbing. Punching and kicking the tear- and snot-slickened seat.

And I dream.

Raina. Older. Heavier. Long, shaggy salt-and-pepper dreads. A gristly scar snaking up her right arm and across her cheek. Black tank, ragged jeans. Fingers sheathed in numerous silver, hematite and pewter rings. Reading by candlelight a worn paperback in a trailer parked somewhere in Murderville—a spot in the backwoods of Coloma where three girls from our high school had been raped and killed.

I awake with a start, take a piss behind the bar, and drive.

"Shit!" she yells, stubbing out her cigarette on the doorframe and flicking it into the dirt. "I should have fucking known you'd find me. Goddamn freak. C'mere."

We hug hard. Raina's body odor is powerful, like she hasn't bathed in at least a couple of weeks, but the smell is perfumed by the balmy summer night smudged with ganja. Inside her hazy, poverty-stricken trailer, the walls are layered with protection symbols. A large flowering Hamsa hand with an eye painted in the palm. Pentagrams. Ankhs. Eyes of Horus. Occult shit I'd forgotten even existed. I gesture to the walls, a hundred eyes staring at us. "I'm afraid to ask how you are."

Dropping into a threadbare loveseat, she pours herself a few fingers of cheap tequila in a grungy glass. Offers me one, too. I decline, sitting on a cracked vinyl kitchen chair across from her.

Hey, Little Sister

"Shit's gotten real, Bear," she says, drinking. "While you've been out fucking Muggles, I've been here wrestling with the haints." Her eyes gleam in the candlelight at that last word, one of her favorites. We dated briefly in school but after a Ouija board session that went totally crazy, I decided two spooky people together felt too much like the big battle scene in *Ghostbusters* on loop. I needed a "normal" person in my life. Someone to remind me to eat, sleep and hydrate. And clean. I later suspected Raina was schizophrenic. These protection symbols could easily be a symptom of paranoid schizophrenia, but I know better. She was raised by Wiccans who'd fallen off the "Law of Threes" bandwagon and indulged in various dark arts. I can see things, but Raina can *do* things. It's probably how she keeps herself in smokes and food. Selling love spells. Banishments. Finding deadbeat dads. Getting revenge on unfaithful lovers.

Not that she can do anything about this.

She doesn't offer specifics, and I'm afraid to ask. So, I tell her about Dad's death and this morning's revelation that wasn't. She leans back in her chair, eyes narrowed.

"What the hell do you want, Bear?" she asks. "I'm not being a bitch. I'm serious. You didn't come here to cry into my tea cups. Or maybe you did, but that's not what you really want. You and I both know that."

My head hangs, eyes squeezed shut against tears. "I want to dig him up and murder him a thousand times," I say quietly.

Raina grins, leaning forward. Dirty yellow teeth, one incisor chipped. A wraith of smoke sways from her cigarette, clouding her face. "What if you could?"

The trailer temperature drops. Every hair stands up on my arms.

Several moments of silence slip by. She rises with a groan—"Goddamn it"—and marches through the tiny kitchen back into the bedroom that swims in candle flame shadows. After a few moments of digging and drawer slamming, she returns with an indigo vial. She hands it to me as she takes a deep drag on her cigarette. "This is the last of it." She drops back down on the loveseat and leans forward again, her expression sharp and dark. "Just pour it on the grave and wait. You'll get your wish." A smile smears across her face that chills me.

Why am I so scared? It isn't like you can raise the dead, especially with a bottle of crazy lady juice."

"Oh, for fuck's sake. Give it back," she grumbles, hand outstretched. "Don't say shit like that unless you mean it."

The eyes in the room seem to judge me for my skepticism. "I mean it," I mutter, closing the bottle in my palm.

Raina smirks. "I know."

"Thanks, Raina. I owe you."

"No, you fucking don't. Just forget it, okay? And forget me now. Seriously. You didn't even ask why I'm living out in this shit hole."

"I figured you wanted to escape the living."

She shakes her head. "It ain't the living," she says. "It's the dead. Now get the fuck out of here."

When I arrive at the massive cemetery, it's almost two in the morning. The gates are locked, but with my cell phone light I find a way in where kids have cut the chain-link fence and peeled it back like a candy wrapper. My eyes are adjusting to the night slowly. I train the light on the ground to keep from stumbling on headstones. Crickets chirp. Leaves rustle like the dead rolling over in their beds.

I recognize the gravesite by its proximity to a tall stone angel that guards a nearby family who passed away in the 19th century. My knees fall on the damp grass at the foot of the grave, cell light beaming on the headstone.

Shit.

I forgot that Mom and Dad are buried together. Not next to each other, but on *top* of each other, coffins stacked. I guess Dad's coffin's on top? What if this works and I'm wrong? A Celtic cross crowns the double headstone. Mom's side reads, "Beloved wife and mother. Forever and after." Dad's merely says, "At last he has found peace." I chose that with Sophia. What I'd *wanted* it to say was "Dick in the Dirt," but even I couldn't do that. Dad still has living relatives. I have to respect their feelings and memories, which are apparently more pleasant than mine.

Mom. Seeing the headstone rips open my heart, releasing a cataract of grief. I've missed her far more than I realized. Her kindness, her simple thoughts. The gentle way she'd kiss my cheek, even when I was being a teenage jerk. Her laugh, which I heard too rarely. She and Sophia were my world, the only ones I loved growing up. But I also grieve her inability in life to leave my father. Her love for a monster. And how my sister's accident shackled her to him for decades as they cared for her. In a way, I'm just as angry at her as I am at him, but he's the one I want to murder.

A thousand times.

Wait. What the hell am I doing? If by some small chance this is real, there could be a terrible price. I stew in my rage for a few minutes. He got away with countless crimes, against his family and others. I don't believe in Hell. I do believe there might be something like reincarnation. But if he's been reincarnated as a cockroach, that's not much of a punishment. He won't be aware of it. If there isn't any kind of eternal retribution, that means I'm the only one who can set this right.

I love Allie and our life together, but my first love and duty is to Sophia. The sister who was always there for me until her accident. The one who bandaged my wounds when Mom wasn't home. Who stuck up for me when Dad lied to Mom and said I'd assaulted him. Sophia never, ever let me down. Yet I let her down when I didn't do everything possible to end the molestation. Price or no, I would never be able to live with myself knowing I could have made up for it but didn't.

Still kneeling on the grave, I open the bottle and pour its contents on the grass, wondering what will happen, if anything.

As the last drop hits the ground, a ropey arm closes around my throat from behind, crushing my windpipe. I struggle, lungs screaming for air, vision fading. Before the other arm can grapple me, both of my fists shoot back, connecting with a face.

"Christ!" an older man yells. I strike him again. He wilts. But as my head slips out of his grip, he shoves me to the ground and lands on top of me, crushing me against the grave. "I should have killed you when you were a kid," he snarls into my ear. "You goddamn little *freak.*"

My Dad. Younger. Maybe when he was ten years older than me. Shorter than I am, but at least now it's a fair fight.

"Fuck you," I gasp, seething with childhood hatred.

He gets up and slams his foot into my side. Pain floods my body. I cry out.

Focus. Breathe.

I roll over out of range. Scramble to my feet. I see him for the first time: a silhouette with clenched fists rushing me. I dodge, slugging him in his kidneys, and wrench one arm up behind him. A mass of darkness in my grasp. I catch his unmistakable profile as he tries to turn his face toward me. Seeing him again releases a torrent of childhood anguish.

Those bad memories, resurrected.

With a sharp pull, I snap his arm out of its socket. His screams echo through the cemetery, air wavering like hundreds of black ribbons swimming through the air. One of my heavy Fluevogs connects with the back of his ankle. Another dimension-shattering shriek.

Even after he falls, I keep kicking—just the way I'd always wanted to as a kid. Mercilessly. Viciously. Delivering bully vengeance with every strike. My foot stomps his face until he stops moving.

A sick shiver racks my body, teeth chattering. The self-loathing is worse than my wounds. He might have been dead already, but I feel like a murderer. I dig my phone out of my pants pocket. Screen cracked. Training the light on the scene, I watch the revenant dissolve into a storm of dust that rises into the star-littered sky. A breeze gusts over the cemetery. The air is still again.

It's done.

Suddenly, a fist connects with my jaw from the side, blood souring my mouth. Stars shooting in my eyes.

Another fight.

His "haint" is more detailed this time. Rheumy eyes. Flabby jowls. That crazed fury tensing his body. My righteous anger curdles to blind violence so that I can survive to kill him again.

But a thousand times? *The last of it*, she said. Unholy shit. Will I eventually have to run like Raina, hiding in a forest hovel crowded with occult symbols to keep out my father's homicidal ghost? Or will I die first? If not from injury, certainly from the venom of revenge . . .

The price.

The fourth time he appears, he plows his fist in my nose. It feels like I've been clocked by a block of ice. White fiery pain explodes across my face, behind my eyes. I stumble backward, crumple to the ground. A lifetime of wreckage.

I have to stop this. But how? I see now in my misery that idiot me didn't really want revenge as much as I wanted to make him realize what he did was wrong. I should have known it wouldn't work. The day he died, I had the crushing realization that there was now no chance he'd ever change. No last-minute requests for forgiveness. No deathbed redemption. He'd never be the father I wanted or needed. Why did I think after death it would be different?

And now he's going to kill me.

Hey, Little Sister

I roll up, hands shielding my head, blood pouring out of my nose, dribbling over my lips and chin. One big ball of pain, coughing into the cool grass.

His old scuffed dress shoes are level with my eyes. A foot draws back to kick me in the face—

—just as a luminous hand erupts from the grave. It grabs his ankle, yanking him back.

My heart races as my mother's shining revenant rises, halting when the dirt meets her narrow waist. Her face is veiled in mists. But those stooped shoulders. Long arms and slender hands. How could I ever forget?

Dad goes down hard. He kicks and screams, clawing the grass to get free. Those eyes blaze with a familiar fury.

Calmly, she pulls him toward her until he lies outstretched before her half-submerged form. She seems to consider him wistfully before her hands curl around his neck and she chokes him, his newly defined features blurring and smoldering as she forces him down, down into the ground. After a moment, he stops struggling and crumbles, devoured by the soil.

She then regards me, head tilted. Questioning? Pleading.

My tears come thick and hot as I grasp the full consequence of my actions. "I can't do it, Mom. I didn't mean to raise you. I . . . forgive me . . . *please*."

A moment passes. She then raises her hand, thumb and fingers splayed, and the two middle fingers bend to touch the palm.

I love you.

I tell Allie I got in a drunken bar fight with a biker

bitching about gay marriage. It's a good thing she doesn't have my dreams.

Whenever we're in Placerville, I go to the cemetery. Sometimes I leave photos of our new baby, flowers or letters on the grave. Sometimes I even bring Sophia. Although I've robbed her of eternal peace, I suspect Mom is at least happy knowing that Sophia is so well cared for. So very loved.

Me? I'll never fucking sleep again.

The One You Live With

JOSH MALERMAN

Mom held her face and said,

"There's two yous, Dana. And there always will be. There's the you that you show to other people. The you who goes to school and goes to parties and meets people and talks a lot or a little, dances or doesn't. Then there's the you that you are inside. Now, since you're just a kid, the two yous are much closer together than mine are. You might not even notice the split. But it's there. You're just not smart enough yet to see it. And the older you get, the more that split is gonna grow, breaking up the two yous, until you hardly recognize the you you are when you're out of the house and the you you are when you're not. Now, I'm not talking about split personalities here, though believe you me, they *do* live separately. The public and the private." To Dana, it looked like a cloud passed across Mommy's eyes, inside her head. "I think it's the best thing a person can do is to try and keep those two yous as close together as they can. It's hard. It's *damn* hard. But you gotta try, right? Cause if you don't try, one of your yous might get up and do her own thing entirely, without permission from the other. I've seen it before. It ain't pretty, Dana. I may even be guilty of having lost sight of one of my mes a time or two, but I've always got it back. Back together. Under control. You know what control is, Dana?"

Dana, five, shook her head no.

"*Control* is being the one who says where the two yous go and who they see and what they do with their day. That's control. None of this money power shit you're gonna hear all about for the rest of your life. Real control is controlling the two yous: the one you show and the one you are, giving them permission. Do you understand what I mean?"

Dana shook her head no.

Mom sighed.

"Well, it's like I said. You're a kid. Your yous are so close together you think it's all one cuddly person. But mark my words, girl." She tapped Dana's forehead with her fingernail. "You are ... *not* ... *alone* ... *in* ... *there*. And the sooner you realize *that*, the sooner you can go about taking control. Now, go fetch Mommy something to drink."

Dana crawled off the couch and crossed the living room. Mom had scared her good. All that talk about two people inside of her and that word, "control." Momentarily, she wondered if it was Mom still sitting on the couch behind her so she paused at the entrance to the kitchen and spun, to get a good look at her. To be sure.

"Orange juice, Hon," Mom said. "With just a wee splash of that vodka. Or the other way around. You're the one fixin' the drink, Dana. Up to you."

The One You Live With

On stage in the school theater, singing soprano with six other sopranos, Dana wondered if this was really her. It didn't *feel* like her. Singing this stupid song with all these other girls, it's not what she'd expected of middle school. Dana, twelve, wondered if the only reason she was in the choir was because Michelle said she should do it and so here she was doing it. It was very Michelle to join the choir and the debate team and the track team and all that other stuff but maybe it wasn't really Dana to do it. And yet . . . here she was.

"Dana!" Mister Terrence called, waving his hands, the signal for practice to pause.

Dana stared back at him, silent.

"You're not *singing.*"

Dana thought she'd been singing. Wasn't she singing? And if she wasn't singing, who was up here on the stage instead?

Whatever this was; Mister Terrence, Michelle, seventh grade . . . it wasn't her.

"I quit," she said.

And the theater was very quiet as she left, as her stupid choir shoes clacked on the wooden stage and echoed all over the place like an exit that was much more dramatic than she was.

She was drinking a beer on the front porch with a depressed maniac, wondering what she was doing here. She didn't necessarily enjoy this guy, yet she'd been coming over every other day for a month. Or two. Might have been two. The numbers and time could get confusing when you were on your back, eyes closed, floating down the Universal River, letting life take you where it would. When you didn't really make any decisions on your own. When you kinda went along with things and acted a certain way in front of other people, a different way than how you acted at home.

"What you thinking about?" the depressed maniac asked. He had a twinkle in his eye. She shook her head, or maybe it was more of an inside head, like she shook her head without him seeing her do it.

"Nothing."

"Nothing?" he repeated. Then he laughed real loud, too loud, and part of Dana thought he was making fun of her. But another side of her guessed it was a funny thing to say. Nothing.

"I was wondering what I'm doing here," she said.

She sipped her beer.

The depressed maniac sighed deep.

"Oh shit," he said. "Are we about to have the talk?"

Dana didn't know what the talk was.

"We could have a talk," she said, but she didn't really want to.

"No," he said. He even held up an open palm. Like straight out of a book on how to say no with your hands. "We're *way* too early into this to start defining things."

Dana smiled. Define things? She didn't think she could define things if she had the rest of her life to do it.

"Look," he said. "If you're thinking we need to start calling each other girlfriend and boyfriend and all that jazz, I don't—"

Dana smiled again and hopped off the porch

banister. Then she crossed in front of where he sat in the outdoor recliner and took the steps down to the grass. There was still some snow lining the streets.

"I'll see ya," she said. Kindly. Relieved, too.

"Hey," the depressed maniac called after her. "Hey! Where you going?"

Dana turned and waved goodbye. Part of her felt good about it. Like she'd seen the ending of the movie and so she didn't need to sit through the middle. But another part of her, like half, wondered at her own behavior. Surely sitting on the porch with that guy, spending time with him, her college years, wasn't her. But what about where she was going, and what she'd do when she got there?

Was that not her either?

Dana was getting real pretty. It seemed to be happening fast. Every time she looked in the mirror she saw someone who was prettier and prettier than the last time she checked and more often than not it was real hard to make sense of the person looking back. So this was her. Alright. A pretty woman. Twenty-four years old. She was aging well. As they say. As Mom said. And Mom had aged well, too. So, all right, this was her and this was who her body was growing into but it was hard not to suppress a nervous smile every time she looked in the mirror, like maybe she was letting the person in the glass know that this wasn't *really* her. And it was nobody's fault really. This was just the public her, the *visible* her, the one she presented to people, the her she showed around the room. But really she may as well have walked a dog and pretended the dog was her for how close this blonde woman in the mirror was to being her.

She liked this idea.

Liked the idea of the dog.

So she went out and got one.

The dog, a golden retriever, was a good one. But he wasn't as simple as everybody said dogs were. It felt like, to Dana, that over the course of the four years she'd had him, he was the only living thing that'd ever noticed another person wedged inside her. He looked at her funny, with a different shine in his eyes, on the days and in the moments she felt like someone else. Sometimes he even sniffed. Like he could smell this other person in the room. Sometimes this scared her. Part of her. Like half. And she'd smile and shake her head and tell him to get lost, that he was freaking her out, that he should go play with a toy or something and stop staring at her like he saw someone else in the room and that this someone else was sitting on top of her.

Sometimes she'd call her Mom when this happened but Mom was always out partying with friends, with a new boyfriend, someone, and she'd sound only mostly like herself on the phone and she'd always ended up whispering the things she didn't want the other people around her to hear. Drunkish whispers. Things like,

I'm foolin' everybody in this place.

And

They have no idea.

Dana would listen to Mom, hear her out, then hang

up without ever really saying what was on her mind, what she was thinking about, that the dog she'd had for four years was getting more and more skittish, barking at nothing, sniffing the air, and staring at her with this stupid tilted head thing he did, as if asking her a question, as if asking who are you that I live with, and who are you that's sitting on top of her?

Aging well. Yes. Prettier at thirty-one than she was at twenty-one. Dana imagined it made some people mad but she just rolled her eyes, inward, thinking how nobody has any say in how big their nose is, how wide their eyes, how high their cheekbones. Some days she made herself ugly on purpose. She'd get some grease from the garage and run it up the sides of her hair, pour ketchup under her nose and over her lips, spin around real fast, then look in the mirror again. These were exciting times when she did this. Because in those moments the person in the mirror truly looked like someone else, or at least someone other than the person she'd been watching growing outside her for thirty-one years. Then the phone would ring or the dog would bark and she would wash her face and get in the shower and clean herself up before returning the phone call or seeing what it was the dog wanted so badly.

She met a man in these days.

The man liked the dog and so he asked if he could pet the dog and Dana said yes, believing she was the kind of person who said yes to questions like these. Then the man stood up and asked what the dog's name was.

"He doesn't have one yet," Dana said, smiling. She could tell the man thought she was pretty.

"No? Did you just get him?"

"Oh no. I've had him for seven years."

How could she know him to name him?

The man laughed so hard that Dana wondered if he was going to be okay and then his eyes settled on hers and she knew he was going to ask her on a date before he did and she decided she would say yes before she did.

"I don't mean to sound like a crazy person," the man said. "But you are the most beautiful woman I've ever seen. I'm Jason."

"Thank you, Jason."

Not *I'm Dana* because . . . who knew?

"What's your name? Do you have one?"

More laughter, mostly on his end, but Dana laughed, too, as it always felt like the right thing to do.

She wondered if the man, Jason, felt like he was talking to two people.

"My mom named me Dana."

"Well," Jason said. "Your mom picked out a lovely name."

Silence then. The dog sniffed close to Dana and she shoved his head gently aside.

"Would you like to get a coffee?" Jason asked.

Dana smiled. She could feel her high cheekbones lift the corners of her lips, as if her mouth were a marionette.

A well-built one.

"Yes," she said. Then she pointed to the coffee shop they were standing in front of. "Here, right?"

Jason laughed again. He looked surprised.

"Well, I didn't mean right now!" he said. "But, yeah. Absolutely. Wanna get coffee right now?"

Dana didn't know if she wanted to. Maybe a part of her did.

The dog sniffed.

"Yes," she said.

Jason held the door open for her to enter.

Married nine years and Jason always seemed like the same person. Sure, sometimes he got angry, sometimes he said things that were out of character, but eventually these things became part of his character and Dana had a hard time believing his continuity. It must take a great effort, she imagined, to keep himself together like that.

Sometimes she spied on him.

When he was watching a movie or fixing himself a sandwich, sometimes Dana would crouch behind the kitchen island and peek up over the marble top and watch him do things. Even in these moments he rarely looked like anybody other than Jason. Sure, sometimes he appeared tired but it was tired *Jason*. The same floppy brown hair and loose lower lip; the kind look in his eyes. Sometimes Dana scared herself when she did this, when she spied. As if not only was she spying on Jason in the kitchen but someone else was in the room spying on her, too. Like someone else was watching her watch her husband and one time the feeling was so great that she actually popped up from behind the couch and said, "Hey there!" Just to not feel alone with whoever was watching her.

Jason was scared good and laughed about it and

asked if she wanted to join him for a movie and she said yes. They hadn't named the dog, a thing Jason cutely ascribed to half the reason they got married, *the Nameless Dog*, but the dog would always join them for movies. And sometimes Dana wondered if Jason called the dog in to protect himself. Protect himself from this other person who was watching Dana watch Jason.

At seventeen years old, the dog died. Dana was forty-one. No more sniffing. No more staring. No one around to make whichever Dana was present feel like the other Dana was the truth.

At fifty Dana looked fifteen years younger than she should have and Jason would point out the younger men who looked at her. He said he liked it and Dana had no reason to think he didn't. Jason was very good at being Jason.

But the cracks were showing and had been for some time.

Maybe it was a lift of one eyebrow. An unnecessary shrug. An exaggerated thing to say.

Like:

Are you sure, Dana?

Always are you sure. Like Jason was just now seeing the open space, the gap in Dana. Like he knew someone else was inside her and he'd decided to love her, too. A good man. Good enough never to bring it up. Good enough never to tell her she wasn't acting like herself. The closest Jason ever said to anything like that was on New Year's Eve.

They were dancing, the very middle of the dance

floor, and all of their friends and family were laughing and chattering and dancing, too, around them, and Jason had her close by the waist and brought his lips to her ear and said, "What did your Mom mean by . . . 'did you meet her yet'?"

Dana could feel invisible fingers, someone else's fingers, lifting up the sides of her perfect smile.

"She's old," Dana said. But she wished she hadn't. For the first time in her life she wished she'd just told Jason exactly what she knew Mom meant.

And yet, it *was* true. Mom *was* old. And drunk.

Jason smiled.

"The way she said it," he said, "I thought she was talking about an old friend."

Then people started to countdown and Dana kissed Jason before the number reached zero, not wanting to be so definite, so defined. And the kiss was a good one. And later that night, long after they'd driven Mom home and eaten fish sandwiches at the all-night diner, they made love. It was good love and Dana could tell Jason was happy. And yet, when he smelled her shoulders, smelled just behind her ear, Dana thought of the dog they once had, and wondered if Jason wasn't looking, searching his wife for that old friend Mom had drunkenly spoke of in public.

A widow at sixty-six, but Mom was still alive. Dana went to the pet store shortly after Jason's death but the cats seemed more perceptive than the dogs and the dogs were too perceptive as it was. It was something of a bad experience for her, that day in the pet store; she felt like all the animals were looking at the other people like they wanted to be taken home but looking at Dana like they were scared or confused. Like they thought it was wrong of her not to tell Jason that night, that New Year's Eve, the truth about what Mom was talking about.

Even the birds seemed to know it, seemed to say,

That was your chance to bridge the gap. Your chance to be a kid again.

A worker at the pet store, a girl about nineteen, asked if she needed any help.

Dana smiled at the question.

"Miss," the girl said before leaving her with the birds. "Can I just say that you are a *beautiful* woman."

Dana smiled again. But she didn't say anything, didn't say thank you because what did this girl know about whether or not Dana was beautiful?

In that moment, quite suddenly, Dana had to hang onto the rack of birdseed for stability, to keep herself from falling.

It was the furthest she'd ever felt the split. The biggest the gap had ever gotten. The feeling was so overwhelming that she believed, momentarily, that her neck might split open, that she might suddenly be torn in two.

"Are you all right, miss?" the girl asked.

And Dana actually waited, innocently, waited with the girl for whomever she'd asked to answer.

Dana was singing in the backyard when a neighbor's gardener heard her and couldn't stop himself from walking over to tell her she had a lovely voice. The gardener was handsome, though Dana wasn't sure she knew what beauty was anymore; wasn't sure she had a concrete opinion on anything; the way life presented all these different scenarios that asked you to be so many different people in return. But something inside herself told her the man was handsome and kind and she asked if he wanted to come talk with her. He said he did and so they sat at the deck table and talked.

"You ever think of joining a choir?" the man asked.

Dana shrugged. It felt good to shrug. Somehow the simple gesture exemplified how she saw herself.

"I did once," she said.

"I sing, too," the man said.

Then he started to sing.

Dana listened and wondered what she thought of his voice. Was it pleasing and romantic? Or was it nasally and overdone? Part of her wondered if it mattered at all what he sounded like. Another part of her, like half, imagined herself telling him to stop.

She wiped her forehead with a napkin.

"How old are you?" the gardener asked.

"I'm seventy-nine years old."

But was she? Yes, she finally agreed. Seventy-nine years old.

The gardener shook his head.

"I'm sixty-seven myself. Had we met in another lifetime, we may have been great friends."

Dana felt a concrete reaction to this statement. It was refreshing; concrete.

"But we are meeting in another lifetime," she said.

The man paused, thought about this, then laughed.

"I like that," he said. "I like 'we are meeting in another lifetime.' Like the one I've been living hasn't been the one I've thought I was living all along."

Dana smiled. Could almost feel a second mouth, behind her own, smiling for her.

She'd been staring in the mirror for too long. Grease in her hair, ketchup under her nose, spinning, then staring into her face, eighty-something years old. She'd definitely been staring for too long because the woman who looked back was frightening. Not because she was ugly; no, never. The woman was indeed pretty, had aged almost unfairly well. What scared Dana was the look in the woman's eyes, as though she was capable of doing different things than Dana was; able to move in a different direction; might blink when Dana, on this side of the glass, did not. At one point, Dana had to bring her wrinkled hands to her face to stop herself from looking. She was so sure the woman in the glass was about to say something, about to move, even the slightest bit, showing herself, completely, for the first time.

Dana crouched to her knees and ran her fingers through the grease in her hair, wiped the ketchup onto her fingers and looked at her fingernails. This was good; better than looking in the mirror. Dana was sure, as sure as she'd ever been of anything ever, that if she looked up, she'd see that other woman peering over the edge of the sink, eyes wide, wider than her own, this her, almost mockingly, as her lips moved independently and formed the words:

Have you met her yet?

She was in a hospital bed and the nurses were very nice. They fawned over her endlessly and loved the story about never naming the dog. They told her that ninety-nine years was an incredible run. To Dana it was more fitting than one hundred. She liked that. What she didn't like was that she was not alone. The unit held two patients and the other one was quiet, too quiet, behind the curtain that divided them.

"Who's there?" Dana called often and once a nurse told her it was woman. The nurses helped in this way, helped Dana forget about this other patient and how the curtain was kind of like a mirror the way it split two images of two people doing the exact same thing in dying.

Maybe because the nurse asked about her childhood, Dana often recalled her mom, long after the nurses left the room.

There's two yous, Mom once said. *And there always will be. There's the you that you show to other people. Then there's the you that you are inside. Now, since you're just a kid, the two yous are much closer together than mine are. You might not even notice the split. But it's there. You're just not smart enough yet to see it. And the older you get, the more that split is gonna grow, breaking up the two yous, until you hardly recognize the you you are when you're out of the house and the you you are when you're not. I think it's the best thing a person can do is to try and keep those two yous as close together as they can. It's hard. It's damn hard. But you gotta try, right?*

Dana thought Mom was right, thought it was the smartest damn thing Mom ever said. She thought about this talk a lot and eventually she didn't want to think about it but it kept coming back. One night, hoping for a distraction, she turned on the television that hung high up on the wall and dropped the remote control before she'd changed the station from static. It hit the floor.

Still nimble at ninety-nine, she turned onto her side to ring for the nurse, to ask them to remove the static from the screen, to put something entertaining on, perhaps a program featuring a woman who was sure of herself. Before the nurses came, in the blue light of the flickering static, Dana saw a ripple in the curtain that separated her from the other patient, the woman, and saw a hand, too, fingers, curl around that curtain's edge.

Have you met her yet?

And as the curtain was pulled aside, Dana smiled, all on her own, smiled because Mom was right when she said it was hard, keeping them together, *damn* hard, but you gotta try.

And Dana believed she knew what she was gonna say, when the parting of the curtain was complete, she was gonna say what she should've said on New Year's Eve forty-nine years ago, that it was hard, damn hard, but you gotta try.

Because there's the you you are at any given time, and the you you get and give with; the one you often are and, always, the one you live with.

And Dana would tell the woman on the other side of the curtain that she believed she'd tried.

The Place of
Revelation

RAMSEY CAMPBELL

At dinner Colin's parents do most of the talking. His mother starts by saying "Sit down," and as soon as he does his father says "Sit up." Auntie Dot lets Colin glimpse a sympathetic grin while Uncle Lucian gives him a secret one, neither of which helps him feel less nervous. They're eating off plates as expensive as the one he broke last time they visited, when his parents acted as if he'd meant to drop it even though the relatives insisted it didn't matter and at least his uncle thought so. "Delicious as always," his mother says when Auntie Dot asks yet again if Colin's food is all right, and his father offers "I expect he's just tired, Dorothy." At least that's an excuse, which Colin might welcome except it prompts his aunt to say "If you've had enough I should scamper off to bye-byes, Colin. For a treat you can leave us the washing up."

Everyone is waiting for him to go to his room. Even though his parents keep saying how well he does in English and how the art mistress said he should take up painting at secondary school, he's expected only to mumble agreement whenever he's told to speak up for himself. For the first time he tries arguing. "I'll do it. I don't mind."

"You've heard what's wanted," his father says in a voice that seems to weigh his mouth down.

"You catch up on your sleep," his mother says more gently, "then you'll be able to enjoy yourself tomorrow."

Beyond her Uncle Lucian is nodding eagerly, but nobody else sees. Everyone watches Colin trudge into the high wide hall. It offers him a light, and there's another above the stairs that smell of their new fat brown carpet, and one more in the upstairs corridor. They only put off the dark. Colin is taking time on each stair until his father lets him hear "Is he getting ready for bed yet?" For fear of having to explain his apprehensiveness he flees to the bathroom.

With its tiles white as a blizzard it's brighter than the hall, but its floral scent makes Colin feel it's only pretending to be a room. As he brushes his teeth the mirror shows him foaming at the mouth as though his nerves have given him a fit. When he heads for his room, the doorway opposite presents him with a view across his parents' bed of the hospital he can't help thinking is a front for the graveyard down the hill. It's lit up as pale as a tombstone, whereas his window that's edged with tendrils of frost is full of nothing but darkness, which he imagines rising massively from the fields to greet the black sky. Even if the curtains shut tight they wouldn't keep out his sense of it, nor does the flimsy furniture that's yellow as the wine they're drinking downstairs. He huddles under the plump quilt and leaves the light on while he listens to the kitchen clatter. All too soon it comes to an end, and he hears someone padding upstairs so softly they might almost not be there at all.

As the door inches open with a faint creak that puts him in mind of the lifting of a lid, he grabs the edge of the quilt and hauls it over his face. "You aren't asleep yet, then," his mother says. "I thought you might have drifted off."

Colin uncovers his face and bumps his shoulders against the bars behind the pillow. "I can't get to sleep, so can I come down?"

"No need for that, Colin. I expect you're trying too hard. Just think of nice times you've had and then you'll go off. You know there's nothing really to stop you."

She's making him feel so alone that he no longer cares if he gives away his secrets. "There is."

"Colin, you're not a baby any more. You didn't act like this when you were. Try not to upset people. Will you do that for us?"

"If you want."

She frowns at his reluctance. "I'm sure it's what you want as well. Just be as thoughtful as I know you are."

Everything she says reminds him how little she knows. She leans down to kiss each of his eyes shut, and as she straightens up, the cord above the bed turns the kisses into darkness with a click. Can he hold on to the feeling long enough to fall asleep? Once he hears the door close he burrows under the quilt and strives to be aware of nothing beyond the bed. He concentrates on the faint scent of the quilt that nestles on his face, he listens to the silence that the pillow and the quilt press against his ears. The weight of the quilt is beginning to feel vague and soft as sleep when the darkness whispers his name. "I'm asleep," he tries complaining, however babyish and stupid it sounds.

"Not yet, Colin," Uncle Lucian says. "Story first. You can't have forgotten."

He hasn't, of course. He remembers every bedtime story since the first, when he didn't know it would lead to the next day's walk. "I thought we'd have finished," he protests.

"Quietly, son. We don't want anyone disturbed, do we? One last story."

Colin wants to stay where he can't see and yet he wants to know. He inches the quilt down from his face. The gap between the curtains has admitted a sliver of moonlight that turns the edges of objects a glimmering white. A sketch of his uncle's face the colour of bone hovers by the bed. His smile glints, and his eyes shine like stars so distant they remind Colin how limitless the dark is. That's one reason why he blurts "Can't we just go wherever it is tomorrow?"

"You need to get ready while you're asleep. You should know that's how it works." As Uncle Lucian leans closer, the light tinges his gaunt face except where it's hollowed out with shadows, and Colin is reminded of the moon looming from behind a cloud. "Wait now, here's an idea," his uncle murmurs. "That ought to help."

Colin realises he would rather not ask "What?"

"Tell the stories back to me. You'll find someone to tell one day, you know. You'll be like me."

The prospect fails to appeal to Colin, who pleads "I'm too tired."

"They'll wake you up. Your mother was saying how good you are at stories. That's thanks to me and mine. Go on before anyone comes up and hears."

A cork pops downstairs, and Colin knows there's little chance of being interrupted. "I don't know what to say."

"I can't tell you that, Colin. They're your stories now. They're part of you. You've got to find your own way to tell them."

As Uncle Lucian's eyes glitter like ice Colin hears himself say "Once . . . "

"That's the spirit. That's how it has to start."

"Once there was a boy . . . "

"Called Colin. Sorry. You won't hear another breath out of me."

"Once there was a boy who went walking in the country on a day like it was today. The grass in the fields looked like feathers where all the birds in the world had been fighting, and all the fallen leaves were showing their bones. The sun was so low every crumb of frost had its own shadow, and his footprints had shadows in when he looked behind him, and walking felt like breaking little bones under his feet. The day was so cold he kept thinking the clouds were bits of ice that had cracked off the sky and dropped on the edge of the earth. The wind kept scratching his face and pulling the last few leaves off the trees, only if the leaves went back he knew they were birds. It was meant to be the shortest day, but it felt as if time had died because everything was too slippery or too empty for it to get hold of. So he thought he'd done everything there was to do and seen everything there was to see when he saw a hole like a gate through a hedge."

"That's the way." Uncle Lucian's eyes have begun to shine like fragments of the moon. "Make it your story."

"He wasn't sure if there was an old gate or the hedge had grown like one. He didn't know it was one of the places where the world is twisted. All he could see was more hedge at the sides of a bendy path. So he followed it round and round, and it felt like going inside a shell. Then he got dizzy with running to find the middle, because it seemed to take hours and the bends never got any smaller. But just when he was thinking he'd stop and turn back if the spiky hedges let him, he came to where the path led all round a pond that was covered with ice. Only the pond oughtn't to have been so big, all the path he'd run round should have squeezed it little. So he was walking round the pond to see if he could find the trick when the sun showed him the flat white faces everywhere under the ice.

"There were children and parents who'd come searching for them, and old people too. They were everyone the maze had brought to the pond, and they were all calling him. Their eyes were opening as slow as holes in the ice and growing too big, and their mouths were moving like fish mouths out of water, and the wind in the hedge was their cold rattly voice telling him he had to stay forever, because he couldn't see the path away from the pond—there was just hedge everywhere he looked. Only then he heard his uncle's voice somewhere in it, telling him he had to walk back in all his footprints like a witch dancing backwards and then he'd be able to escape."

This is the part Colin likes least, but his uncle murmurs eagerly "And was he?"

"He thought he never could till he remembered what his footprints looked like. When he turned round he could just see them with the frost creeping to swallow them up. So he started walking back in them, and he heard the ice on the pond start to crack to let all the bodies with the turned-up faces climb out. He saw thin white fingers pushing the edge of the ice up and digging their nails into the frosty path. His footprints led him back through the gap the place had tried to stop him finding in the hedge, but he could see hands flopping out of the pond like frogs. He still had to walk all the way back to the gate like that, and every step he took the hedges tried to catch him, and he heard more ice being pushed up and people crawling after him. It felt like the place had got hold of his middle and his neck and screwed them round so far he'd never be able to walk forward again. He came out of the gate at last, and then he had to walk round the fields till it was nearly dark to get back into walking in an ordinary way so his mother and father wouldn't notice there was something new about him and want to know what he'd been doing."

Colin doesn't mind if that makes his uncle feel at least a little guilty, but Uncle Lucian says "What happens next?"

Colin hears his parents and his aunt forgetting to keep their voices low downstairs. He still can't make out what they're saying, though they must think he's asleep. "The next year he went walking in the woods," he can't avoid admitting.

"What kind of a day would that have been, I wonder?"

"Sunny. Full of birds and squirrels and butterflies. So hot he felt like he was wearing the sun on his head, and the only place he could take it off was the woods, because if he went back to the house his mother and father would say he ought to be out walking. So he'd gone a long way under the trees when he felt them change."

"He could now. Most people wouldn't until it was too late, but he felt . . . "

"Something had crept up behind him. He was under some trees that put their branches together like hands with hundreds of fingers praying. And when he looked he saw the trees he'd already gone under were exactly the same as the ones he still had to, like he was looking in a mirror except he couldn't see himself in it. So he started to run but as soon as he moved, the half of the tunnel of trees he had to go through began to stretch itself till he couldn't see the far end, and when he looked behind him it had happened there as well."

"He knew what to do this time, didn't he? He hardly even needed to be told."

"He had to go forwards walking backwards and never look to see what was behind him. And as soon as he did he saw the way he'd come start to shrink. Only that wasn't all he saw, because leaves started running up and down the trees, except they weren't leaves. They were insects pretending to be them, or maybe they weren't insects. He could hear them scuttling about behind him, and he was afraid the way he had to go wasn't shrinking, it was growing as much longer as the way he'd come was getting shorter. Then all the scuttling things ran onto the branches over his head, and he thought they'd fall on him if he didn't stop trying to escape. But his body kept moving even though he wished it wouldn't, and he heard a great flapping as if he was in a cave and bats were flying off the roof, and then something landed on his head. It was just the sunlight, and he'd come out of the woods the same place he'd gone in. All the way back he felt he was walking away from the house, and his mother said he'd got a bit of sunstroke."

"He never told her otherwise, did he? He knew most people aren't ready to know what's behind the world."

"That's what his uncle kept telling him."

"He was proud to be chosen, wasn't he? He must have known it's the greatest privilege to be shown the old secrets."

Colin has begun to wish he could stop talking about himself as though he's someone else, but the tales won't let go of him—they've closed around him like the dark. "What was his next adventure?" it whispers with his uncle's moonlit smiling mouth.

"The next year his uncle took him walking in an older wood. Even his mother and father might have noticed there was something wrong with it and told him not to go in far." When his uncle doesn't acknowledge any criticism but only smiles wider and more whitely Colin has to add "There was nothing except sun in the sky, but as soon as you went in the woods you had to step on shadows everywhere, and that was the only way you knew there was still a sun. And the day was so still it felt like the woods were pretending they never breathed, but the shadows kept moving whenever he wasn't looking—he kept nearly seeing very tall ones hide behind the trees. So he wanted to get through the woods as fast as he could, and that's why he ran straight onto the stepping stones when he came to a stream."

Colin would like to run fast through the story too, but his uncle wants to know "How many stones were there again?"

"Ten, and they looked so close together he didn't have to stretch to walk. Only he was on the middle two when he felt them start to move. And when he looked down he saw the stream was really as deep as the sky, and lying on the bottom was a giant made out of rocks and moss that was holding up its arms to him. They were longer than he didn't know how many trees stuck together, and their hands were as big as the roots of an old tree, and he was standing on top of two of the fingers. Then the giant's eyes began to open like boulders rolling about in the mud, and its mouth opened like a cave and sent up a laugh in a bubble that spattered the boy with mud, and the stones he was on started to move apart."

"His uncle was always with him though, wasn't he?"

"The boy couldn't see him," Colin says in case this lets his uncle realise how it felt, and then he knows his uncle already did. "He heard him saying you mustn't look down, because being seen was what woke up the god of the wood. So the boy kept looking straight ahead, though he could see the shadows that weren't shadows crowding behind the trees to wait for him. He could feel how even the water underneath him wanted him to slip on the slimy stones, and how the stones were ready to swim apart so he'd fall between them if he caught the smallest glimpse of them. Then he did, and the one he was standing on sank deep into the water, but he'd jumped on the bank of the stream. The shadows that must have been the bits that were left of people who'd looked down too long let him see his uncle, and they walked to the other side of the woods. Maybe he wouldn't have got there without his uncle, because the shadows kept dancing around them to make them think there was no way between the trees."

"Brave boy, to see all that." Darkness has reclaimed the left side of Uncle Lucian's face; Colin is reminded of a moon that the night is squeezing out of shape. "Don't stop now, Colin," his uncle says. "Remember last year."

This is taking longer than his bedtime stories ever have. Colin feels as if the versions he's reciting may rob him of his whole night's sleep. Downstairs his parents and his aunt sound as if they need to talk for hours yet. "It was here in town," he says accusingly. "It was down in Lower Brichester."

He wants to communicate how betrayed he felt, by the city or his uncle or by both. He'd thought houses and people would keep away the old things, but now he knows that nobody who can't see can help. "It was where the boy's mother and father wouldn't have liked him to go," he says, but that simply makes him feel the way his uncle's stories do, frightened and excited and unable to separate the feelings. "Half the houses were shut up with boards but people were still using them, and there were men and ladies on the corners of the streets waiting for whoever wanted them or stuff they were selling. And in the middle of it all there were railway lines and passages to walk under them. Only the people who lived round there must have felt something, because there was one passage nobody walked through."

"But the boy did."

"A man sitting drinking with his legs in the road told him not to, but he did. His uncle went through another passage and said he'd meet him on the other side. Anyone could have seen something was wrong with the tunnel, because people had dropped needles all over the place except in there. But it looked like it'd just be a minute to walk through, less if you ran. So the boy started to hurry through, only he tried to be quiet because he didn't like how his feet made so much noise he kept thinking someone was following him, except it sounded more like lots of fingers tapping on the bricks behind him. When he managed to be quiet the noise didn't all go away, but he tried to think it was water dripping, because he felt it cold and wet on the top of his head. Then more of it touched the back of his neck, but he didn't want to look round, because the passage was getting darker behind him. He was in the middle of the tunnel when the cold touch landed on his face and made him look."

His uncle's face is barely outlined, but his eyes take on an extra gleam. "And when he looked . . . "

"He saw why the passage was so dark, with all the arms as thin as his poking out of the bricks. They could grow long enough to reach halfway down the passage and grope around till they found him with their fingers that were as wet as worms. Then he couldn't even see them, because the half of the passage he had to walk through was filling up with arms as well, so many he couldn't see out. And all he could do was what his uncle's story had said, stay absolutely still, because if he tried to run the hands would grab him and drag him through the walls into the earth, and he wouldn't even be able to die of how they did it. So he shut his eyes to be as blind as the things with the arms were, that's if there wasn't just one thing behind the walls. And after he nearly forgot how to breathe the hands stopped pawing at his head as if they were feeling how his brain showed him everything about them, maybe even brought them because he'd learned to see the old things. When he opened his eyes the arms were worming back into the walls, but he felt them all around him right to the end of the passage. And when he went outside he couldn't believe in the daylight any more. It was like a picture someone had put up to hide the dark."

"He could believe in his uncle though, couldn't he? He saw his uncle waiting for him and telling him well done. I hope he knew how much his uncle thought of him."

"Maybe."

"Well, now it's another year."

Uncle Lucian's voice is so low, and his face is so nearly invisible, that Colin isn't sure whether his words are meant to be comforting or to warn the boy that there's more. "Another story," Colin mumbles, inviting it or simply giving in.

"I don't think so any more. I think you're too old for that."

Colin doesn't know in what way he feels abandoned as he whispers "Have we finished?"

"Nothing like. Tomorrow, just go and lie down and look up."

"Where?"

"Anywhere you're by yourself."

Colin feels he is now. "Then what?" he pleads.

"You'll see. I can't begin to tell you. See for yourself."

That makes Colin more nervous than his uncle's

stories ever did. He's struggling to think how to persuade his uncle to give him at least a hint when he realises he's alone in the darkness. He lies on his back and stares upwards in case that gets whatever has to happen over with, but all he sees are memories of the places his uncle has made him recall. Downstairs his parents and his aunt are still talking, and he attempts to use their voices to keep him with them, but feels as if they're dragging him down into the moonless dark. Then he's been asleep, because they're shutting their doors close to his. After that, whenever he twitches awake it's a little less dark. As soon as he's able to see he sneaks out of bed to avoid his parents and his aunt. Whatever is imminent, having to lie about where he's going would make his nerves feel even more like rusty wire about to snap.

He's as quick and as quiet in the bathroom as he can be. Once he's dressed he rolls up the quilt to lie on and slips out of the house. In the front garden he thinks moonlight has left a crust on the fallen leaves and the grass. Down the hill a train shakes itself awake while the city mutters in its sleep. He turns away and heads for the open country behind the house.

A few crows jab at the earth with their beaks and sail up as if they mean to peck the icy sky. The ground has turned into a single flattened greenish bone exactly as bright as the low vault of dull cloud. Colin walks until the fields bear the houses out of sight. That's as alone as he's likely to be. Flapping the quilt, he spreads it on the frozen ground. He throws himself on top of it and slaps his hands on it in case that starts whatever's meant to happen. He's already so cold he can't keep still.

At first he thinks that's the only reason he's shivering, and then he notices the sky isn't right. He feels as if all the stories he's had to act out have gathered in his head, or the way they've made him see has. That ability is letting him observe how thin the sky is growing, or perhaps it's leaving him unable not to. Is it also attracting whatever's looming down to peer at him from behind the sky? A shiver is drumming his heels on the ground through the quilt when the sky seems to vanish as though it has been clawed apart above him, and he glimpses as much of a face as there's room for—an eye like a sea black as space with a moon for its pupil. It seems indifferent as death and yet it's watching him. An instant of seeing is all he can take before he twists onto his front and presses his face into the quilt as though it's a magic carpet that will transport him home to bed and, better still, unconsciousness.

He digs his fingers into the quilt until he recognises he can't burrow into the earth. He stops for fear of tearing his aunt's quilt and having to explain. He straightens up in a crouch to retrieve the quilt, which he hugs as he stumbles back across the field with his head down. The sky is pretending that it never faltered, but all the way to the house he's afraid it will part to expose more of a face.

While nobody is up yet, Colin senses that his uncle isn't in the house. He tiptoes upstairs to leave the quilt on his bed, and then he sends himself out again. There's no sign of his uncle on the way downhill. Colin dodges onto the path under the trees in case his uncle prefers not to be seen. "Uncle Lucian," he pleads.

"You found me."

He doesn't seem especially pleased, but Colin demands "What did I see?"

"Not much yet. Just as much as your mind could take. It's like our stories, do you understand? Your mind had to tell you a story about what you saw, but in time you won't need it. You'll see what's really there."

"Suppose I don't want to?" Colin blurts. "What's it all for?"

"Would you rather be like my sister and only see what everyone else sees? She was no fun when she was your age, your mother."

"I never had the choice."

"Well, I wouldn't ever have said that to my grandfather. I was nothing but grateful to him."

Though his uncle sounds not merely disappointed but offended, Colin says "Can't I stop now?"

"Everything will know you can see, son. If you don't greet the old things where you find them they'll come to find you."

Colin voices a last hope. "Has it stopped for you?"

"It never will. I'm part of it now. Do you want to see?"

"No."

Presumably Colin's cry offends his uncle, because there's a spidery rustle beyond the trees that conceal the end of the path and then silence. Time passes before Colin dares to venture forward. As he steps from beneath the trees he feels as if the sky has lowered itself towards him like a mask. He's almost blind with resentment of his uncle for making him aware of so much and for leaving him alone, afraid to see even Uncle Lucian. Though it doesn't help, Colin

The Place of Revelation

starts kicking the stone with his uncle's name on it and the pair of years ending with this one. When he's exhausted he turns away towards the rest of his life.

Acknowledgements

Doug Murano:

To my wife, Jessica: But for your love and support, this book would not exist. Thank you for carrying me through nights, weeks, months of doubt. Thank you for celebrating each quiet victory along the way. Thank you for giving me the time I need. I love you.

To our authors: Thank you for taking a chance on us—and on our rather difficult idea for a book. You've been wonderful, all of you, and I hope we get a chance to work together again soon.

To Joe Mynhardt: You turned us loose to make this book what we wanted it to be, which is a rare and priceless thing. Thank you for your faith in us, and for taking this project under the Crystal Lake Publishing banner.

To David: Thank you for indulging me, and joining me, in the pursuit of this tricky, amorphous concept. Thank you for banging your head against the wall with me when things went wrong, and for standing in awe with me as things went more right than we ever dreamed they could.

To our readers: Your readership is, well, everything. Thank you for dropping by our dark and disturbing corner of the universe. We hope to see you around these parts again.

To GJW: Thank you for leaving me all that store credit. You know why.

D. Alexander Ward:

To all of the authors who contributed stories to this book, I offer my heartfelt thanks. Through your stories, you have shaped something beautiful and terrible.

To Joe Mynhardt and Crystal Lake Publishing, it truly has been a pleasure.

To Doug, who, with an idea, plucked this strange bit of fruit from the ether.

And to the readers. Keep those tissues handy.

About the Editors

Doug Murano is an author and editor who lives somewhere between Mount Rushmore and the mighty Missouri River. A proud South Dakota native, he earned his Master of Arts in English Literature (creative writing track) at The University of South Dakota. In addition to co-editing the collection you're holding right now, he is the co-editor of the best-selling and critically acclaimed small-town Lovecraftian horror anthology, *Shadows Over Main Street* and the forthcoming *Shadows Over Main Street, Volume 2* (Cutting Block Books).

An Affiliate Member of the Horror Writers Association, he was the organization's promotions and social media coordinator from 2013-15, served as the communications chair for the 2014 World Horror Convention in Portland, Oregon, and has served as a jurist for the Bram Stoker Awards. He is a recipient of the Horror Writers Association's Richard Laymon President's Award for Service.

Follow him on Twitter: @muranofiction.

D. Alexander Ward is an author and editor of horror and dark fiction and an involved participant in the independent horror community.

In addition to *Gutted: Beautiful Horror Stories*, he co-edited the Lovecraftian horror anthologies, *Shadows Over Main Street*, Volumes 1 and 2 from Cutting Block Books.

His novels include *Beneath Ash & Bone* and *Blood Savages* from Necro Publications and Bedlam Press.

Along with his family and the haints in the woods, he lives near the farm where he grew up in what used to be rural Virginia, where his love for the people, passions and folklore of the South was nurtured.

He is active on social media and you can find out more on his website: www.dalexward.com.

About the Authors

Richard Chizmar is the founder/publisher of *Cemetery Dance* magazine and the Cemetery Dance Publications book imprint. He has edited more than 20 anthologies and his fiction has appeared in dozens of publications, including *Ellery Queen's Mystery Magazine* and *The Year's 25 Finest Crime and Mystery Stories*. He has won two World Fantasy awards, four International Horror Guild awards, and the HWA's Board of Trustee's award.

Chizmar (in collaboration with Johnathon Schaech) has also written screenplays and teleplays for United Artists, Sony Screen Gems, Lions Gate, Showtime, NBC, and many other companies. Chizmar is the creator/writer of *Stephen King Revisited*, and his next short story collection, *A Long December*, is due in 2016 from Subterranean Press. Chizmar's work has been translated into many languages throughout the world, and he has appeared at numerous conferences as a writing instructor, guest speaker, panelist, and guest of honor.

You can follow Richard Chizmar on both Facebook and Twitter.

Stephanie M. Wytovich is an instructor of English by day and a horror writer by night. She is the poetry editor for Raw Dog Screaming Press, a book reviewer for *Nameless Magazine*, and the assistant to Carlow University's international MFA Program for Creative Writing. She is a member of the Science Fiction Poetry Association, an active member of the Horror Writers Association, and a graduate of Seton Hill University's MFA program for Writing Popular Fiction.

Her Bram Stoker Award-nominated poetry collections, *Hysteria: A Collection of Madness*, *Mourning Jewelry*, and *An Exorcism of Angels* can be found at www.rawdogscreaming.com, and her debut novel, *The Eighth*, will be out in 2016 from Dark Regions Press.

Follow Wytovich at stephaniewytovich.blogspot.com and on twitter @JustAfterSunset.

Brian Kirk is an author of dark thrillers and psychological suspense. His short fiction has been published in many popular magazines and anthologies, and his debut novel, *We Are Monsters*, was released in July 2015. In addition to being nominated for a Bram Stoker Award® for Superior Achievement in a First Novel, *We Are Monsters* was included on many of the industry's most illustrious "Best of the Year" lists, and has been optioned for film development by the Executive Producer for movies such as *The Messengers* starring Dylan McDermott and Kristen Stewart, *Role Models* starring Paul Rudd, and *Lone Survivor* starring Mark Wahlberg.

Feel free to connect with him at www.briankirkfiction.com or on Twitter @Brian_Kirk. Don't worry, he only kills his characters.

Lisa Mannetti's debut novel, *The Gentling Box*, garnered a Bram Stoker Award and she has since been nominated four times for the prestigious award in both the short and long fiction categories: Her story, "Everybody Wins," was made into a short film and her novella, "Dissolution," will soon be a feature-length film directed by Paul Leyden. Recent short stories include, "Esmeralda's Stocking" in *Never Fear:*

Christmas Terrors; "Resurgam" in *Zombies: More Recent Dead* edited by Paula Guran, and "Almost Everybody Wins," in *Insidious Assassins*. Her work, including *The Gentling Box*, and "1925: A Fall River Halloween" has been translated into Italian.

Her most recently published longer work, *The Box Jumper*, a novella about Houdini, has not only been nominated for both the Bram Stoker and Shirley Jackson Awards, it won the "Novella of the Year" award from This is Horror in the UK.

She has also authored *The New Adventures of Tom Sawyer and Huck Finn*, two companion novellas in her collection, *Deathwatch*, a macabre gag book, *51 Fiendish Ways to Leave your Lover*, as well as non-fiction books, and numerous articles and short stories in newspapers, magazines and anthologies. Forthcoming works include more stories and a dark novel about the dial-painter tragedy in the post-WWI era, *Radium Girl*.

Lisa lives in New York in the 100 year old house she originally grew up in with two wily (mostly) black twin cats named Harry and Theo Houdini.

Visit her author website: www.lisamannetti.com. Visit her virtual haunted house: www.thechanceryhouse.com.

Neil Gaiman was born in Hampshire, UK, and now lives in the United States near Minneapolis. As a child he discovered his love of books, reading, and stories, devouring the works of C.S. Lewis, J.R.R. Tolkien, James Branch Cabell, Edgar Allan Poe, Michael Moorcock, Ursula K. LeGuin, Gene Wolfe, and G.K. Chesterton. A self-described "feral child who was raised in libraries," Gaiman credits librarians with fostering a life-long love of reading: "I wouldn't be who

I am without libraries. I was the sort of kid who devoured books, and my happiest times as a boy were when I persuaded my parents to drop me off in the local library on their way to work, and I spent the day there. I discovered that librarians actually want to help you: they taught me about interlibrary loans."

Christopher Coake is the author of the novel *You Came Back* (2012) and the story collection *We're in Trouble* (2005), which won the PEN/Robert Bingham Fellowship for a first work of fiction. In 2007 he was named one of Granta's Best Young American Novelists. His short fiction has been anthologized in *Best American Mystery Stories 2004* and *The Best American Noir of the Century*, and published in journals such as *Granta*, *The Southern Review*, *The Gettysburg Review*, *Five Points*, and *The Journal*. A native of Indiana, Coake received an MA from Miami University of Ohio and an MFA from Ohio State University. He is an Associate Professor of English at the University of Nevada, Reno, where he directs the new MFA program in creative writing.

Mercedes M. Yardley is a dark fantasist who wears red lipstick and poisonous flowers in her hair. She writes short stories, nonfiction, novellas, and novels. She is the author of *Beautiful Sorrows*, *Apocalyptic Montessa and Nuclear Lulu: A Tale of Atomic Love*, *Nameless*, *Little Dead Red*, and her latest release, *Pretty Little Dead Girls: A Novel of Murder and Whimsy*. Mercedes lives and works in Sin City, and you can reach her at www.abrokenlaptop.com.

Paul Tremblay is the author of the novels *A Head Full of Ghosts*, *The Little Sleep*, *No Sleep Till*

Wonderland, and coming in June 2016, *Disappearance at Devil's Rock*. He is a member of the board of directors of the Shirley Jackson Awards, and his essays and short fiction have appeared in the *Los Angeles Times* and numerous "year's best" anthologies. He is tall, hates pickles, and has no uvula. www.paultremblay.net.

Damien Angelica Walters is the author of *Paper Tigers* (Dark House Press, 2016) and **Sing Me Your Scars** (Apex Publications, 2015). Her short fiction has been nominated twice for a Bram Stoker Award, reprinted in *The Year's Best Dark Fantasy & Horror* and *The Year's Best Weird Fiction*, and published in various anthologies and magazines, including *Nightscript, Cemetery Dance Online, Nightmare Magazine*, and *Black Static*. She lives in Maryland with her husband and two rescued pit bulls. Find her on Twitter @DamienAWalters or on the web at http://damienangelicawalters.com.

Richard Thomas is the award-winning author of seven books—*Disintegration* and *The Breaker* (Random House Alibi), *Transubstantiate, Herniated Roots, Staring Into the Abyss, Tribulations* and *The Soul Standard* (Dzanc Books). His over 100 stories in print include *Cemetery Dance, PANK, storySouth, Gargoyle, Weird Fiction Review, Midwestern Gothic, Arcadia, Qualia Nous, Chiral Mad 2 & 3*, and *Shivers VI*. Visit www.whatdoesnotkillme.com for more information.

A visionary, fantasist, poet and painter, **Clive Barker** has expanded the reaches of human imagination as a novelist, director, screenwriter and dramatist. An inveterate seeker who traverses between myriad styles with ease, Barker has left his indelible artistic mark on a range of projects that reflect his creative grasp of contemporary media—from familiar literary terrain to the progressive vision of his Seraphim production company. His 1998 "Gods and Monsters", which he executive produced, garnered three Academy Award nominations and an Oscar for Best Adapted Screenplay. The following year, Barker joined the ranks of such illustrious authors as Gabriel Garcia Marquez, Annie Dillard and Aldous Huxley when his collection of literary works was inducted into the Perennial line at HarperCollins, who then published *The Essential Clive Barker*, a 700-page anthology with an introduction by Armistead Maupin.

Barker began his odyssey in the London theatre, scripting original plays for his group The Dog Company, including "The History of the Devil," "Frankenstein in Love" and "Crazyface." Soon, Barker began publishing his *The Books of Blood* short fiction collections; but it was his debut novel, *The Damnation Game* that widened his already growing international audience.

Barker shifted gears in 1987 when he directed *Hellraiser*, based on his novella *The Hellbound Heart*, which became a veritable cult classic spawning a slew of sequels, several lines of comic books, and an array of merchandising. In 1990, he adapted and directed *Nightbreed* from his short story "Cabal." Two years later, Barker executive produced the housing-project story *Candyman*, as well as the 1995 sequel, *Candyman 2: Farewell to the Flesh*. Also that year, he directed Scott Bakula and Famke Janssen in the noir-esque detective tale, *Lord of Illusions*.

Barker's literary works include such best-selling

fantasies as *Weaveworld*, *Imajica*, and *Everville*, the children's novel *The Thief of Always*, *Sacrament*, *Galilee* and *Coldheart Canyon*. The first of his quintet of children's books, *Abarat*, was published in October 2002 to resounding critical acclaim, followed by *Abarat II: Days of Magic, Nights of War* and *Arabat III: Absolute Midnight*; Barker is currently completing the fourth in the series.

As an artist, Barker frequently turns to the canvas to fuel his imagination with hugely successful exhibitions across America. His neo-expressionist paintings have been showcased in two large format books, *Clive Barker, Illustrator, volumes I & II*.

In 2012 Barker was given a Lifetime Achievement Award from the Horror Writer's Association, for his outstanding contribution to the genre.

John F.D. Taff is a Bram Stoker Award-nominated author with nearly 30 years experience in all sorts of writing . . . public relations, marketing, sales, journalism and creative. He's a published author with more than 75 short stories and soon to be six novels in print. His writing tends to be categorized as "horror," though most of it has a weird, pulpy *Twilight Zone* vibe to it. He also writes fantasy, suspense and some science fiction. Over the years, six of his short stories have been awarded honorable mentions in Datlow & Windling's *Year's Best Fantasy & Horror*.

John is a fascinating human being (yes, he's writing this), with diverse interests in history (ancient Egypt and the Civil War, particularly), spiritualism, the paranormal, cooking, movies, music and reading. He resides in a lovely house down by a river that likes to, every so often, overflow its banks and spread alarmingly over the countryside, sweeping aside mobile homes, swine and meth labs. He shares the house with his three wonderfully cute pugs, Sadie, Tovah & Muriel. He shares his life with his wonderful wife, Deborah, who puts up with a great deal from him.

Amanda Gowin lives in the foothills of Appalachia with her husband and son. Her work has appeared in a variety of print and online publications, including everything from *Warmed and Bound* and the *Burnt Tongues* anthology to *NAILED* magazine. She co-edited the *Cipher Sisters* anthology, and her first collection, *Radium Girls* (Thunderdome Press), is now available. More can be found at her blog: www.lookatmissohio.wordpress.com. She has always written and always will.

Kevin Lucia is the reviews editor for *Cemetery Dance* magazine and he writes the quarterly column, "Horror 101," for *Lamplight Magazine*. His short fiction has appeared in several anthologies. He is the author of *Hiram Grange & The Chosen One*, *Things Slip Through*, *Devourer of Souls*, *Through A Mirror Darkly* and *A Night at Old Webb*. He's currently working on his first novel.

Maria Alexander's debut novel, *Mr. Wicker*, won the 2014 Bram Stoker Award for Superior Achievement in a First Novel. Her short stories and nonfiction have appeared since 1999 in critically acclaimed anthologies and publications such as *Chiaroscuro Magazine*, *Nightmare Magazine*, *Paradox: The Magazine of Historical and Speculative Fiction* and many others. Champlain College uses her nonfiction to teach about female warriors in popular culture. Since 2010, she's been studying samurai swordsmanship. Don't ask her which is mightier. You'll probably regret it. Instead, visit www.mariaalexander.net.

Josh Malerman is the author of the novel *Bird Box* and forthcoming novella *A House at the Bottom of a Lake*. He lives in Ferndale, Michigan with his fiancée Allison Laakko and their two cats, Dewey and Frankenstein.

The Oxford Companion to English Literature describes **Ramsey Campbell** as "Britain's most respected living horror writer". He has been given more awards than any other writer in the field, including the Grand Master Award of the World Horror Convention, the Lifetime Achievement Award of the Horror Writers Association, the Living Legend Award of the International Horror Guild and the World Fantasy Lifetime Achievement Award. In 2015 he was made an Honorary Fellow of Liverpool John Moores University for outstanding services to literature. Among his novels are *The Face That Must Die*, *Incarnate*, *Midnight Sun*, *The Count of Eleven*, *Silent Children*, *The Darkest Part of the Woods*, *The Overnight*, *Secret Story*, *The Grin of the Dark*, *Thieving Fear*, *Creatures of the Pool*, *The Seven Days of Cain*, *Ghosts Know*, *The Kind Folk*, *Think Yourself Lucky* and *Thirteen Days by Sunset Beach*. He is presently working on a trilogy, *The Three Births of Daoloth*. *Needing Ghosts*, *The Last Revelation of Gla'aki*, *The Pretence* and *The Booking* are novellas. His collections include *Waking Nightmares*, *Alone with the Horrors*, *Ghosts and Grisly Things*, *Told by the Dead*, *Just Behind You* and *Holes for Faces*, and his non-fiction is collected as *Ramsey Campbell, Probably*. His novels *The*

Nameless and *Pact of the Fathers* have been filmed in Spain. His regular columns appear in *Dead Reckonings* and *Video Watchdog*. He is the President of the Society of Fantastic Films.

Ramsey Campbell lives on Merseyside with his wife Jenny. His pleasures include classical music, good food and wine, and whatever's in that pipe. His website is at www.ramseycampbell.com.

About the Artists

Cover Art

Caitlin Hackett's passion for the natural world has inspired her art since she first put pencil to paper as a child. She grew up on the northern coast of California, between the cold Pacific Ocean and the redwood forests. It was there that her love for nature and wilderness flourished. As she has grown, she has combined her love for animals with her interest in both wildlife biology and mythology to create artwork that speaks to the current biological mythos that constructs the barrier between what is considered Human, and what is considered Animal.

Mirroring ancient myths of transformation in often grotesque ways, we find in contemporary times that animals are being transformed biologically due to interactions with human pollutants; there are frogs with triplicate legs and blind eyes, cows with shriveled sets of legs growing out of their backs, two-faced piglets being born on factory farms and radioactive fish rotting from the inside in poisoned seas, the list goes on. She is interested in the power of these mutations both for their mythological allusions as well as their dire environmental implications. She hopes to remind those who view her artwork that we, too, are animals, embedded in this fragile world even as we poison it.

Her work alludes to the boundaries that separate humans from animals both physically and metaphysically, and the way in which these boundaries are warped by science, mythology, and religion alike.

Like the gods of so many myths, Humanity has

warped the world into our own image, and it is this often frightening image she hopes to reflect in her work.

Learn more at https://caitlinhackett.carbonmade.com.

Interior Art

Luke Spooner currently lives and works in the South of England. Having graduated from the University of Portsmouth with a first-class degree, he is now a full-time illustrator working under two aliases; **Carrion House** for his darker work and **Hoodwink House** for his work aimed at a younger audience. He believes that the job of putting someone else's words into a visual form, to accompany and support their text, is a massive responsibility as well as being something he truly treasures.

Learn more at www.carrionhouse.com.

If you enjoyed this book, I'm sure you'll also like the following titles:

The Final Cut by Jasper Bark—Follow the misfortunes of two indie filmmakers in their quest to fund their breakthrough movie by borrowing money from one dangerous underground figure in order to buy a large quantity of cocaine from a different but equally dangerous underground figure. They will learn that while some stories capture the imagination, others will be the death of you.

Blackwater Val by William Gorman—a Supernatural Suspense Thriller / Horror / Coming of age novel: A widower, traveling with his dead wife's ashes and his six-year-old psychic daughter Katie in tow, returns to his haunted birthplace to execute his dead wife's final wish. But something isn't quite right in the Val.

Devourer of Souls by Kevin Lucia—In Kevin Lucia's latest installment of his growing Clifton Heights mythos, Sheriff Chris Baker and Father Ward meet for a Saturday morning breakfast at The Skylark Dinner to once again commiserate over the weird and terrifying secrets surrounding their town.

Tales from The Lake Vol.1—Remember those dark and scary nights spent telling ghost stories and other campfire stories? With the *Tales from The Lake* horror anthologies, you can relive some of those memories by reading the best Dark Fiction stories around. Includes Dark Fiction stories and poems by horror greats such as Graham Masterton, Bev Vincent, Tim Curran, Tim Waggoner, Elizabeth Massie, and many more.

Tales from The Lake Vol.2—Beneath this lake you'll find nothing but mystery and suspense, horror and dread. Not to mention death and misery—tales to share around the campfire or living room floor from the likes of Ramsey Campbell, Jack Ketchum, and Edward Lee.

Eidolon Avenue: The First Feast by Jonathan Winn—where the secretly guilty go to die. All thrown into their own private hell as every cruel choice, every deadly mistake, every drop of spilled blood is remembered, resurrected and relived to feed the ancient evil that lives on Eidolon Avenue.

Wind Chill by Patrick Rutigliano—What if you were held captive by your own family? Emma Rawlins has spent the last year a prisoner. The months following her mother's death dragged her father into a paranoid spiral of conspiracy theories and doomsday premonitions. But there is a force far colder than the freezing drifts. Ancient, ravenous, it knows no mercy. And it's already had a taste . . .

Children of the Grave—Choose your own demise in this interactive shared-world zombie anthology. Welcome to Purgatory, an arid plain of existence where zombies are the least of your problems. It's a post-mortem Hunger Games, and Blaze, a newcomer to Purgatory, needs your help to learn the rules of this world and choose the best course of action.

Little Dead Red by Mercedes M. Yardley—The Wolf is roaming the city, and he must be stopped. In this modern day retelling of Little Red Riding Hood, the wolf takes to the city streets to capture his prey, but the hunter is close behind him. With Grim Marie on the prowl, the hunter becomes the hunted.

Flowers in a Dumpster by Mark Allan Gunnells—The world is full of beauty and mystery. In these 17 tales, Gunnells will take you on a journey through landscapes of light and darkness, rapture and agony, hope and fear. Let Gunnells guide you through these landscapes where magnificence and decay co-exist side by side. Come pick a bouquet from these Flowers in a Dumpster.

The Dark at the End of the Tunnel by Taylor Grant— Offered for the first time in a collected format, this selection features ten gripping and darkly imaginative stories by Taylor Grant, a Bram Stoker Award® nominated author and rising star in the suspense and horror genres. Grant exposes the terrors that hide beneath the surface of our ordinary world, behind people's masks of normalcy, and lurking in the shadows at the farthest reaches of the universe.

Tribulations by Richard Thomas—In the third short story collection by Richard Thomas, *Tribulations*, these stories cover a wide range of dark fiction—from fantasy, science fiction and horror, to magical realism, neo-noir, and transgressive fiction. The common thread that weaves these tragic tales together is suffering and sorrow, and the ways we emerge from such heartbreak stronger, more appreciative of what we have left—a spark of hope enough to guide us though the valley of death.

If you ever thought of becoming an author, I'd also like to recommend these non-fiction titles:

Horror 101: The Way Forward—a comprehensive overview of the Horror fiction genre and career opportunities available to established and aspiring authors, including Jack Ketchum, Graham Masterton, Edward Lee, Lisa Morton, Ellen Datlow, Ramsey Campbell, and many more.

Horror 201: The Silver Scream Vol.1 and *Vol.2*—A must read for anyone interested in the horror film industry. Includes interviews and essays by Wes Craven, John Carpenter, George A. Romero, Mick Garris, and dozens more. Now available in paperback, as well.

Modern Mythmakers: 35 interviews with Horror and Science Fiction Writers and Filmmakers by Michael McCarty—Ever wanted to hang out with legends like Ray Bradbury, Richard Matheson, and Dean Koontz? *Modern Mythmakers* is your chance to hear fun anecdotes and career advice from authors and filmmakers like Forrest J. Ackerman, Ray Bradbury, Ramsey Campbell, John Carpenter, Dan Curtis, Elvira, Neil Gaiman, Mick Garris, Laurell K. Hamilton, Jack Ketchum, Dean Koontz, Graham Masterton, Richard Matheson, John Russo, William F. Nolan, John Saul, Peter Straub, and many more.

Writers On Writing: An Author's Guide—Your favorite authors share their secrets in the ultimate guide to becoming and being and author. Writers On Writing is an ongoing eBook series with original 'On Writing' essays by writing professionals. A new edition will be launched every few months, featuring four or five essays per edition, so be sure to check out the webpage regularly for updates.

Or check out other Crystal Lake Publishing books for your Dark Fiction, Horror, Suspense, and Thriller needs.

Connect with Crystal Lake Publishing

Website:
www.crystallakepub.com

Be sure to sign up for our newsletter and receive
a free eBook:
http://eepurl.com/xfuKP

Books:
http://www.crystallakepub.com/books.php

Twitter:
https://twitter.com/crystallakepub

Facebook:
www.facebook.com/Crystallakepublishing
https://www.facebook.com/Talesfromthelake/
https://www.facebook.com/WritersOnWritingSeries
/
Google+:
https://plus.google.com/u/1/107478350897139952572

Pinterest:
https://za.pinterest.com/crystallakepub/

Instagram:
https://www.instagram.com/crystal_lake_publishing/

Tumblr:
https://www.tumblr.com/blog/crystal-lake-publishing

Patreon:
https://www.patreon.com/CLP

With unmatched success since 2012, Crystal Lake Publishing has quickly become one of the world's leading indie publishers of Mystery, Thriller, and Suspense books with a Dark Fiction edge.

Crystal Lake Publishing puts integrity, honor, and respect at the forefront of our operations.

We strive for each book and outreach program that's launched to not only entertain and touch or comment on issues that affect our readers, but also to strengthen and support the Dark Fiction field and its authors.

Not only do we publish authors who are destined to be legends in the field (and as hardworking as us), but we also look for men and women who care about their readers and fellow human beings. We only publish the very best Dark Fiction and look forward to launching many new careers.

We strive to know each and every one of our readers, while building personal relationships with our authors, reviewers, bloggers, pod-casters, bookstores and libraries.

Crystal Lake Publishing is and will always be a beacon of what passion and dedication, combined with overwhelming teamwork and respect, can accomplish: unique fiction you can't find anywhere else.

We do not just publish books, we present you worlds within your world, doors within your mind, from talented authors who sacrifice so much for a moment of your time.

This is what we believe in. What we stand for. This will be our legacy.

Welcome to Crystal Lake Publishing.

We hope you enjoyed this title. If so, we'd be grateful if you could leave a review on your blog or any of the other websites and outlets open to book reviews. Reviews are like gold to writers and publishers, since word-of-mouth is and will always be the best way to market a great book. And remember to keep an eye out for more of our books.

THANK YOU FOR PURCHASING THIS BOOK